MARION LANE

LANE

RAVEN'S

REVENGE

Also by T.A. Willberg

Marion Lane and the Midnight Murder
Marion Lane and the Deadly Rose

MARION LANE

AND THE

RAVEN'S REVENGE

T.A. WILLBERG

PARK
ROW
BOOKS

PARK
ROW
BOOKS™

PLEASE RECYCLE
THIS PRODUCT IS RECYCLABLE

Recycling programs
for this product may
not exist in your area.

ISBN-13: 978-0-7783-3419-4

Marion Lane and the Raven's Revenge

Copyright © 2023 by T.A. Willberg OU

Park Row Books
22 Adelaide St. West, 41st Floor
Toronto, Ontario M5H 4E3, Canada
ParkRowBooks.com
BookClubbish.com

Printed in U.S.A.

For Hayley and Laura,
who've been with Marion from day one.

MARION LANE

LANE

AND THE

RAVEN'S

REVENGE

THE HUNTED
Sunday, April 10, 1960
Middlesex, London

DARCY GIBSON PULLED ON HER FAVORITE PAIR of lambskin gloves, fastened a chalky pearl bracelet to her wrist and pinched her cheeks. She straightened her belted shift dress in the mirror, smoothing the cotton against her thighs over and over until the creases had diminished. It was a long while since she'd been this on edge. In fact, the only other time she'd felt so sick with nerves was the day she realized she was about to be thrown in the slammer for a crime she didn't commit.

These, however, were a different kind of nerves—the type you get on Christmas morning, seeing a red stocking dangling over the fireplace and wondering if the present inside was the one you'd been wishing for. But really, there was no need to be so twitchy about things, was there? She'd picked the right dress, the perfect accessories, she'd scouted out the location beforehand and even checked the weather forecast (mild with a chance of rain). He *would* show up. He *would* tell her what she'd been wanting to hear. Everything was going to be fine.

Heavy footsteps thumped up the staircase, down the corridor and soon there was a knock on the bedroom door.

"Oi, Gibson," barked the boardinghouse mistress—Mrs. Titherington. "Need a word. Open up."

"On my way out, sorry."

"Out?"

"Yes, *out*," Darcy said, jaw tight. "As in I'm about to leave and don't have time for a chat."

There was a quick pause. "Where to?"

Darcy felt no obligation to tell the old hag the truth. Then again, Mrs. T was surprisingly good at catching lies when she heard them. She sighed. "To see my fella. He might propose today."

Mrs. T guffawed so loudly the floor seemed to shake. "Propose! To you? Must be a real idiot, then."

Darcy clenched her fists.

"Anyway, wonderful, that's lovely," Mrs. T went on, gathering herself, "but before you run off into the sunset with your lover boy, you pay up. Got it? Five pounds from last week and ten from the fortnight before. I ain't forgotten."

Darcy rolled her eyes. Mrs. T could hardly read or write but blimey, she could count like the best of them. "Don't fret, I'll get it to you by Friday. Like I promised."

"You better, little miss. Or you're out. This ain't a charity and I ain't your mother."

Thank God for that. Darcy waited until the portly old crow had stormed back down the staircase before wandering over to the window. While the cluttered room was as cold and cheerless as a graveyard, outside the city was bathed in crisp spring sunlight, the London skyline dazzling in the distance. Double-deckers trailed past, coughing out fumes, their cherry-colored coats shining like gems in the afternoon sun. Darcy was by no means a dreamer, and certainly not an optimist, but it was easy to imagine that a day such as this could bring only glad tidings and good fortune.

Darcy arrived at Petticoat Lane in the East End to find the Sunday market teeming. Countless stalls had been assembled on either side of the crowded street, exposing a threadlike path through the center. Keen-eyed shoppers, dressed meticulously in patterned sports coats and slim-fit trousers, strode to and fro, examining the assortment of merchandise—everything from cheap lace and nylon stockings to tarnished jewelry and nondescript trinkets. Among the punters, patrons haggled with salesmen while children played hopscotch and marbles wherever they found a clearing.

Indeed, it was a bustling place, but Darcy's sharp gray eyes scanned the throng of bodies with precision and focus, searching for the face she longed to see. If he wasn't here already, though, there was a small chance he wasn't coming at all.

She shook out her hands and wandered farther down the lane, pausing at a stall adorned with an array of colored cloth, a sign nailed to the front: *Himalayan Cashmere. Scarves, Ties and More!* A plump man paced behind the piles of garments, dabbing a handkerchief to his brow. A group of women moseyed past, glancing with little interest at the stall, while discerning shoppers discussed the cashmere's value and price.

Darcy's limbs tingled as the minutes ticked by, her eyes scanning, searching. But the crowd was dense, faces crammed together, bodies shifting this way and that, and for one gut-churning second she thought she saw...

She cocked her head, narrowed her eyes. Why was *he* here?

She took a quick step backward, bumping into a woman who was examining the swathes of cashmere. The woman yelped, scowled. Darcy ignored her as she shouldered her way through the crowd and toward the low-roofed, unoccupied storeroom that stood just behind the cashmere stand.

Inside, the room glowed with the feeble light of a single gas lamp, standing on a rickety table that looked as though it hadn't been used in years. The plain concrete floor was chipped and stained, but the walls were adorned with hooks ripe with cashmere, silk and velvet. Darcy turned down the gas lamp to just a flicker. She needed to think.

What the hell was he doing here? Was he looking for her? The thought made her sick.

She dug around in her handbag, pulled out a small silver case containing a collection of white tablets, swallowed two. Almost immediately, she felt lighter, warmer. The old pains in her neck eased and her thoughts cleared. She sucked in a lungful of air, steeling herself, then peered out through a slit in the door.

Oscar Biggar had certainly aged since she'd seen him last, but his boxy jaw and stupid wide-set eyes were as prominent as ever. He was dressed in a lime-green sweater vest and checkered trousers and was pushing his way through a group of sellers toward the storeroom. His face was creased in an expression of impatience and irritation, his sleeves damp with sweat. He paused as he came to the cashmere stall, his gaze searching. Terrified, Darcy scanned the crowd behind him, wondering if he'd brought along his entourage of plier-wielding thugs, the ones who'd pinned her to the ground nine years ago and ripped clean her fingernails. If yes, she was done for.

She watched now, breath hitching in her throat, as Oscar's gaze finally settled on the storeroom.

Rap-rap-rap.

Darcy waited a moment, fiddling with the belt of her shift dress, wringing her hands. It was too late now to run, and the tiny room offered no place to hide. But if she was going to face the bastard alone and unarmed, best she did it with at least a lick of confidence.

She heaved a breath, stepped back and opened the door.

Oscar placed a hand on the wall, steadying himself. His lips parted, spine straightened in shock. He stared at her unblinking, and she could see the memories burn inside his mind. So, he hadn't been expecting her as much as she hadn't been expecting him.

"Oscar. Fancy meeting you here," she said, as coolly as she could manage.

He risked a glance over his shoulder, then straightened the collar of his sweater. He set his filthy eyes back on Darcy and tried to conceal the catch in his voice. "What the hell is this, Gibson?"

She pressed her tongue against her cheek, allowing fury to rise in her chest, obscuring everything else. Memories swarmed like flies from a corpse, all those times she'd stood like this in front of him, waiting for instruction, for reprimand or reward, for permission to eat, to sleep, even to breathe. But it was nearly a decade since they'd seen each other and so much had changed. She was stronger now, braver. And he'd better know it.

"Was it you?" Oscar asked, changing tack.

"Was what me?"

"That…that *thing*." He jammed a finger under his shirt collar and ripped it downward. "The package. Delivered two weeks ago. A raven. Dead. It was you, wasn't it?"

Darcy waited several beats before answering. *"The Raven,"* she breathed.

"What?"

"It's a warning, then, ain't it?" Her words hit their mark; she could tell by the way his eyebrow twitched, something that happened when he was nervous but desperate not to show it. That made two of them, then. "But you closed down the factory, didn't you? You closed it down ages ago?"

He frowned, nodded. "Yeah, so? What's that got to do with anything?"

"Still, don't matter," she rambled on, as if talking to herself. "With all the bees and honey you've been thieving from your fellas year after year, it shouldn't be too hard to imagine you've gone and got yourself a couple of enemies, should it?"

His Adam's apple bobbed up and down as he swallowed. "Are you threatening me, Gibson?"

She stepped back into the gloom of the storeroom so that Oscar might not see the tremor returning to her hands. "In the old days, you lot had the fuzz on your side, and could do with me what you pleased. Not so sure it'd be that easy now. Things have changed, you know. I've heard they're cracking down mighty hard on organized crime these days. And fellas like you are top of their 'to do' list."

Oscar dove forward, hands reaching, eyes burning dark as coal. He gripped Darcy by her coat collar and pressed his lips to her ear. She didn't scream, or even try to wriggle free. The one thing men like Oscar Biggar loved almost more than anything else was watching women squirm and beg for mercy. She wasn't going to give him either.

"You want to play games, eh? Then let's play." He removed a razor from under his shirt sleeve. "I got no problem cutting you to ribbons right here and now, Gibson." He pressed the edge of the razor into the delicate skin at the corner of her eye.

She felt the sting, then the warm trickle of blood down her cheek.

"So, tell me," he breathed, "what is this about?"

"How would I know?" she spat back. "I got one, too!"

Oscar hesitated a second, then released her, though he kept the razor pointed in her direction. "What?"

"A raven. About a week ago. Delivered to my doorstep. I thought it was—" She shook her head, said no more.

Oscar studied her for a moment. Did he think she was lying? Would he really risk killing her right here in the middle of a busy Sunday market?

"Did it come with a letter?" he asked.

"A letter? No. No. I didn't get anything like that but—" She stopped, turned away from him, wrapped a gloved hand around her neck and felt the urgent hammer of her pulse beneath her fingers.

"But what? Spit it out!" Oscar swiped the razor through the air impatiently.

"I don't think they're connected. Can't be." She faltered, then continued when she saw the look on Oscar's face. "The letter came *after* the raven. Same day, but later. It was from my fella, though, saying we should meet here at the market on Sunday because he had something to ask me." She turned back, looked Oscar in the eye. Oh God, how hard it was to look him in the eye. "You don't think it was a trap, do you?"

Oscar nodded, slipped the razor back under his sleeve. "Yeah, it was a trap all right. Mine said about the same. But it wasn't addressed to me, it was addressed to Alan from Elinor. Said she had something important to say about the business. Alan's out of town, though, so I came instead."

Alan was Oscar's brother and Elinor, Alan's wife. Darcy swallowed. "Someone wanted us both here, then. Me and Alan. Same time, same place."

"That makes no sense. Why you? Why Alan?" He rubbed his chin, then the back of his neck. "And why a damn raven?"

"How the hell am I supposed to know?" She stared at the door, and the slit in the wall beside it. Someone shifted past, footsteps crunching on the gravel. A pause, then silence. She lowered her voice. "Someone's talking, ain't they? It's got to be. Someone from the old days."

"Like who?"

"I told you, I don't know! But like I said, you and your brother got loads of enemies now. Could be anyone. Suppose they've got something to leak about your new clothing venture. And maybe they think I'm involved, too. Who knows."

Oscar didn't look convinced. "If you're having me on, Gibson, I swear to God—"

"Having you on?" she barked, almost hysterical now. "You think I'd make this up? For what? I want nothing to do with any of you gutter rats. Nothing! I've a new life now, a perfect life. I ain't going to throw it away, not for anything."

Oscar gnashed his teeth, took a step forward. "Likewise. So, I think we're done here, yes?"

She rolled her shoulders and hissed back, *"Yes."*

Nearly an hour later, Darcy made her way back down Petticoat Lane toward the bus stop, swaying under the influence of the three pints she'd chugged down to wash away the memory of Oscar's hands on her throat.

The plump man behind the cashmere stall eyed her warily as she passed, then whispered to an elderly woman at his side. The pair scuttled off, down the lane, leaving the stall unattended and its patrons puzzled. Darcy sensed a shift in the atmosphere as she crossed the market, like a ripple of agitation that was quickly building up to something worse. Nothing felt safe, and she had a sudden urge to leave the market.

She reached the end of Petticoat Lane, the bus stop visible just ahead. She paused.

Someone screamed. The market-goers stopped in their tracks, heads spinning, eyes searching for the source of the commotion. Some began to run, bumping into stalls and each other, tripping, cursing, gasping.

Darcy turned around, back toward the cashmere stand, where a small crowd had gathered in a circle near the entrance to the attached storeroom. Through a break in the line of bodies, she could just make out a group of people crouched at the threshold, whispering, their faces pale with shock.

She shuffled closer, pulse racing, pushing her way through the circle of onlookers.

Oscar Biggar sat limp and gray, propped up against the storeroom door, his head lolling.

Her breath hitched. Her skin tingled.

The Raven had struck. And thing was, she knew exactly who was next.

AT THE MAYFLOWER
Good Friday, 1960

MARION LANE, TWENTY-FIVE-YEAR-OLD AP-
prentice detective at the ever-elusive *Miss Brickett's Investigations and Inquiries*, arrived at the Mayflower at dusk. The pub
was perched precariously above the swirling gray waters of the
Thames, now glistening under the sinking sun like a thread
of silver yarn spiraling into the distance. Londoners moved
about the surrounding cobblestone streets in their colorful
frocks and suits, cigars, pints and gossip abound, ready for a
weekend of Easter festivities. The air was thick and heavy,
tainted with petrol fumes and perspiration. It was London at
her best. Bright, crisp, loud and *alive*.

Coming to the jetty that extended out from the pub's entrance, Marion opened her knit handbag and pulled out a pair
of faded baby blue wedges that were only marginally more pre-
sentable than her work boots, which were scuffed and clunky
and reinforced with unsightly steel toecaps. The boots, mind
you, had come in mighty useful three weeks ago when—after
five hours of toiling over a malfunctioning Wire Catcher (a

nifty device for detecting covert recording devices, i.e., bugs) she'd dropped a box of the Catcher's weighted magnets on her toes. But try telling *that* to someone who'd never set foot inside the glorious subterranean labyrinth that was *Miss Brickett's Investigations and Inquiries.*

She fitted her wedges and straightened her panel skirt and rayon blouse—both too loose for her narrow, short frame. Ignoring her calloused palms and brittle fingernails stained with engine grease, she peered—almost fearfully—at her watch. While her punctuality was once a thing of legend, keeping track of time the past few months had become nearly as impossible a task as repairing the ceaseless stream of clock-work contraptions that had been flying across her workbench in *Miss Brickett's* famed Gadgetry Department. Indeed, life as a final-year apprentice detective (and first assistant to the agency's chief gadget engineer) had never been busier, which was why she realized, with a heavy sigh, that there just wasn't enough time to do anything about the monstrosity of frizzed brown hair on the top of her head.

"Bugger," she cursed under her breath. Frazzled and unkempt would have to do.

As expected, the Mayflower was buzzing, packed to the rafters with patrons of every shape and sort (though mostly the drunken sort). The air inside reeked of perspiration and tobacco smoke, alleviated only slightly by a cool breeze coming off the tumbling river.

"Hello, miss," panted a harried waiter, sweat gleaming on his forehead and peeking through his white undershirt. "I hope you've booked a table? Please say yes!"

She grinned. "Yes. For six o'clock. Under Hugo, I think."

The waiter consulted a register at the reception, then guided Marion over to a snug corner booth near the bar. Already seated at the table was a young man with a thicket of wild, dark hair and a tall, feeble frame. William Alexander Hobb, or Bill—as he and everyone who knew him preferred. To Marion, Bill was a dear friend and fellow apprentice detective at *Miss Brickett's*, someone who'd proven himself to be unwaveringly loyal, particularly brilliant at cracking complex cases and had an encyclopedic knowledge of historical facts, rules and regulations. However, to everyone else inside the Mayflower (or indeed aboveground), Bill was a long-suffering bookshop attendant whose only claim to fame was that he'd once worked as an archivist for the British Library.

Seated next to him was a woman, several years older and wider set than Marion, with hair the color of champagne, hanging in perfect curls about her heart-shaped face. The pair were intertwined, foreheads pressed together, oblivious to absolutely everything, including Marion's abrupt arrival.

She cleared her throat loudly. "Is three a crowd?" she asked with a grin. "Or can I join?"

"Oh, Mari," Bill said somewhat awkwardly, getting to his feet. He straightened his shirt, then gestured to the woman at his side, who remained seated, her elbows on the table, chin resting on interlaced, gloved fingers. "Darcy, this is Marion. Mari, Darc."

It was just a fortnight since Bill and Darcy had met at the pictures, though they now seemed, quite literally, joined at the hip. Or the shoulder.

"Wonderful to meet you at last!" Marion said enthusiastically, taking a seat on the opposite side of the booth while Darcy fixed her with a pair of striking silver-gray eyes. "Bill's been driving us mad, gushing about you every minute of every day," she added as she tried to keep her focus on Darcy's eyes, instead of the rather obvious affliction above her right cheek— a clean, shallow flesh wound about two inches long.

Darcy shuffled into the crook of Bill's arm and peered up at him lovingly, batting her unnaturally long lashes. "Oh I know, he's a right gusher," she agreed with a thick East End accent. "But I've got to admit, so am I."

"The perfect match, then," Marion concluded with a brisk nod. She meant it, too. If there was one thing Bill deserved but had never found—up until now, it seemed—it was a woman to appreciate his incomparable loyalty and unwavering benevolence. That is to say, a woman who loved him as much as Marion did, and just a little more.

"The good ones are hard to come by these days," Darcy went on, "so you've got to thank the saints when you snag one." She wrapped her arms around Bill's waist and leaned even further into him. He smiled sheepishly in response, his cheeks reddening. "Ain't that right, Marion?"

Marion laughed, warming to Darcy's unpolished, easy charm. "I suppose it is. But it goes both ways, doesn't it?"

Darcy clipped the table with vigor, the tarnished silver bracelets on her wrist clinking. "Too true. Us grade-A gals are as rare as hen's teeth, no doubt about it." She winked at Bill, who, reddening further, glanced at his watch and changed the subject.

"Speaking of rare things. Where the hell is Hugo?" he asked, referring to Kenny Hugo—American private detective turned reluctant *Miss Brickett's* Inquirer, who'd joined the agency shortly after Marion to help solve the brutal murder of one of their colleagues, Michelle White.

"Working late, I think," Marion said, tactfully omitting the fact that he was delayed only because he had to catch up on work after an unscheduled romantic rendezvous in the back of the Intelligence Department—the hot, sweaty details of which Marion would take to the grave. "Something about a special project he has to wrap up."

Bill gave her a funny look and it was only then that she remembered, her face turning as hot as a bonfire, that he too had been on duty in Intelligence around that time. "Funny," he said, one side of his mouth curling into a grin, "I could've sworn he gave that 'special project' a thorough going-through this afternoon."

Marion picked an imaginary fleck of dirt from her collar and tried not to smile.

Just then, the waiter arrived, bearing a tray cluttered with drinks—two glasses of white wine, two pints of Guinness—and several bowls of finger snacks.

Bill passed Marion and Darcy a glass of wine each. Marion—feeling suddenly parched—took an enormous sip, draining half her glass. It really had been a long day.

Darcy noticed this and grinned widely. "I like you, Marion Lane," she announced, nodding to herself. "Just like Bill said I would. Oh! That reminds me—" She slumped a handbag on the table and drew out a slender black leather belt with a delicate brass buckle in the shape of a crescent moon. "This is yours, I think," she said, handing it to Marion across the table.

Marion examined the belt, confused. It was definitely hers, a vintage piece she'd bought at a thrift shop several years back, but which she hardly ever wore owing to the fact that the fanciful buckle dug uncomfortably into her waist whenever she bent over or sat down. What was Darcy doing with the thing?

"I spotted it at Bill's," Darcy explained nonchalantly, twisting a yellow twine bracelet around her wrist. "And I'm sorry, love, but I just *had* to borrow it." She flashed Bill a look that seemed to hold some sort of warning. "Knew it must be yours since he promises you're the only bird who ever sets foot inside his bedroom."

Marion rolled the belt around her hand, placed it in her bag, watching Bill's expression flit from puzzlement to something she couldn't quite read. Now that she thought about it, she'd last worn the belt several weeks ago while on a field assignment. And although she couldn't remember doing so, it was likely she'd left it at Bill's place when they'd returned to his flat afterward for lunch.

"I should've asked, I'm sorry," Darcy admitted, chewing her lip. "I grew up with five sisters, see, and we were always wearing each other's things. I suppose it's just a habit. Forgive me?"

Marion whisked her fingers through the air with a flare of indifference, hoping to break the slightly awkward tension that was simmering now. "No, please. I don't mind, really. In fact—" She dipped her hand into her bag and pulled out the belt once more. "You can have it. I hardly ever wear the thing anyway."

Darcy waved the offer away and clicked her tongue. "That's kind of you, sweet, but it was a bit tight." She grasped her ample hips and laughed, while Bill shifted in his seat with a forced grin. "Once you hit the thirties, let me tell you, things only grow sideways!"

There was a beat of muffled silence between the trio, then Darcy added, "So, Bill tells me I ain't the only one head over heels these days. How long have you and this Hugo fella been steady for?"

"What, Kenny?" Marion fumbled, already sweating. "I wouldn't say we're going steady. It's more like a…" A what? Fling? Affair? Trial period? She had no idea.

Bill rolled his eyes. "They're steady, trust me. Marion just doesn't like to admit it."

Darcy smiled mischievously and asked, "Oh, so you've got someone else on the side, then, sweet?"

"God no, no. One man's more than enough to handle, thank you very much." She started to pick her nails, then realized what she was doing and placed both hands down on the table. *Damn the old habit!*

It was four months now since she and Kenny had shared their first kiss, a divine but fleeting moment on Christmas Eve. And while things had progressed since then (case in point their meetup that very afternoon in the Intelligence Department), she still wasn't entirely sure where their relationship was going. They *were* together, in all senses of the word, and spent nearly every night twisted up in each other's arms—hair tousled, skin flushed. It'd been a heart-fluttering escapade the likes of which, she suspected, would make even a courtesan blush. So why was it, then, that every time someone asked her to explain their relationship, she felt so exposed and ill at ease? Kenny, being Kenny, appeared to experience no such turmoil or confusion. In fact, since that glorious Christmas Eve, he'd mentioned the word *marriage* on at least five separate occasions. All in passing, all nonchalantly. But still—*marriage.* Yes. Perhaps *that* was the problem.

"Apologies, gang," Kenny said, jolting her from the thought as he appeared at her side. He slid in next to her, broad shoulders touching hers. Dressed in beige chinos and a slick blue golfer's shirt, he looked—as ever—devastatingly handsome. "Had a slight hitch in the Filing De—" He stopped short, extended his hand across the table, as though noticing Darcy for the first time. His eyes traveled, as Marion's had done, to the split skin above her cheek. He frowned, though remedied this quickly with a wide, warm grin that was surely impossible for any woman, man (or living creature) to distrust. "Kenny Hugo, a pleasure."

Darcy flashed him a sly smile in return, revealing a pair of flawless dimples. "Darcy Gibson, and the pleasure's *definitely* mine."

Kenny took a long sip from the pint of Guinness Marion

had set in front of him. He pulled a pack of cigarettes from his pocket and lit up. "So, Bill says you're a secretary for a financial services company in Mayfair." He offered Darcy a smoke. She accepted, leaning across the table as Kenny struck a match and brought the flame toward her. "You enjoy it?"

Darcy's full lips formed a perfect O as she puffed out a thread of smoke and sent it drifting skyward. "Can't say I do. But what choice does a woman like me have? I was born in the arse end of London, no education past the basics, no acquaintances in higher places. You lot know how it is." She sighed. "Suppose I was lucky, if you really think about it. At least I've got something to pay the bills, though it ain't keeping the gray matter twirling, that's for sure." She tapped some ash into an empty water glass and took another drag. "But enough about me." Her eyes flickered from Marion to Kenny to Bill. "Tell me more about this bookshop you work at."

Bill swallowed. "It's, er, well, nothing special really—"

"And what's all this yak about an employee-only surprise later tonight?" she cut in, referring to the *Miss Brickett's* "event" scheduled for eleven o'clock that night. "A work dinner or something? Bill's so coy about it all, I'm beginning to think you lot work for the secret service."

"Ha!" Bill laughed nervously, poured the last ounce of Guinness down his gullet. This was clearly not the first time Darcy had quizzed him about their occupation, nor the first time he'd floundered while replying. "I'm not trying to be coy. It's just that there's nothing to tell you. Nothing interesting, anyway." He waited a moment, a little tongue-tied. Unfortunately, his pause only seemed to intensify Darcy's interest. "We sell books and, um, knickknacks. I say sell but... you know, hardly. And I've got no clue what tonight's surprise is but trust me, you won't be missing anything."

Darcy tapped a finger against her glass, lips pursed. "Okay, so if it's *that* humdrum, why have you been working there for nearly three years? Sounds like you'd be better off back at the library."

Bill muttered something incoherent, which was Marion's cue to take over.

"He's trivializing it, really," she said. "Selling books and knickknacks is the bulk of our business, but it's not the best part." Having lived with an overly inquisitive, spectacularly suspicious grandmother for the first six months of her top-secret apprenticeship, Marion considered herself a master at deflecting interest into the nature of her work at *Miss Brickett's*. And what she'd learned first and foremost was that you didn't fool someone by being vague, but rather by the opposite. Lying, she'd come to realize, was in the details.

"Pawning," she explained, reaching into her bag, once again pulling out the belt Darcy had handed her at the beginning of the night. "That's what we're really known for."

Kenny and Bill shared a glance, confused.

"See, I bribed this belt off a dealer in town," Marion went on, ignoring them. "I probably could've sold it for a considerable amount of money at our shop, had I not fancied keeping it for myself. Which I now regret, mind you."

Darcy didn't look entirely convinced, but at least she was satisfied enough to put the matter aside. She ground out her cigarette and nodded. "Well, then…maybe you're more industrious than I had you for, all of you." She paused for just a split second, then raised her glass. "To new friends."

"She's trouble," Kenny said resolutely, once Bill had left to walk Darcy home.

"Oh, I don't know. She's a firecracker, that's all. And having someone like that is good for Bill. He'd never fall for a wallflower."

Kenny led her onto the jetty outside the pub, lit a cigarette and took a thoughtful drag. The way he slipped the thing between his lips made Marion's cheeks burn. "No. *You're* a firecracker, she's trouble. There's a difference, and I'm old and ugly enough to know it."

"Ugly is one thing you're definitely not."

He offered her a lopsided grin. "Thank you, but I'm serious, Lane. She's got him hook, line and sinker."

"What's wrong with that?"

"Nothing, if it went both ways. But it doesn't."

"How could you possibly know that?"

Kenny took one last puff of his cigarette, dropped it into a nearby ashtray. "Just can."

Marion didn't want to admit it, but there *was* something about Darcy that didn't fit right. Then again, first impressions weren't always to be trusted. Take Kenny for example: at first glance an arrogant Yank with too much charm and too little tact. Second glance, everything she'd ever wanted in a man, and then some. "Let's just be happy he's happy," she said, somewhat uncertainly. "If she's not good for him, he'll see it soon enough."

"And why's she so interested in what we do at the bookshop?" he asked, as if he hadn't heard a word.

Marion rolled her eyes. "A better question might be, why are *you* so interested in Bill's love life?"

He shrugged. "I've grown to like the kid. That a crime?"

"It's a peculiarity."

"Anyway," he said, "we've got to head back to the bookshop soon, but there's something I want to show you first."

"Okay…"

He rubbed the back of his neck. "You know how the other day when we were working in the Filing Department together, and I asked what you wanted to do for the summer holidays and you got all weird and said you had to leave?"

"I was late for my shift in Gadgetry."

"No, you weren't. You're never late for anything." (*Until recently*, she considered mentioning.) "But I get it. Really. You didn't want to answer because you're not sure we'll still be together by the summer. You don't trust me yet, you don't trust *us* yet. And why should you? That thing I did last year... with Kate—"

"Oh, not this again, please," she interrupted. The last thing she wanted to think about right then was the moment she'd found Kenny and junior Inquirer Kate Bailey naked in bed together just moments after Marion had admitted to herself she had feelings for him.

"I just—"

"Kenny, we've talked about this a hundred times. It doesn't matter. We weren't even together then. No harm, no foul."

"I'm going to prove myself to you, all right? I'm going to prove to you every damn minute of every day how serious I am. Starting now."

She frowned, but let him take her hand, twirl his fingers through hers.

"Come," he said.

They clambered down from the jetty and onto the narrow strip of tarmac that separated the pub from its somewhat unsightly neighbor—a four-story tower of gray-green brick.

"What's this?" she asked as Kenny gestured to a flimsy metal ladder that crept up the side of the Mayflower.

He placed his hands on either side of her waist and nudged her toward the ladder. "After you."

She considered protesting but was silenced by the look of eagerness on his face. She placed a foot on the lowest rung and hauled herself upward. Kenny followed, climbing swiftly despite his colossal frame.

"What do you think?" he asked once they'd reached the roof, extending an arm to the view—one of chimneys and spires, and a black velvet river twinkling in the moonlight.

"I've never seen it like this," she murmured, wide-eyed, gazing at the gleaming skyline—a world away from the endless miles of pneumatic pipes and gloomy passageways of *Miss Brickett's*. That was *her* London. And this? "It's just so…bright."

Kenny laid out a blanket, two cups, a bottle of wine and box of snacks. He then dug around in his haversack and pulled out a small metallic sunbird. A Distracter—used by Inquirers in the field to circumvent tricky situations and suspicious civilians.

"Are we expecting an ambush?" Marion teased, watching with curiosity as he tinkered incompetently with the gadget.

"No, I just—" He yanked at one of the bird's tail feathers. There was a strange clanking sound.

Marion winced. "Um, what exactly are you trying to do?"

"Just hold on, you know how bad I am at handling these things…" With some difficulty and a certain amount of groaning, he eventually found the key hidden under the bird's wing and began to wind it up. "Professor Bal set it up for me," he added as the bird came to life—feather by glistening feather—twitching and squirming within his grip. At last, he set it loose and it fluttered skyward for several seconds, then stopped mid-air and began to hover, wings buzzing so fast they were nearly invisible. Marion marveled at the creature, her favorite gadget, now so familiar it was as though the bird's tiny ticking insides were a part of her own.

"*Come on!*" he said impatiently, counting under his breath. "Three, two, one…" He clicked his fingers and, at that precise moment, a muffled tune drifted down from the bird's speakers. Some sort of waltz.

He held out his hand, and Marion let him spin her twice under his arm.

"Just so you know," she said flippantly as he spun her faster, "this 'proving yourself' plan isn't working. I'm not falling for it."

He placed a hand in the center of her spine, dipped her backward. She laughed despite herself as he lifted her to her feet and twirled her once again under his arm. They swayed across the rooftop, under the crisp night sky, and Marion imagined what it must have looked like from above, their silhouettes spinning, cutting through shards of city light, slipping into their own perfect world.

She cast an eye to the hovering bird, beating its wings silently above them a little more slowly than before, its battery waning. Kenny leaned in, pressed his lips to hers.

"Still not working," she mumbled as she breathed him in, her hands crawling through his hair.

When they separated, on cue, the bird fell silent and fluttered back down to the roof, wrapped its wings around itself and became still. Kenny scooped Marion up under the knees, swung her round. She laughed breathlessly, closed her eyes, her head spinning, as dizzied by the movement as the meteoric beat of her heart.

Two hours later they were lying on their backs, staring up at a starless blue sky, a thick woolen blanket over their knees, feet curled up together, a bottle of port between them. The booming music and laughter from the Mayflower below still filled the air, though softer than before. Marion held the metallic sunbird on her chest. Her fingers traced its jagged wings, catching a loose joint near the windup key, no doubt triggered by Kenny's overzealous attempt to get the thing started. She'd have to repair that tomorrow.

"Penny for your thoughts?" he asked. He turned onto his

side, so that his head rested on his elbow and the muscles in his neck twitched.

God, he was perfect. His flaxen mane, brown eyes. Not a flaw in sight.

"Actually, let me guess." He looked at the Distracter, laughed. "You're analyzing the mess I made of that thing and wondering how long it's going to take to fix it?"

"It's just a loose joint. You've done far worse," she chirped. "Besides, I've missed working in Gadgetry." She really had. Repairing gadgets at *Miss Brickett's* had always been more than a job to her. It gave her a sense of purpose, and gave her days structure. Most of all, it made her feel as though she belonged. Not just to the agency, but to the community of people who worked there. *Her* people. She sat up and bundled the blanket around her knees. "I can't believe you people have locked us out of there for over two weeks now."

"Me? I had nothing to do with it."

"Oh, come on! You're a terrible liar and horrid at keeping secrets," she said with a laugh. "Bill and I have known all about your little 'surprise' for days now."

Not completely true, she thought to herself. Two weeks ago, Marion and her fellow apprentices (including Bill) had been told that the Gadgetry Department would be closed until Good Friday for "maintenance." But everyone with half a brain cell had put two and two together and come up with five. Tonight was the third-years' long awaited Induction Ceremony, when they would at last be handed a polished silver badge and named Inquirers—an event that marked the start of their careers as full-fledged private detectives.

"And why does it have to be a surprise for *just* the apprentices?" she went on.

He spread his hands as if to say *No clue, babe.*

"Last year's inductees weren't kept in the dark, were they?"

she asked. "Also, what on earth are they doing setting the ceremony up in Gadgetry? It's supposed to be held in the ballroom. Gadgetry's... It's just...what if someone breaks something? I had six crates of Distracter wings sitting on my workbench when they shooed me away. Do you have any idea how fragile Distracter wings are?"

He sighed. "First off, it's not *my* secret. I'm just on the organizing committee. Second, I made triple sure your beloved Distracter wings and everything else on your workbench were locked up safely. Third, who ever said it was your Induction Ceremony?"

Marion frowned. If it wasn't their Induction Ceremony, then what on earth...?

They hauled themselves down from the Mayflower's rooftop, swaying like willow branches, glassy-eyed. Kenny offered an arm. Marion hooked hers through his and hiccoughed. In the background, a church bell chimed and high above, the sky was a black pearl, stars glittering like dew drops. Never had she dreamed that landing a job as an apprentice Inquirer at *Miss Brickett's* would lead to this, to happiness so pure it cut through all doubt, all her scars, all her past mistakes.

It was approaching eleven when, after a detour to Marion's flat in the East End to change (still fairly convinced she was about to attend her own Induction Ceremony, she now wore her formal work attire—a slim-fitting gray pencil skirt and white blouse), they finally arrived at the old Gregorian shop—*Miss Brickett's Secondhand Bookshop & Curiosities*, the agency's facade. The last light of day had long since vanished. The air was crisp, growing cold, and a strong breeze now rattled the windowpanes.

"One sec," Kenny said as Marion drew out her keys and

slipped them into the bookshop door. "My car's parked around the corner. Mind if I fetch something quick?"

"Please don't tell me it's another surprise?" she quipped.

"I guess you could say that."

"Go on, then."

He planted a kiss on her lips, then vanished like a wraith around the bend.

As usual, the cul-de-sac was deserted, its only buildings the old bookshop and two dilapidated structures; defaced with fractured walls and shattered roofs. It was rare for anyone to traverse the street, besides the odd pedestrian who'd wandered aimlessly off from the nearby Eel Brook Common, or, of course, the Inquirers and apprentices who worked at *Miss Brickett's*. And yet, right then, Marion noticed a shadow move at the far end of the street.

Click. Snap. Snap.

A white light flashed, like a torch or a single headlamp. She blinked, craned her neck at the pocket of darkness from which the light had emerged, but just as swiftly as it had come, it disappeared. What had it been? She was tempted to investigate, but a peal of shrill laughter changed her mind.

She turned westward, toward the mouth of the cul-de-sac. Three figures drifted into view, their arms linked together as they tumbled down the street. The laughter grew, voices becoming distinct, recognizable. Marion let out a breath of relief as Bill, Kenny and Jessica Meel—another third-year apprentice—materialized in front of her. Bill and Jessica, like Marion, were dressed in formal work attire. But Kenny...

"What on earth are you wearing?" Marion asked, gawking at Kenny's getup: a ridiculous red-and-gold doublet and knee-high leather boots.

Jessica laughed, green eyes glinting at Kenny. "I agree. Bit extravagant, even for you, darling."

Kenny, not in the least insulted, pushed back his strapping shoulders and smoothed down a lick of mislaid flaxen hair. "I think the word you're looking for is *style*."

"Nineteen twenties' style, maybe," Jessica retorted. It wasn't like her to offend anyone, even playfully, but Kenny's ridiculous attire was just something else. "Although I'm not sure anyone in those days used whatever it is you put in that hair of yours." Standing on her toes, she reached up, attempting to run a hand through Kenny's most prized feature. Noticing her effort, he obliged, lowering his head, but was quick to whip away before she could "wreck the wave."

Marion stared at him, aghast. "No, but really, what *is* this?" She flashed Bill an incredulous look, expecting he might provide some explanation.

"Eh, I'm hoping it's a gag," he said, grinning as he spoke. "Unless this—" he gestured to Kenny "—is *en vogue* stateside?"

Kenny gave him a shrug, as if to suggest it might be. "We were encouraged to arrive in costume," he explained nonchalantly. "Or wear a mask, if we're one of them."

"One of whom?" Marion and Jessica asked in chorus.

Kenny held the door as Jessica and Bill entered the bookshop. "You'll see," he said, pressing a hand to the small of Marion's back.

FIGHT CLUB

MARION, KENNY, BILL AND JESSICA ARRIVED AT the Gadgetry Department, several corridors and stairwells beneath the bookshop and city streets. The gloom here, on the agency's bottommost level, was always thicker, and the atmosphere almost sinister. This was undoubtably thanks to the spiraling passageways that curved off to the left, forming the border of *Miss Brickett's* restricted section—a confusing maze filled with deadly trapdoors and countless deterrents Marion preferred not to think about.

But it wasn't what lay beyond The Border that now had her spine tingling.

She frowned at the old gargoyle that guarded the entrance to the Workshop—the Gadgetry Department's main hall. The grotesque creature, a freakish blend of man and goblin, looked more menacing than ever tonight, clad in a black hooded veil that hung to the floor and flapped mysteriously in an unfelt breeze.

Kenny grinned at Marion, Bill and Jessica as he gave the gargoyle's muscly arm a tug and the creature—cloak and all—sunk obediently into the floor, revealing the sealed door beyond.

"Ready for your *Induction Ceremony*?" he asked with a smirk.

Marion rolled her eyes heavenward. "Step aside, Hugo. The joke's up." She nudged him firmly in the ribs and pushed open the door.

She stepped over the threshold, gasped and froze midstride.

As Kenny had predicted, at least a quarter of the event's attendees were dressed in extravagant costume—plague doctors, footmen, Victorian lords and ladies, knights and maids and devils and demons. Fewer wore Venetian masks, expanding their disguise. The usually barren, dim hall—where the agency's bespoke gadgets of espionage and surveillance were crafted and repaired—was decorated with perimeter lamps wrapped in ribbons of green and copper. The ceiling was dotted with hundreds of twinkling emerald lights and the entire department, from the entrance to the far western wall, was scattered with a forest of birch samplings in terra-cotta pots. Each tree was adorned with glossy mechanical embellishments—birds, butterflies, bees and flowers—and a long buffet table had been set up in the center of the hall, covered in mountains of steaming hot cross buns, spiced biscuits and mouthwatering caramels and nougat.

Strung across the ceiling from one side of the hall to the other was an enormous green and copper banner.

Welcome to the First Annual Fight Club:
Miss Brickett's Investigations and Inquiries
vs
Der Schatten

Marion, Bill and Jessica stared up at the banner, slack-jawed and wide-eyed while Kenny watched them with wicked delight.

Jessica began to mutter incoherently. "I don't understand… What…what is *Der Schatten*?" She peeled her eyes from the banner and glanced around the hall more thoroughly, as did Marion, who only then realized that the number of attendees exceeded the number of *Miss Brickett's* employees by at least fifty.

"No!" Marion said, smiling, though she was beginning to feel mildly ill with shock. "The people in masks, they're not—"

"Not us, no," Bill said, nodding.

Jessica's eyes popped. "Pardon?"

"They're from *Der Schatten* in West Berlin," Kenny explained smugly. "You know, our sister agency."

"Our *what*?" Marion gasped.

"In *where*?" Jessica added.

"Knew it!" Bill said excitedly. "I bloody well knew we weren't the only ones. But Germans? Blimey…"

"You knew? Really?" Jessica said, casting him an incredulous look. "I don't remember you ever mentioning that. Mari, do you remember Bill mentioning *our sister agency*?"

Marion was too distracted to answer. A petite blonde had appeared at her shoulder, wearing a flashy gold and silver pantalone mask and floor length red silk gown. She raised a glass of champagne in greeting, and for a moment looked as though she wished to join the conversation. But for whatever reason, she changed her mind and disappeared back into the crowd.

"Her name's Anneliese, I think. But don't try asking her anything," Kenny advised sternly. "At least not anything related to *Der Schatten*. If you think *we're* secretive…"

"How long are they here for?" Marion asked, still trying to wrap her head around what was going on.

"Just tonight. Though the head of their agency is staying for a week or so to 'exchange trade ideas'…or something like that."

"The head?"

Kenny scanned the crowd as he spoke. "Lance Zimmerman. The only member of *Der Schatten* who's not in disguise." He nodded at a well-proportioned gentleman with a shock of graying hair standing at the farthest end of the hall, dressed in a white collared shirt and simple black trousers. He wasn't wearing a mask, and didn't seem at all concerned that everyone was staring at him. "He's also their agency's chief gadget designer. I got a look at his collection. You wouldn't believe the technology. Puts us to shame."

Marion shot him an affronted look.

"And...*bingo!*" Kenny said, clicking his fingers. "That's exactly the attitude we're hoping for." He pointed again at the banner across the ceiling and said, "'*Miss Brickett's Investigations and Inquiries* versus *Der Schatten*.' Nothing like a little friendly competition to unite the ranks. In fact, that's exactly why the High Council organized the thing."

"Well," Jessica said thoughtfully, "I suppose that makes sense. Heaven knows we need it, after, you know...last year."

It was true, now that Marion considered the fact. Last year, *Miss Brickett's* had been split in two by a traitor from the east, who'd infiltrated the agency on behalf of the KGB. But instead of opposing the turncoat as a united front, *Miss Brickett's* had found itself ripped down the middle by lies and propaganda that eventually led to the murder of one of Marion's fellow apprentices—Amanda Shirley. It was the closest the agency had ever come to falling apart, and while things were generally back to normal, an undercurrent of mistrust lingered between those who'd been swayed by the propaganda and those who hadn't.

Contemplating how tonight's events might help seal that rift, Marion trailed Bill, Jessica and Kenny through the forest of saplings, eyes wide with delight, fingers splayed in the hopes of catching one of the menagerie's flying mechanical creatures—a bird, a butterfly or a glittering bee.

"I just have one quick question about this so-called 'Fight Club,'" Jessica said, voice wavering slightly as she ducked out of the way of something that had zapped rapidly across her path, emitting a drone that Marion guessed was the whirl of a miniature internal combustion engine. "Who exactly will be doing the fighting? Please don't say the apprentices. If you do, I'm quitting on the spot."

"Same," Marion said.

Bill looked down at his spindly arms, flexed a nonexistent muscle, then gulped, "Ah, yeah, that makes three of us."

"You'll see," Kenny said, and laughed as they sidestepped the new first-year apprentices: a lad from Glasgow, another from Cork and two young women from London.

Marion and Bill continued their exploration of the hall, trailing—awestruck—behind Kenny, while Jessica split off to examine what appeared to be some sort of aviary filled with modified Distracters.

"Truly bizarre…" Marion murmured, gawking at an individual dressed as a Viking, and another as a pirate, arm wrestling each other over a pint of ale while a large scarlet butterfly hovered silently above their heads.

"Pretty brilliant, eh?" said Preston Dinn—a fellow third-year apprentice—strolling over from the buffet table. "Funny they managed to keep it a secret from us. I didn't catch a whiff 'till two days ago, when they started lugging the trees down here." He nudged a nearby sapling as though testing whether it were real. "Anyway, what time's the first matchup?" he asked, accepting the cigarette Kenny had passed to him. He took a drag. "All my brass is on the spider, sorry to say."

Kenny puffed out a curl of smoke thoughtfully. "Should be in minutes. But the odds are three to one, pal. Not worth it. And I heard the scorpion did a number on the spider last night in the trials. Who's to say it'll even be fit to compete."

"Nah, I've seen the daggers on that thing," Preston insisted. "There's no way the scorpion will get a claw in edgeways. Unless—"

"Oh, for goodness' sake!" Marion interrupted, glaring up at the pair of them. "What are you blabbering about? What spider? What scorpion?"

"Yeah," Bill said with a suspicious frown as he jabbed a finger at Preston. "You're supposed to be in the dark like the rest of us."

Preston let his cigarette hang from the side of his mouth as he answered, "I just told you. I got suspicious a few nights ago so, like any self-respecting future Inquirer should, I shimmied on down to have a look-see for myself. Birch saplings for an Induction Ceremony? Nah. I wasn't buying that one."

No one replied.

"Anyway, I got caught when I walked slap-bang into one of those mechanical butterfly things, which double up as alarm bells, by the way. The High Council wasn't too happy with me but in the end, they decided it didn't matter, so long as I didn't spoil the surprise for anyone else."

"Right," Marion said, answering for Bill who seemed to have lost his tongue. "Now can you get back to explaining what the blast all this is about a spider with daggers?" As a steadfast member of the agency's gadgetry team, she didn't like the idea that her forced two-week leave of absence had led to the creation of a host of deadly mechanical arachnids—which was exactly what it sounded like.

Kenny laughed so smugly she ground her teeth. He slung an arm over her shoulder. "Come come, my little firecracker, I'll show you."

After weaving their way through the maze of saplings, pillars and bizarre decorations, they finally found themselves in the northern wing of the Workshop—a spot normally lined with benches piled high with gadget parts and disassembled clockwork engines. Tonight, the area had been cleared for what appeared to be a mini boxing ring, elevated on a wooden dais. Surrounding the ring was a pack of onlookers, sweaty, loud, fists pumping the air. Kenny took Marion's hand as they pushed their way through to a small clearing with a view of the ring.

Marion gasped, peering up. "Are those—"

"Brilliant!" Bill said, slapping Kenny on the back as he caught up. "You sneaky bastard, keeping this all to yourself."

In the center of the ring was a shimmering chrome spider the size of a small cat with articulated (and disproportionately long) legs, an undulated thorax and ten awful black eyes that seemed to spin within their sockets like marbles in oil. Facing it, as though prepared to duel, was a slightly larger, though less polished and certainly more archaic looking scorpion with pincers like tweezers and a razor-sharp tail that curled menacingly above its body.

Marion's eyes traveled upward to a banner that hung over the ring—suspended in midair by a bizarre swarm of metal fireflies—*Place Your Bets! Place Your Bets! Der Schatten's Spider, Or Miss Brickett's Scorpion? Winner Takes All!*

"We've been taking bets all week," Kenny shouted over the din of the crowd. "The scorpion's the favorite, since last night's trial. But I'm not so sure. I've a feeling Zimmerman's been tinkering with his design since then, which is *verboten*. But you know the Germans, they really hate to lose."

A thousand questions sprang to Marion's mind, but she blurted out the first and foremost. "So Bal designed the scorpion? By himself? In two weeks?" She couldn't imagine it, honestly. Professor Uday Bal was the head of the Gadgetry Department and the agency's chief gadget engineer, but even for him, this would've surely been a gargantuan task. Especially without his first assistant, Marion, to help. Not to mention the cost of designing such a creature, which could've easily run into the thousands.

"Correct," Kenny said nonchalantly. "Though not in two weeks. He's been working on it for months. In secret. The spider, though, that was made by Zimmerman and his team."

"Blimey," Bill gushed, his focus pinned unwaveringly on the creatures in the ring, which hadn't moved an inch and seemed, in fact, rather...dead.

Marion would've loved to quiz Kenny further, but it was now impossible to hear a word over the feverish chanting from *Der Schatten's* members that had rung up all around them.

Spider, spider up the wall
Spider, spider beats them all

"I'm presuming there's a prize for the winner?" Marion shouted, to no one in particular.

A junior Inquirer, who'd shoved his way to the front, a pint in each hand, nodded briskly. "The winning agency gets all the dosh."

Marion gave him a questioning look.

"The pooled loot. I've heard it's a heap load, too."

"Right," she said, no less perplexed. She looked up to see Kenny, now standing in the center of the ring. He doffed his hat, pressed two fingers to his lip and let out a shrill whistle, commanding the attention of every onlooker.

"And now for what we've all been waiting for—spider versus scorpion," he boomed. "I hope you've placed your bets, lads, ladies, because time's up."

The Inquirer at Marion's side clinked his pints together in celebration. "Aye! Aye! Let's have it!"

A rattle came from above, like drums beating. Marion's gaze followed the sound to where, on a partially concealed platform that was suspended just below the ceiling, she caught sight of Professor Bal and three other members of the *Miss Brickett's* High Council—the agency's governing body. The professor was staring down at the ring, a fob watch tight in his grip, his posture hunched, as though he were hoping not to be seen. Marion was about to look away when she noticed Zimmerman, lingering behind the professor with what appeared to be a pair of binoculars pressed to his face.

"Fight! Fight! Fight!" bellowed the Inquirer at her side, distracting her. She looked again to see the spider and scorpion shiver as though coming to life. Kenny climbed out of the ring just as the spider's legs began to twitch. Its thorax clinked, stretched. The scorpion's pincers clacked together loudly.

The hall fell into a quick, feverish silence.

There was a strange hissing sound, though Marion couldn't tell which creature it had come from.

Without warning, the spider charged forward, darted around the scorpion and leapt onto its back. The scorpion raised its tail and plunged an arrow-shaped stinger directly into one of the spider's legs. The spider let out a high-pitched mechanical whine, followed by a clicking sound that Marion noticed accompanied the unsheathing of something that looked like a dart from within the spider's mouth. There was a loud clang as the two creatures tossed and turned, merging into a tight ball of glimmering metal.

Flash, scrape, clink and a wisp of black smoke rose from the center of the ring. The scorpion pulled itself free with an odd stagger, revealing a badly disfigured pincer and one broken leg.

The spider darted left, backing into a corner, then launched itself at the scorpion. There was a quick scuffle, accompanied by an ear-splitting shriek, and the scorpion rolled over, creaked and was sill.

The hall erupted in a cacophony of applause and an equally raucous string of boos.

Several hours later, with the crowd of spectators now dispersed and Kenny, Preston and Bill long since lost to an indepth postduel analysis, Jessica and Marion hooked up to share a bottle of wine. They slumped down at one of the workbenches, decorated with a gingham tablecloth and mechanical flower centerpiece. Marion popped the cork as a medley of The Beatles filtered through the hall.

"The Shadow," Jessica said, pouring them each a measure of wine.

"Hmm?" Marion muttered, distracted as her eyes scanned the thinning crowd.

"It's English for *Der Schatten.* A bit sinister, don't you think?"

"Maybe they are. I mean, we know nothing about them, other than they're very good at gadget design." She watched the petite blonde from earlier stroll past Professor Bal's office—which was locked, she hoped.

"We know nothing about them, true, but I'll bet Nancy knows everything," Jessica said, referring to Nancy Brickett, the indomitable head and founder of the agency who, now that Marion came to think of it, she hadn't seen all evening. Was she, too, wearing a disguise?

"Right, I suppose. But if they're allowed to visit us, do you think they'd repay the favor some time?"

"No, definitely not," Jessica replied, massaging the stem of her glass. "Word is, *Der Schatten's* level of concealment and secrecy puts *Miss Brickett's* to shame. Apparently, that's part of the reason Zimmerman is staying with us for a while. A security adviser, of sorts."

"Huh, a bit like closing the stable door after the horse has bolted," Marion mused, thinking of her first two years of employment at *Miss Brickett's*, and the string of accidents and murders that had occurred during that time.

Jessica, sensing the shift in mood, placed a comforting hand on Marion's wrist. "You know, I've a good feeling about this year. I really do."

Marion wasn't sure she felt the same but before she could say so, third-year apprentice, Maud Finkle—a stout individual with cropped, auburn locks and a general air of brusqueness—appeared at the table. She sat down next to Marion, one leg on either side of the bench and a bulging purse in her hands.

"Let me guess," Jessica said dryly, eyeing Maud's purse and the ridiculous grin on her face. "You bet everything you had on the spider, and thus won handsomely, and now you're here to boast about it."

Maud jangled her purse in front of Jessica's face. "Something like that. I was also going to offer to buy you both a round. Think I've just changed my mind, though."

Marion laughed, offering Maud her half-empty glass of wine. She accepted, downing the leftovers in a single gulp.

"Anyway," Jessica said, swirling her drink in her glass. "Enough about bets and mechanical arachnids." There was a gleam in her iridescent eyes now, which she'd set solely on Marion. "Tell me, quick. What's he like?"

"Sorry?"

Jessica gnawed her lip impatiently. "What's he like in the sack?" She nodded unsubtly to her left, where Kenny and Bill were standing, heads pressed together, chatting enthusiastically.

"Boring, I bet," Maud piped up. "I had a man about his

size once and it was as exciting as shagging a tree. Always the macho ones who can't seem to get things going."

Jessica pursed her lips. "Lovely."

Marion gave them both a cavalier shrug. "He's good enough, I suppose."

Jessica shrieked with frustration. "Oh come on, don't spare me the details! I haven't had a lick of romance this year. If I can't live vicariously through you, I'm going to shrivel up and die."

Maud nodded at Marion. "That's true. She's bleeding desperate."

Marion pushed her wineglass aside, suddenly realizing just how fast her head was spinning. Her mind flashed back to last week, during her lunch hour, when Kenny had laid her down on this very workbench.

"Well, I'm sorry to disappoint," she said, trying not to smile, "but—"

"On top or missionary?" Jessica asked. "Or do you prefer—"

"Right, that's it," Maud interrupted. "You in the mask, come here." She yanked the arm of a long-limbed, dark-haired member of *Der Schatten* wearing a silver wolf mask. "Do you have a girlfriend?"

He blinked once, shook his head.

"Good. And are you free tonight?"

"Ja aber—"

"Perfect," Maud concluded, extending a hand to Jessica. "Okay, now let me explain how this is going to go…"

While Maud launched into a lengthy description of how Jessica and her masked lover were going to spend the night, Marion surveyed the hall. Apart from the last remaining members of *Der Schatten*, who were—barring Jessica's masked friend—gathered in a circle, their suitcases at their feet, several groups of *Miss Brickett's* employees mingling among them, the place was empty. She watched as the petite blonde in the pantelone mask said her farewells, emptied her champagne glass and made for the exit, followed closely by Bill.

"Just a moment," Marion said to Jessica, getting to her feet and grabbing her bag. She dashed across the hall and caught up with Bill just beyond the gargoyle at the base of the long stone staircase.

"You're heading home?" she asked. "Already?"

"Yeah." He sighed. "Darcy is waiting for me and, yeah, you know…"

"Oh, right. Of course." She faltered at the look on Bill's face. Was he sad, or just uncertain of something? If it was the latter, then surely that was normal. Bill and Darcy had only been going steady for two weeks—not nearly long enough to really get to know each other. So, keen to help, she said brightly, "All right, tell me. The three things you like most about her. Go."

Bill frowned at first, then, slowly, smiled. "Well, she's independent. I like that the most. She has a job, she does her own thing, she knows what she likes."

"Okay, that's four," Marion laughed as they reached the top of the staircase.

"Nah, that's one. Number two, she's funny. Snippy, almost, but I like it." He paused, then added, "And she makes me feel, I don't know…wanted, I guess. Is that pathetic? To want to feel wanted?"

Marion thought about Kenny, and how he made her feel: comfortable, safe and yes, wanted. *Very* wanted. "No. Definitely not. Wanting to be wanted is good. Normal."

They turned right into a short, dank corridor, their footsteps echoing loudly.

"The thing is though," Bill said a little while later, "something's been bothering her, and I don't know what it is. Maybe I'm just imagining it but she seems, I don't know, on edge."

Marion recalled the fresh cut on Darcy's face. Had she told Bill how she got it? Should Marion ask?

"And not just tonight," he went on. "The past few days, too. I don't know, maybe it's me? I've tried to ask her, but she just brushes me off."

Marion linked her arm through his as they traversed the long corridor that led past the library bar, out of which she could hear the beat of blues music, drunken laughter and the clink of glasses. An after-party, perhaps.

"I wouldn't overthink it," she said. "Maybe it's just an issue at her work or something. And anyway, things are always shaky in the beginning of a relationship. I won't point out any obvious examples, but cast your mind back to the spring of '58 and a certain well-groomed American who might've got under my skin a couple of times."

She had hoped her cheeky remark would lighten Bill's mood, but it seemed to make no difference at all. In fact, it seemed he hadn't heard a word.

They trudged on in silence, navigating the warren of passageways and chambers that made up the agency. It was certainly busier than it should've been at this time of night, pockets of employees gathered at nearly every turn, chattering, laughing, settling debts scored during the Fight Club.

At last, they climbed through the trapdoor and into the bookshop. Marion flicked on the light, illuminating the tight rows of disorganized, unsightly shelves littered with books and oddities that no one would ever buy.

"Plans for the weekend?" Bill asked as he detached himself from her side and pulled a coat over his shoulders. He opened the door and stepped into the street. The wind had picked up and was howling as it whipped through the cul-de-sac, rattling the bow-fronted windows and shrieking through the rooftops.

"Work, probably. Gadgetry officially reopens on Monday, but Professor Bal will almost certainly be getting started with the backlog this weekend. I might join him. You?"

He straightened his collar, glanced quickly over his shoulder. Marion had heard it too, the clip of footsteps, a swish of fabric.

"Ah, not sure," he said, turning back to Marion. "I promised Kenny I'd go with him to the football game tomorrow, but Darc wants to go to the pictures."

"Well, how about I keep Kenny busy so you don't have to pick?"

"Ha, yeah, sounds good." He gave her a weak smile. "You heading back to Gadgetry now?"

She nodded. "Maud's got Jess roped into, eh, I don't actually know. But I should go check on her."

"All right. Well, night, Mari. I'll see you Monday."

She raised a hand in parting and followed him out into the cul-de-sac. It was a moonless night, and he vanished into the gloom within seconds.

She waited for a moment, then turned back to the door, her keys jingling at her side and a strange prickling sensation rising up the back of her neck. What did she see there, at the opposite end of the cul-de-sac. A dog? A person? The same shadow from earlier? Or was it just her mind playing tricks on her?

Glass crashed to the pavement. She squinted into the dimness, and thought she saw the figure shift behind a flickering streetlight. She edged closer.

One yard.

Two.

A beer bottle lay shattered on the ground, shards scattered amid the fallen leaves and bits of rubbish that had washed up from the storm drain. She surveyed the shadows with keen eyes, waiting for movement, the sound of footsteps, but nothing came.

Quickly, she padded back to the bookshop and locked the door behind her.

4

THE TAIL AND THE KNIFE

MARION WATCHED WITH MILD REVULSION AS
Professor Uday Bal inserted a finger into the eye socket of his
(now defeated) mechanical scorpion. He winced, something
deep within the socket catching his flesh, and Marion was certain one of the scorpion's legs twitched in response. She shivered.

It was Easter Sunday, and while the rest of the live-in staff
were gorging themselves on a spread of baked ham with apricot
stuffing, mashed potatoes and buttered bread (or dousing themselves in rum and port in the library bar), Marion was, as she'd
predicted, back in the Gadgetry Department with Professor Bal.

"All right, now I'll need to loosen this joint before we take
a look inside," the professor croaked, holding out his left hand
while his right remained firmly locked within the scorpion's
eye socket. "Screwdriver, please."

"A flathead?" Marion suggested, holding out the delicate,
thin-limbed screwdriver. She was certain, one hundred per-
cent certain, that this was the only tool for the job.

The professor gave her a doubtful look, but accepted the flathead all the same. And within seconds, as Marion had guessed, the screw came loose.

"Ah, well there we are, perfect!" He removed his beloved checkered beret and shook his head, a beaming smile spreading across his face. "It's not so much the professor and the apprentice anymore, is it? This really is where you belong, my dear Marion."

She glanced around the workshop—its eerie flickering lamps, secret alcoves, benches scattered with tools of every shape and sort, the scent of oil heavy in the air. There was only one word for it: *home*. But as she watched the professor continue to tinker with his peculiar contraption, deep in concentration, Marion was reminded that a home was nothing without the people you shared it with.

The professor gave his mechanical charge a gentle shake as he continued his examination of its eye socket. *"Hmm..."*

"What?" Marion asked.

"There was a pellet lodged inside. It must have come from Zimmerman's spider during the match, some sort of projectile." He tut-tutted. "Ha, if I'd known we were going to play dirty like that, I'd have added a little heat to that arachnid's fancy-pants alkaline battery."

Marion sighed. "Well, you know, spilt milk."

"Ten thousand pounds of spilt milk," the professor cut in. "We really could've done with the money, you know."

"Ten thousand? Good grief! I didn't realize the prize money was *that* much."

He nodded sadly, and in response she patted him sympathetically on the shoulder.

"Anyway," she said, still frowning at the scorpion, "what are we going to use it for? Now that it's all patched up."

The professor placed the creature back on the workbench,

wiped his grease-lined hands on his trouser legs. "Surveil-lance, of course. I'll insert a camera or two into those eyes, and maybe a voice recorder in its tail."

"Right, like the snakes, then." She shuddered, glancing over at a small spherical cage behind the workbench, which housed five clockwork serpents—all seemingly inert and ut-terly still. The snakes, wrought of translucent silver scales that were nearly invisible unless placed under direct light, could detect movement with their tongues and record it with their eyes. They were occasionally employed by the agency as a se-curity measure of sorts, to patrol the out-of-bounds corridors and chambers. And while Marion had had one too many close encounters with the creatures, at least she knew they were, in essence, harmless. But an oversize arachnid with a razor sharp tail? Now *that* was crossing a line. She was about to say as much when the Workshop door creaked open.

She blinked several times at the intruder before she real-ized who it was. Frank Stone—head of the apprenticeship program and field office—long-stepped across the Workshop. He was dressed in a thick travel coat and gray woolen scarf, and a polished leather suitcase was swinging at his side. It defi-nitely *was* Frank. Only, he didn't look anything like himself. As he neared, he pulled a thick, flesh-colored strip from his chin, then one from his jawline. Next, he tore a bristly brown mustache from above his lip and a strange, padded contrap-tion from around his waist.

"Brilliant, *brilliant!*" Professor Bal said, clapping his hands together as Frank removed the last of his disguise—a pair of blue contact lenses that obscured his pale gray eyes. "So con-vincing, I was about to whack you over the head."

"Me too," Marion added incredulously. "What on earth is all this?"

Bal turned to her with an impish grin. "My latest designs,

which some of our staff have been testing out aboveground. What do you think?"

"Impressive, certainly. And useful, I suppose." She picked up the silicone waistband Frank had discarded and examined it thoughtfully. Historically, the Inquirers relied on stealth and skill alone to mask their identities while negotiating the streets of London on business. But with anonymity the most crucial element to the survival of the agency and all its staff, it could be argued that a nifty set of disguises was well overdue.

"I've more ideas up my sleeve, just need the time to get around to them," the professor went on, warming to his theme, "wigs, slimmers, muscle pads, false teeth. Anything you can think of, anything!"

"I look forward to trying them all," Frank said, giving Marion a discreet wink. "Though perhaps not the false teeth."

It was nearly a week since Marion had last laid eyes on Frank, and despite his peculiar entrance, she felt a sudden glow of excitement at the list of things she was due to update him on: the progress she'd made on the missing persons case she'd been working on in the Intelligence Department, the preparations she'd made for her final apprenticeship assessment (which was to take place next month) and, most importantly, the selection of gadgets she and the professor were drafting for construction in the coming weeks. Since her mother had died nine years ago, Frank—an old family friend—had drifted in and out of Marion's life, appearing when she needed him most, such as that wondrous day two and half years ago when he'd arrived at her front door with a letter written in invisible ink, offering her a position at *Miss Brickett's*.

"You wouldn't believe what you've missed!" she raved, then went on to spill every last detail of Friday's Fight Club, even though she was sure he already knew it all. "Oh, and happy Easter, by the way."

Frank removed his coat and slung it over his arm. "Happy Easter, my dear." He placed his suitcase on the workbench with an exhausted thud. "And yes, I'm very sorry I missed it, but I had business in Middlesex that just couldn't wait." He looked as though he wanted to say something more, then changed his mind. "How did you find our guests from *Der Schatten*?"

"Aloof, frankly." She put her hands on her hips and added in an earnest tone, "I can't believe you've never told me about them. Two and a half years and not a peep."

Frank smiled, taking her comment more frivolously than she would've liked. "Who says I knew about them myself?"

She raised an eyebrow.

He smiled again, neither confirming nor denying the accusation. Then, as though noticing it for the first time, nodded at her yellow sleeveless V-neck dress—a far cry from her usual gray, grease-stained work attire.

"I'm off for drinks in a minute," she explained.

"Aboveground?"

"At the Mayflower. Bill's gone and landed himself a lady friend."

The professor's eyes widened. "Bill has a girlfriend? My my…"

Marion nodded. "We're meeting up tonight, just us two."

"Ah." A troubled expression crossed Frank's face, but he shook it off almost immediately. "Well then, this seems like perfect timing." He unclipped his suitcase and drew out a Spinner Knife, which, in contrast to nearly every other agency gadget, possessed no ornate disguise or complicated parts, barring a large notch on its handle and an accompanying silver wrist strap. "I wanted to give you this as an early induction gift." He handed the knife to Marion, its blades folded backward, and tightened the strap around her wrist. It fit perfectly, the contraption lying flush against her ivory skin.

"A Spinner Knife?" she said, bewildered, removing the strap from her wrist. She spun the notch on the handle clockwise. Click. A thin serrated blade, about half the length of a butter knife, sprung up from the gadget's inner folds. She swiped the blade carefully through the air, then spun the notch clockwise once more. Click. A longer, heavier blade was ejected.

"As I said, you're going be an Inquirer soon, out in the field," Frank explained, "and I'd like you to carry this on you. Always. For protection."

"Oh…okay." Marion turned the dial on her Spinner Knife counterclockwise and the blades folded in on themselves, disappearing once more. It was perhaps true that Inquirers in the field required protection from targets and assailants. Indeed, many carried gadgets that could distract and hinder. But actual weapons, such as the Spinner Knife (which, according to *the Basic Workshop Manual*, had been recalled ten years ago), were fiercely discouraged. But the main reason Marion felt slightly unsettled by the gift was because it seemed that Frank had suddenly become paranoid about her safety. Just last month, he'd encouraged her to take extra self-defense and evasion classes from senior Inquirer, Aida Rakes, and the month before that he'd gone through a very bizarre phase of following her around whenever she left the agency after hours.

She patted her pocket awkwardly and smiled. "Well, again, thank you. Still, I don't really think I'll need—"

"Just keep it on you," Frank interrupted brusquely. "Better to be safe than sorry." He closed his suitcase with a snap, slipped it under his arm and was gone.

A couple of hours later, Marion found herself at the bus stop in Fulham. It was a clear night, windless and unseasonably warm, perfect weather to be aboveground. And while she was bemused as to exactly why Darcy wished to meet with her alone, after the day she'd had with Bal in Gadgetry, she realized she could do with a glass of wine. Besides, she told herself as she climbed onto the bus that would deliver her to the Mayflower, if Darcy was going to be in Bill's life for the foreseeable future, she might as well make an effort to get to know her better. Not just because that's what best friends did, but because Kenny's warning had been playing over in her mind ever since Friday. If Darcy *was* trouble, Marion felt it her duty to find out. And soon.

She stepped off the bus at Rotherhithe, walked the short distance to the pub and found Darcy seated at a small table on the jetty, immaculately dressed in a gray wool dress and black leather gloves, her golden hair falling in effortless curls about her shoulders. She looked up, noticing Marion, and was on her feet in seconds. She threw a handful of coins onto the table, grabbed her bag.

"Follow me," she said breathlessly, leading the way across the jetty, down onto the cobbled street.

"We're not having a drink? I could really do with one…"

Darcy marched on without a word, stopping only once they were standing on the pavement of the short, quiet street that bordered the Mayflower. She touched the cut above her cheek absently. It was still raw, even seeping now, as though the edges had been ripped afresh. "I know who you are," she began, her East London lilt more pronounced than ever.

The muscles in Marion's neck tightened, but she kept her face deadpan.

"You're an Inquirer. Bill is too." She paused to judge Marion's reaction, but Marion gave her none. "That's why I called you here. I need your help. The Inquirers' help." She twisted her gloved hands together, the leather squeaked. "I know I should've just sent you a letter through the mail slots, like everyone else does. Or I should've asked Bill instead, but I'm afraid he'd think less of me once he knew the truth."

Still, Marion held her tongue, reluctant to acknowledge Darcy's assumptions. But was there any point in lying? However Darcy had found out, through Bill's ramblings and pillow talk, or her own investigations, the truth was out. And while the matter would have to be remedied (though heaven alone knew how), perhaps now was not the time.

"Someone's been following me," Darcy went on. "Someone from my past that—" She swallowed hard, tilted her head. A car revved in the neighboring street, its headlights flickering in the distance. "See, I used to work as a secretary at a steelworks factory down in Hackney. It was easy work, answering the telephone, typing up invoices, making tea, that sort of thing. Or at least that was how it seemed in the beginning, before I found out what them boys were really up to."

"Boys?"

"The Biggar brothers," Darcy said abruptly. "Big shots in gangland. You might've heard of them."

Marion shook her head. *Gangland.* She steeled herself.

"Oscar Biggar, the oldest, someone had it out for him. Maybe one of his clients, someone he did wrong—"

Frustrated, Marion placed her hands on Darcy's shoulders, squeezed tight. "Darcy, please. You called me here to help you, but I can't help unless you tell me *everything.*" She waited for her to take a breath. "Start from the beginning."

Darcy shook her head anxiously, as though she wasn't sure they had time. "The factory was a front," she said. "I wasn't supposed to know that, of course, but I ain't no fool. I figured it out soon enough, that they were trafficking drugs, cocaine mostly, right from the factory and across Europe. And not little bits here and there, tons of it. I was going to quit, soon as I found out, honest, but before I got the chance, something…

something happened. I don't know what, exactly, maybe the police were tipped off about the operation, maybe a rival gang came after them. But whatever it was, it had Oscar and the boys scattering like rats. They left the factory and haven't gone back since."

A car door slammed somewhere in the distance. Marion scanned the street ahead and behind. Nothing

"That was almost a decade ago now," Darcy added, "so I figured things had cooled off. But it looks like… I think—" She glanced over her shoulder, spoke under her breath. "I don't know what's going on but it's a muck up. He's dead, see, and I think I'm next."

"Wait, wait. Dead? Who's dead?"

"Oscar Biggar! He was strangled, you must have heard about it? Right in the middle of a crowd of people at Petticoat Lane. But that's how they do it in the underground, see. They like to make a show of things, to send a warning, scare off their enemies."

Marion looked up, her mouth dry. *Gangland. The underground. Murder.* She didn't like the sound of this one bit. "Okay, so…why do you think you're next?"

She averted her eyes, moved from foot to foot. Marion was certain there was something Darcy was omitting.

"I don't know," Darcy said hurriedly. "All I know is someone's been following me since the day Oscar was killed and that ain't no coincidence."

A car screeched around the corner at the end of the street, headlights off, too far away to tell the make or model. It slowed, then reversed out of sight. Moments later, a man appeared at the end of the street, his face partially obscured by the shadows, his figure broad and slouched.

"Do you know who it is, this person who's been following you?"

Darcy muttered something. It sounded like *The Raven*. She froze, her eyes wide with terror, hands trembling, her back to the car. "Don't let them get me, Marion, please."

The man drew out a cigarette, leaned up against the wall. He clicked a lighter; an amber flame flickered upward.

"You have to help me," Darcy said, more urgent now. "If they take me, I'll be worse than dead. You don't understand how cruel they can be...especially with..." Again, she touched the cut on her cheek.

Marion gripped her by the wrist so firmly Darcy winced. "We'll be fine. Just follow my lead and don't panic. No one will attack us here."

"They will! I just told you, that's how they operate!"

Marion silenced her by rolling up her shirtsleeve, exposing the Spinner Knife at her wrist. Strange, she thought, that Frank had given it to her just hours ago, as though he'd predicted this. She unhitched the safety catch, turned slowly on her heels. *"Follow me,"* she whispered as she began to move. "Calm and slow. We'll lose him around the block."

They walked side-by-side, casually, slowly, back toward the Mayflower. The pub's windows glimmered, and for a moment Marion was tempted to slip inside and wait out their tail. But it was a gamble, backing themselves into a corner with no escape. She faltered for a moment, then turned left into a neighboring street, picking up her pace.

Darcy panted at her side. "Where to now?"

"It doesn't matter. The point is to lose our tail." She turned right at the next street, then left and right again, until they found themselves in a long residential road bordered by row houses, lush sycamores and parked cars.

Marion chanced a glance behind her as they came to a stop. No sign of their tail. She rolled her shoulders and pulled her sleeve back over the Spinner Knife. "Do they know where you live?"

"Yes, yes, I think so. Or maybe not. I've been hearing and seeing things everywhere I go. I don't know what's real, or just my imagination."

Marion recalled the incident in the cul-de-sac outside the bookshop on Friday night, the moving shadows, the flash of light, the broken glass. She hoped it was a coincidence.

"I'm just… I'm terrified, Marion," Darcy admitted. She stopped to contemplate something, then unzipped her handbag and pulled out a Smith & Wesson revolver.

Marion flinched.

"It's my sister's." Darcy held the weapon incompetently by the barrel, her grip loose, fingers shaking. "But I don't know how to use it." She forced the revolver into Marion's hands. "Please, show me. Just in case, in case they come back."

Marion felt the cold metal heavy in her palms and wished to rid herself of it immediately. "You won't need that," she assured, placing the gun carefully back into Darcy's bag. "We'll figure this out. Together, okay?"

Darcy's eyes scanned the houses on either side of them, the cars, even the trees. It was quiet, eerily so. "How?"

Marion hesitated. She couldn't let Darcy go home, nor could they stand around like this all night, exposed and vulnerable. "You'll come with me," she said, decision made. "To the bookshop. It'll be safe, and might buy us some time until we come up with a plan."

"No," Darcy snapped, clutching her bag—and the revolver inside—tighter to her side. "I need *you*, no one else. Not the Inquirers. Not the police."

"I didn't say anything about the Inquirers or the police. Just you, me and—"

"Bill won't understand. I can't face him knowing who I worked for."

Marion took her hand and tried to smile, though it must have looked more like a frown. "He will understand, trust me. This is Bill we're talking about. And besides, we need his help."

They reached the bookshop unscathed. Marion guided Darcy inside, switched on the light.

Darcy glanced curiously around the space, fingering the crowded shelves while Marion picked up the telephone behind the desk and dialed Bill's home number. He answered on the third ring, and their conversation was brief and to the point. She replaced the receiver, looked up. Darcy was slumped down on the floor, her back pressed up against a bookshelf and her head in her hands.

"I know Bill," Marion soothed, crouching beside her, "and I promise you, he'll understand."

It felt like only minutes later when the door clicked open and Bill stepped inside, dressed in trousers and a creased shirt, sleep lines crisscrossing his face. He embraced Darcy without hesitation, and rubbed her back while she sobbed quietly into his chest and Marion explained the situation as delicately as she could.

"I'm so sorry," Darcy said, peeling herself away from him and wiping her eyes. "I should've told you. I was just so ashamed. The factory, the drugs. I thought you'd think I had something to do with it all." She muttered a string of further apologies while Bill fell into an anxious tic—finger to thumb, tap-tap-tap—and Marion peered through the window at the darkened street.

"We've got to find out who's been tailing you," she said abruptly, addressing Darcy as she checked (for the second time) that the door was locked. "It's the only way we'll be able to figure out what they want and how to stop them."

Darcy averted her eyes and mumbled something.

Marion looked at Bill. He ceased his tapping and raised his eyebrows. "Yeah, yeah, okay." He picked up the backpack he'd only recently cast to the floor, slung it across his chest. "But first—" he took Darcy's hand "—we need to get you somewhere they won't find you. Ideas?"

"Your flat?" Darcy suggested. "They don't know it, I'm sure."

"They might," Marion retorted, "if they've been tailing you."

Darcy was resolute. "They don't. I've been careful."

Marion wasn't entirely sure Darcy's affirmation sufficed, but was distracted from the thought as her eyes landed on a pile of old newspapers bundled near the wastepaper basket. She sifted through silently until she found last week's issue of *The Daily Telegraph*, which contained the article Darcy had mentioned earlier that night—a short piece detailing the curious events that surrounded Oscar Biggar's death at Petticoat Lane market.

London Shaken as Local Businessman and Philanthropist, Oscar Biggar, Found Dead. Cause of Death Yet to Be Determined.

"I'll ring first thing tomorrow," Bill said, tapping Marion on the shoulder. "Then we'll fix a plan, okay?"

"Yes, right, of course," Marion said, distracted. "And be careful at the flat. You never know."

Bill nodded, looked at the paper, pausing for a moment. "Just keep this between the three of us for the time being, yeah?"

The second they were out the door, Marion turned back

to the newspaper, her eyes skimming through the sentences, mind spinning.

Mr. Biggar was found dead just moments after arriving at the market...initial reports claim the cause of death is unknown, although police have alluded to a significant piece of evidence found at the scene...

She folded the paper, tucked it into her handbag. Something about the article bothered her. Two things, actually.

5

THE OTHER BROTHER

DARCY WATCHED BILL DRIFT OFF AND WAS struck with an unexpected pang of regret. She'd never thought he'd fall for her—not like this, anyway. He was supposed to be a means to an end, nothing more. But then their "serendipitous" date at the pictures two weeks ago had taken a turn she hadn't anticipated. What she'd prepared for was a man who was easy to sway and wouldn't ask questions. But Bill was kind, gentle, loyal, honest—nothing like the vile, rotten blokes she'd been with before. If only things were different, if only she could've met him in a different life, or in the old days when her heart was still open and unblemished.

It was one week since she'd met Oscar Biggar at Petticoat Lane, and in those seven days, she'd hardly slept a wink. Despite the lies she'd told Marion, she knew exactly who was following her. And make no mistake: he *would* find her. Soon. Which was why she had to pack up her things and leg it. Not tomorrow, not in a few days. Right now.

She kissed Bill's cheek, careful not to wake him, placed the note on his bedside table, then slipped out into the street, the loaded Smith & Wesson tucked away in her handbag. She made the journey by foot, dashing down the shadowed alleyways and dim avenues as fast as her trembling legs would carry her, flinching at every passing car, every sound. If he found her now—exposed and vulnerable—she was dead. She had to hurry.

She reached the boardinghouse minutes later. The scandalously ugly three-story hovel loomed out of the smog like the monster it was. God, she *hated* the place. Every brick, every windowpane and every miserable, bottom-feeding soul that existed within its walls.

Nevertheless, there were two very good reasons she'd spent the past several months here, enduring the atrocities of communal living. One—it was the only form of accommodation she'd been able to afford. And two—on account of the abominable riffraff the place attracted, the landlady—Mrs. T (a special breed herself)—had sensibly adopted a "no-questions-asked" policy. As long as you paid your rent and didn't piss in the hallways or bludgeon your roommates to death, you were welcome to stay as long as you could bear it. Which, in Darcy's case, was four months, five days and not a minute longer.

Tonight, she was leaving for good.

She opened the front door, padded silently across the musty hallway, up the creaking staircase. At the landing, she turned right, down a gray, glum corridor that reeked of cigarette smoke, mold and the general odor of misery.

"Blooming hell!" Darcy cursed as she opened her bedroom door, alarmed to see a pale face with bulging black eyes staring back at her like some sort of nasty insect.

"Oh, good," said Pearl, Darcy's roommate, a waiflike thing

who worked in a shoddy nightclub three evenings a week selling drinks (and, Darcy suspected, herself). She was standing in
the threshold in a pink satin nightdress, mascara caked to her
lashes and a pair of sewing scissors in her hand "It's just you."

"Who else would it be?" Darcy said with a snap. She nodded at the scissors. "And what are you doing with those? Put
them down before you skewer yourself."

Pearl lowered her weapon, stepped aside, allowing Darcy to
enter the tiny room, furnished with two single beds, a wash-
basin, a wardrobe and one writing desk.

"Where you been all night?" Pearl asked suspiciously.

"Picking flowers," Darcy said as she opened the wardrobe,
dragged out a large suitcase and began filling it with everything she owned (which amounted to three dresses, three pairs
of lace-up boots, two moth-eaten scarves, some unflattering
undergarments and a handful of tarnished jewelry).

Pearl eyed the suitcase with a scowl but couldn't seem to
put two and two together. "Don't lie to me, Darc. We're supposed to be friends, ain't we?"

Friends? Darcy tried not to scoff at this. Pearl was about the
furthest thing from a friend she could imagine. And besides,
the last real friend Darcy had made had betrayed her in the
worst possible way. She'd learned the hard way: friends were
just enemies in disguise.

"All right, well, let me just say this," Pearl went on, hands
on her bony hips. "I don't want no more of your fellas coming by here scaring the daylights outta me. It ain't right. This
is the first night I've been off in five days, and I want some
bloody sleep."

Darcy slammed her suitcase shut, looked up. She'd been
living with Pearl for sixteen excruciating weeks, but these last
few minutes might try her patience more than all the rest put
together. "What are you talking about? What fella?"

"The one who came by tonight. About an hour ago. Said he wanted to speak with you." She fidgeted nervously with her scissors while Darcy rubbed the yellow twine bracelet around her wrist. "Just barged in here like a madman screaming for you. He had a knife, too, and said he'd slit my throat if I made a peep. Lucky Mrs. T was out shopping, or he'd have sliced her to bits, I reckon."

Darcy swallowed. "What did he look like?"

Pearl looked up at the ceiling momentarily. "Tall, good-looking, scruffy hair. And he's come by before, you know. I recognized him."

Darcy felt a tremble start up in her hands. *Tall, good-looking, scruffy hair.* It had to be *him.* Just as she'd predicted, he'd found her.

She slipped two white tablets into her mouth and swallowed them dry.

"Point is, I've had enough," Pearl continued. "If he or anyone else comes back here ever again, threatening me like that, I'm going to tell Mrs. T and get you thrown out."

"What friends are for, eh?"

"I'm done covering for you," Pearl persisted, her feeble voice rising. "And I'm done being dragged into your mess." She paused a long beat. "I saw you the other night, you know, with that…that *thing.*"

Darcy dragged her suitcase toward the door, the handle slipping in her sweaty grip.

"Now I know it ain't none of my business—"

"You're right," Darcy snapped, without stopping. "It ain't. So go back to sleep and keep your mouth shut, you hear me?"

"I'm just saying, I don't like all this seedy business happening on my doorstep." Pearl followed Darcy into the corridor, nightdress flapping. "Oi, where you off to now? Mrs. T wants to see you when she wakes up. She made me promise to keep an eye on you. Oi, Darcy! When you coming back?"

Without turning, Darcy raised a hand and fluttered her gloved fingers in farewell. The only way she was ever coming back to this hovel was as a ghost, to haunt the living daylights out of Pearl, and all the rest of them.

She marched down the stairs and out the front door, feeling the weight of past mistakes lift from her shoulders. She knew it was fleeting, that she'd never truly be free, but it was a damn lot better to suffer among strangers, where no one knew her story. Feeling lighter with every step, she strutted down the street, her suitcase bobbing reassuringly at her hip, her handbag slung loosely over her shoulder.

She hadn't got farther than ten yards when a hand was pressed over her mouth and a blade to her throat.

She dropped her suitcase, but kept the handbag tight against her shoulder.

"Well, well," a suave voice whispered in her ear, one she recognized immediately. "If it ain't my darling Darcy Gibson. I was hoping I'd catch you before you left." He moved closer, his hips pressing into her buttocks, sending a nauseating chill up her spine.

She tried to open her mouth, but the scent of cologne on his wrist, so familiar, made her gag instead. It was no good screaming, mind, since her best mate Pearl would happily watch her being cut into ribbons.

"You certainly are a difficult little fox to catch," he drawled on, his breath now wet in her ear.

"Let me go," she hissed through his fingers, her spit mingling with his rancid sweat, making her gag a second time. She squirmed, wriggled and cursed, and eventually he released her and spun her around to face him.

Alan Biggar was dressed in a black suit, sleek and clean.

His full dark hair flowed to his shoulders in glossy curls that gave him a deceptively chivalric appearance.

"What?" he said, grinning. "You're not interested in hearing why I've been tracking you down?"

Darcy took a step back. "Stay away from me!"

He raised his hands in surrender. "Oh, I intend to. Just as soon as you answer a question or two about my poor old bruv's last minutes on earth." He sighed theatrically. "You were there, weren't you?"

She drew a shallow breath. Was it worth lying, saying no? With Oscar, a lie like that might've worked but unlike his brother, Alan was sly, even-tempered and nearly impossible to deceive. *Nearly*.

"Yes," she mumbled.

"So?" He smiled again, the smile that had once charmed her, though now only made her sick. "Who killed the dirty scumbag, then? Do tell."

"I don't... I just—"

"Now careful, careful," he interrupted. "Because if you're about to say you have no idea—you saw nothing, heard nothing—well then, I won't have much reason to keep you alive. Will I?" He wiped the knife's blade on his shirtsleeve, then twirled it in his hand threateningly.

Darcy bit back the rage clawing up her throat, triggered by the sight of him. It was so long ago now, but still her body throbbed in all the places he'd hit her, day after day, year after year. But she had to keep her cool, she had to play her cards right. It was a game of life or death, like always.

"Fine. I'll tell you what I saw." A streetlight above them winked, as though listening in. "But not like this. If you want me to talk, you put that knife down."

Alan faltered, but as the silence dragged on and Darcy

held her ground, he relented. He lowered the knife, slipped it under his belt.

"You and I were supposed to be at that market together," Darcy explained. "Oscar told me you were sent a raven, same as I was. Then a note, a fake note, luring us there. Yours was supposed to be from your wife, mine from my fella. I escaped, but Oscar wasn't so lucky." A muscle in Alan's jaw began to twitch. "Thing is, it wasn't Oscar they wanted. It was *you*. You *and* me."

A dog barked at the end of the street. Someone called out.

Alan's eyes surveyed the street, then settled back on Darcy. "You know who this person is, then? The person who wants us dead?"

Darcy's mouth was so dry now she could hardly get the words out. She rolled her tongue over her teeth. The answer, of course, was yes. But she knew Alan well enough to know that if she told him now, she'd be of no use to him anymore and he'd ram that knife right through her chest. If she didn't tell him, same outcome.

So, instead, she said, "Nah. I don't know who they are, but I know how to find them."

THE VANISHING

THE FOLLOWING MORNING, A MONDAY, MARION found a seat in the library bar, usually one of her favorite rooms at the agency, with its low-hanging ceiling, cozy wooden furnishings and puttering candles. But now a record played mournfully from a hidden corner, filling the space with a strange disquiet. Or perhaps the disquiet was just in her head.

She massaged her temples, staring blankly at the bar's only other occupant, Lance Zimmerman—the enigmatic head of *Der Schatten*—who was hunched over a plate of breakfast, several cups of tea and his savage mechanical spider. Zimmerman let out a guttural moan as the spider suddenly and unexpectedly wriggled to life and jabbed its master in the arm with one of its many daggerlike legs. He sucked on the wound and grumbled something in German while giving Marion a scowl, as though the gadget's outburst was her fault.

"You should check the auxiliary burner," she said, nodding

at the spider's thorax. "Might have turned itself on by mistake. Ours do that sometimes."

Unsurprisingly, he said nothing.

Either Zimmerman didn't understand a word of English, or he was a mute because—as far as she knew—he hadn't uttered a single word to anyone since his arrival. She assumed his reticence didn't extend to Nancy or the members of the High Council, but it certainly did to everyone else at the agency. The same went for the rest of *Der Schatten*, with whom several of *Miss Brickett's* employees had tried to converse on Friday night to no avail. Except Jessica, apparently, who was seen chatting amicably with that dark-haired gentleman Maud had introduced her to (chatting amicably and then disappearing into one of Gadgetry's many concealed rooms).

Zimmerman slammed the spider onto the table where it squirmed and flailed until he unscrewed its head from his body and drew out a tiny battery pack. Then, tentatively, he picked up the spider by its tail, sans battery pack, got to his feet and left the bar without so much as a wave.

Marion would've loved to distract herself further by mulling over Zimmerman's odd behavior and what really went on at *Der Schatten*. Unfortunately, she had a more pressing concern currently occupying her thoughts: Darcy.

She ordered a cup of coffee from Harry—the agency's head cook and barman—who, come to think of it, would've fitted in perfectly well at *Der Schatten*, since he seldom spoke or smiled but loved to eavesdrop. She slid a stack of grubby coins across the table toward him.

"Black, please. And one sugar. What?" she asked when he failed to hand over the cup. "The price gone up again or something?"

He grunted, shoved the loot into his pocket and lumbered

off, forcing her to clamber over the counter and fetch the freshly brewed cup herself.

She returned to her table, swallowed a mouthful of bitter, grainy coffee, then another and another. Eventually, the caffeine began to clear a path through the tangle of thoughts that had been plaguing her since last night. She unfolded the copy of The Daily Telegraph she'd brought with her and paged through until she found the article on Oscar Biggar.

She pulled out five more national and regional newspapers from her bag and meticulously pored over each, searching for further mention of the incident. And while the papers contained varying degrees of speculation on the nature of Biggar's demise, the conclusion was always the same.

"*'Cause of death yet to be determined,'*" she repeated to herself, drumming her fingers on the table with a growing sense of unease. "And he was a philanthropist?"

Was there more to the story of Oscar's death at Petticoat Lane market than Darcy had led Marion and Bill to believe? Marion was almost certain the answer was yes and yet she didn't understand why. Why would Darcy be reluctant to reveal the truth? What was she hiding?

The grandfather clock in the adjoining library tolled loudly, striking eight. She pushed her (now empty) cup of coffee aside, pulled a hefty suitcase in front of her. The agency's general Monday meeting would be taking place in the auditorium in just over an hour, where she hoped to catch up with Bill and formulate a plan for later that afternoon. Bill was obviously dead set on trawling the streets in search of Darcy's stalker (and, potentially, Oscar Biggar's killer). Marion, less so. Wouldn't it be more sensible to pass the matter on to Frank? Nancy? The police? Or even someone like Kenny, who at least had some experience in the field?

She sighed, staring down at the suitcase she'd brought along from Gadgetry. There was a minuscule chance she'd be able to convince Bill they needed outside help, but in the likely event that didn't work, she decided it was best to be prepared for a full-scale investigation.

The first contraption she laid out on the table was one of the agency's finest tools—a beautiful brass Vagor compass, capable of tracking a subject fitted with a paired Vagor stone. Of course, the compass wouldn't be of much use until they identified and located the tail. And to do that, they would need Darcy's help.

It was a huge risk to take—and Bill wasn't going to like it—but using Darcy to draw out the stalker was really their only hope. Thus, Marion and Bill would require the pair of night coats she had stashed in her suitcase—special silk garments that worked as camouflage under poor light, especially at night. Lastly, assuming Darcy's tail revealed themselves and Marion and Bill were able to fit the target with a Vagor stone, they'd then need a further set of tools to infiltrate the target's home, bug the telephones and collect evidence. For this, Marion had grabbed a lockpick, a light orb, a handful of wiretaps and several other contraptions designed for the task.

"And you, of course," she added, touching her wrist and the Spinner Knife Frank had given her. "Just in case."

She stared at the gadgets, her mind working through plans and pitfalls and possible entrapments. But if Darcy's tail really *was* a cold-blooded killer, then perhaps they'd need to arm themselves with more than one Spinner Knife.

She looked up to see Kenny sauntering across the bar, carrying a stack of case files, trailed by Jessica and Maud, both of whom were carrying their breakfast trays, layered with bacon, kippers and something else that made Marion's stomach growl in protest.

Before she'd had the chance to stop him (not that she

would've), Kenny lifted her to her feet, dipped her backward and planted a kiss on her lips.

"Well," she said, regaining her breath and momentarily forgetting whatever it was she'd been so worried about just seconds ago. "Good morning to you, too."

Unintentionally, she caught a glimpse of herself in the mirror hanging over the bar counter and cringed inwardly. How Kenny found her desirable in this state was frankly baffling. She'd hardly slept a wink last night and as a result, her hair was frizzed (more than usual) and sticking up in all the wrong places. Her eyes were puffy and dull, her lips cracked and pale, and she wasn't wearing a lick of makeup. Also, as usual, there was grease under her fingernails.

Kenny, on the other hand—despite having just come off a six-hour night duty stint—looked as though he'd spent several hours preening himself to a high shine. It was possible he *had* been preening himself, instead of working, but either way...

He pushed a lock of hair behind her ear and beamed.

"This new?" he asked, touching her creased beige blouse that was anything but new. Two and a half years of apprenticeship wages did not leave much money for clothes. Not a penny, in fact. "Looks good on you."

She tried to smooth it out, then gave up and tucked her grease-stained hands behind her back. "Thanks. I wore it on Wednesday, though. And at dinner on Thursday, I think."

He leaned in and whispered in her ear. "You weren't wearing anything at dinner on Thursday."

"Oh. My. God," Maud said, rolling her eyes heavenward. "I think I'm going to be sick."

"That'll be the kippers," Jessica retorted, settling opposite Maud so that she was directly facing Marion and Kenny. "Please, as you were," she added with voyeuristic thrill, winking at Marion. "Don't mind us."

"You really do need to find yourself a fella," Maud insisted, slicing into her kipper. "Pronto."

Jessica gave her a one shoulder shrug. "Anyone in mind?"

"What about the German?"

"I'm not interested in long distance, darling. So no."

"All right. Then Don from Intelligence? Heard he's looking for a summer fling."

"He's fifty-two!"

"Yeah, and you're desperate."

Jessica fixed her with a withering glare, then turned back to Kenny just as he produced a…well, a *something* from behind his back.

"Made this for you," he said to Marion, holding it out in front of her.

Marion squinted at the brass stick—about three inches long—embellished on one end with a ball of reddish metal the size of a grape. "Oh, thanks. What, um, what is it, exactly?"

"Pull the latch down," he said, smiling slightly nervously. "There, just under the head."

Marion found said latch and pulled gently downward. There was a grinding noise, and a leaf-shaped extension popped out from the center of the ball of reddish metal. She still had no idea what it was supposed to be.

"Ah…um." His brow furrowed. "Maybe just, just try again. Little harder."

"The latch?"

He groaned, took it from her, fiddled with the latch. It clinked, and something oval-shaped dropped to the floor. "Dammit!" He picked *the something* up, screwed it back in place. "Hold on. Here we go." Several attempts later, what could perhaps (very generously) be described as a metal rose popped out from the end of the brass stick. Kenny sighed, handed it back to Marion.

"Oh! Oh. Gosh, it's lovely," Marion said, caressing the jagged petals and almost slicing open her thumb in the process. "Thank you."

"You like it, really?"

She nodded enthusiastically, ignoring Maud's chuckling and Jessica's aww-ing.

"I was set on going for a real rose but that's so *normal* and you're definitely not normal. I don't mean you're... I just mean you're, ah, *special*. Anyway—" he drew a deep breath, rubbed the back of his neck "—join me for breakfast?"

Marion really, *really* wanted to say yes. In fact, she almost did. Then she glanced down at her suitcase and remembered: Darcy. Bill. Oscar. Tracking. Murder investigation. "Sorry, I can't. Not today. Tomorrow, maybe?"

He pushed his hands into his pockets. "Can't do tomorrow. I'm off to Manchester later. Got a case lead I need to follow up on."

"When will you be back?"

"Probably tomorrow. Depends how easy the lead is to follow." He swept in for another heart-rattling kiss, causing Maud to whistle and Marion to go flush in the cheeks.

After Kenny, Maud and Jessica left the library bar, Bill burst through the door, carrying nothing but a crumpled note and his house keys.

"We've got a problem," he said, lowering his voice so that the hum of the gramophone—now playing Sinatra's *"Come Fly With Me"*—nearly drowned him out.

Marion stood, gathered her suitcase (Kenny's metallic rose tucked safely inside), took a breath. She couldn't bear the thought of *another* complication, considering she had one to add to the list herself. Best she get hers in first.

"Yes, we do," she said quickly. "Look, I don't know how to

say this without sounding offensive, but I think Darcy's lying to us. I think she knows more about Oscar Biggar's death than she's letting on. There were two things I noticed last night when I was going through the newspapers. One, Darcy said Oscar was a drug dealer but the papers call him a philanthropist. And sure, that's not a big deal on its own but the other thing I realized—"

"Darcy's gone."

Sinatra had stopped turning in the gramophone, and Harry the barman paused halfway through polishing the glass he was holding. Marion nodded to the exit, then led the way out into the adjoining library. This was definitely *not* a conversation that should be overheard.

"What do you mean she's gone?"

Bill didn't bother repeating himself. "Some time in the night. Or early this morning." He ran a hand over his face, his skin turning from pallid to blotchy red. "I didn't hear a thing, but I'm a deep sleeper so I suppose it's not surprising." He presented her with the crumpled piece of paper he'd been turning over in his hand and which was now almost unreadable. "This was the only thing she left behind."

Bill,
I've made a lot of mistakes in my life but bringing you into my mess is one of the worst. I'm sorry. I'll fix everything. Just give me a chance.
Please don't come looking for me. I'll meet you back here soon as I can and explain everything. Trust me. Please.
Darc

Marion could hardly stand the look on Bill's face, which was somewhere between utter devastation and complete confusion. It made her sick to imagine what he must be feeling, but she found no words to console him.

"I've already been to the boardinghouse she was living at," he added. "The landlady said she hadn't seen Darc all week. She took me to her room, though, and all her things were packed up, gone. Everything."

"Which means she's not planning on coming back."

Bill tapped his finger and thumb together, which made Marion regret pointing that out, even though it was stating the obvious.

"Not to the boardinghouse, yeah," Bill said. "But it's more complicated than that. The landlady also told me a man came by last night looking for Darc. He had a knife and threatened her roommate. Apparently, he was someone the roommate's seen before, though no one could give me a name." He paused, as though deciding something, then looked at the suitcase in Marion's hand. "You got a tracking compass in there?"

"Yes."

"And a lock pick?"

"Yes, but—"

"Then let's get going. She couldn't have left my place more than five hours ago, and I think she went straight from there to the boardinghouse to pack up her things. So, we've just got to figure out where she might've gone after that."

"Well, I don't know," Marion said. "You really think this is a good idea? She *did* say not to look for her." Once again, she felt that strange disquiet descend like a storm cloud. Something very bad was lingering just out of sight, and she got the feeling they were heading straight for it.

"She's in trouble, Mari. I can't just sit around and not do anything. Even if that's what she wants. I'd never forgive myself if something happened to her."

"I understand that but just...*wait*." She grabbed his wrist, yanked him backward. "There's something else." She knelt, opened her suitcase on the floor and pulled out a copy of *The Daily Telegraph*. "Have you read this yet? About Oscar Biggar's death at Petticoat Lane?" He grunted impatiently in reply, but she went on regardless. "Darcy told us Oscar was strangled. But, thing is, all the papers say the cause of his death is still being investigated. Even the police don't know how he died. So, how does Darcy?"

"I don't know," he snapped. "I'll ask her when I find her."

"Bill, come on." She stared him down, one eyebrow arched. "If Darcy's telling the truth about Oscar and his factory that was really a front for a drug trafficking operation, then there's far more going on here than either of us are prepared for. We can't go after her, at least not on our own. It's too dangerous and too complicated. If you really want to do this, I'll help you, of course I will. But only after we talk to Frank. And Kenny."

"No. We promised her we'd keep it between the three of us."

"Yes, but that was before—"

"I'm going after her. With or without you."

"Bill! Come on—" She stopped midsentence, interrupted by a group of senior Inquirers who'd just burst into the library, dark coats billowing behind them as they marched swiftly across the marble floor, weaving between the towering bookshelves in perfect single file.

"You're certain it was meant for us?" the Inquirer at the lead said to another, several steps behind her. Both looked wary, afraid even.

"*One* of us, yes."

"Is it dead?"

The second Inquirer nodded solemnly as they swept past. "*Very* dead."

"What on earth was that about?" Marion asked, turning back to Bill, only to find herself alone among the bookshelves.

THE SEER

MARION FALTERED FOR A MOMENT, CAUGHT between her duty to sprint after Bill and her urge to follow the Inquirers down to the Filing Department. The decision was made for her though, when she spotted several members of the cleaning staff (including Delia Spragg—an ex-High Council Member, recently demoted) lumber up the staircase, a bucket and two bloodstained mops between them.

Marion raced down the staircase, through the arched doorway. A line of chattering apprentices, staff members and Inquirers were crowded in front of the wall that housed the agency's post collecting devices, known as receiver boxes— termini of the intricate web of pneumatic tubes that delivered letters and tip-offs from the citizens of London via a hundred-and-something letter cases scattered throughout the city.

Marion shouldered her way through the onlookers, pausing as she came to the front, where the air smelled of bleach and the floor glistened with a layer of moisture.

"Sick bastard…" mumbled someone to her left, pointing to the only open receiver box, number ninety-three, on which lay a curiously shaped mound, tangled in a bloodied reel of string.

"What *is* that?" she asked, holding a hand over her mouth.

"*Was*, you mean," answered someone behind her.

"The sickest jack-in-a-box I've ever seen," someone else added. "Apparently it exploded when it was opened, sending blood and feathers everywhere. Can you imagine that, first thing in the morning? We're not paid enough, honestly."

Blood and feathers. Marion craned her neck, held her breath, the floor shifting beneath her feet, a queasy feeling already clawing up her throat.

"Move aside, please!" called a stern voice from the back of the department. "Come on, move aside. Out the way, out the way." The onlookers parted swiftly, allowing Nancy Brickett to the front, trailed closely by a rotund and contemptuous looking figure with thinning blond hair and pinprick eyes, whose gaze seemed to be everywhere all at once—Rupert Nicholas, the agency's rather incompetent head of security.

Mr. Nicholas, as usual drawing great pleasure from his nebulous position of authority, ushered the rubberneckers aside while Nancy whipped a penlight and pair of tweezers from the breast pocket of her slim all-gray trouser suit. Coolly, and without any expression on her face, she leaned over the open receiver box and extricated a feathery corpse from a mass of twine.

Yellow twine, Marion noted with a flash of recognition. Could it be a coincidence? It *had* to be a coincidence.

"When did this come through, exactly?" Nancy asked, directing her question at no one in particular.

"One hour ago," an Inquirer near the front answered readily.

"I see."

Nicholas, despite himself, was now as intrigued as the rest of them. "Frightful! Who would do such a thing?" He shuffled closer to Nancy, head tilted, small eyes narrowed. "But, eh, I can't seem to make out what…what it is, exactly?"

Nancy held the corpse at eye level, directly under the beam of her penlight, illuminating gristly feathers, streaks of crimson, claws, a mangled beak. "A bird of some sort, I believe."

"A raven," Marion murmured, mostly to herself. "It's a raven."

It took Marion over an hour to reach Bill's home in Blackwall. She'd hoped to find him here, waiting for Darcy, everyone fine. But the front door was locked and the ground floor curtains drawn. The lights were off. No signs of life. No Bill. No Darcy. She crouched, examined the lock. Indistinct scuff marks encircled the keyhole, and tiny flecks of paint lay on the pavement directly underneath. Sure signs that someone had tried to pick the lock. And recently.

She rapped against the door and called to the bedroom window, two levels up.

"Bill! It's me. Something's happened at Filing. I'm trying to understand but…we need to talk. Quickly. Open up. Please."

Nothing.

She surveyed the street—a wide, double-lane road lined with rubbish bins and thick with the stench of the nearby docks—fish, saltwater, sewage. She knocked again, but when no answer came, she curled around the side of the building where she found a single greasy, uncurtained window. She cupped her hands around her face and pressed her nose to the glass. Beyond was a small entrance hall cramped with a hatstand, stacks of boxes and one wilted fern in a stone pot. At the far end of the entrance hall was a short stairwell with a chipped banister and a grubby fitted carpet that led to the second floor and Bill's part of the building—a small bedsit with a window that looked down onto the street (and now, she noticed, stood ajar).

She paced in front of the building, limbs tingling with impatience and indecision. She *could* pick the lock on the building's front entrance, easily, but then she'd have to pick the lock on Bill's bedsit door as well. That would take time. Ten minutes, maybe fifteen. She looked at her watch, realizing it was now nearly two hours since Bill had left the library alone. She *had* to hurry.

So, instead, she knelt on the pavement, opened her suitcase and drew out a long chrome-colored tube that appeared to be a telescope: The Seer. Recalling the instruction she'd had in second-year classes on how to operate the gadget, she unscrewed the telescope's "seeing end," then pulled down hard, drawing out a foot-long, malleable extension. Next, she placed The Seer against the wall, pressed the latch on the control panel. The scope shivered to life. Tiny metallic legs, like those of a centipede, sprung up from inside the tubing and gripped the wall. With another turn of the lever, the peculiar contraption began to crawl upward, one segment at a time, growing in length as it went. Using the guiding wheel, Marion ushered the gadget through the crack in Bill's window. She pressed her eyes to the scope's looking glass and adjusted the focus.

The Seer slithered around the settee, over the threadbare carpet. Marion worked the guiding wheel left and right, eyes still fixed to the looking glass, surveying every inch of the cramped bedsit. Two cooking pots stood on the stovetop in the kitchen. Several dirty dishes were piled in the sink. The bedsheets were unmade, lying on the mattress in knots. Nothing was broken or appeared out of place. There were no intruders. This, at least, was a relief.

She removed The Seer from her eye, drew a long breath,

pulled the latch toward her and guided the gadget back through the window, down the wall and into her arms.

If Bill wasn't home, it could only mean he was still out there looking for Darcy. But where had he gone? Back to the boardinghouse? Somewhere else? Or had he run into Darcy's stalker on the way and...

She worked the handle of her suitcase nervously, stared blankly at the bedsit window, dark thoughts flittering across her mind, the image of the raven in the receiver box, so familiar it made her sick.

Just a coincidence, she tried to tell herself for the umpteenth time. It *had* to be.

A strange sound, like wings drumming, rang in her ears, part of the memory or...

She looked up, squinting against the midmorning sun. Something was dancing across the mottled sky, moving rhythmically through the rooftops, silent save for a curious, mechanical flapping sound.

It glinted, reflecting the sun, fluttering closer and closer, lower and lower, until it was right above her head.

The Distracter beat its glittering metallic wings as it hovered just out of reach. One mechanical vertebrae at a time, it curled its neck into a perfect arch and peered down at her with black, unseeing eyes.

"What are *you* doing here?" she asked, rising onto her toes. She lengthened her spine, stretched her fingers, reaching for the bird's tail feathers. But just as she attempted to yank it down toward her, it beat its wings harder, ripping itself from her grip, soaring upward and across the street.

She watched it go, bewildered. Distracters were brilliant specimens of engineering, but they could not fly around of their own accord. Someone had to be operating it with a remote control—and from no farther than several hundred yards away.

She looked back over her shoulder at Bill's bedsit. Something tickled the nape of her neck. No one else was nearby, not even a passing pedestrian. The curtains at Bill's window fluttered outward in a breeze. The window slammed shut.

She flinched, looked back up at the Distracter, which was now just a shimmering speck in the distant sky. She picked up her suitcase and, with nothing else to go on, followed the sunbird across the street.

Several yards onward, the Distracter paused midflight at the entrance to a large and tired looking block of flats. It circled aimlessly above her head, the beat of its wings slowing steadily. A grating, whirling sound rose from somewhere within its tiny battery-powered heart, and a drip of oil leaked from its beak as it began to die. She caught it just before it crashed, pitifully, to the ground.

"Gotcha, little fella!" She tucked the bird's wings neatly against its body before the sharp edges could slice through her flesh (it had happened before). "All right, now spill," she said, staring up at the large chipped wooden door in front of her. "Who's been operating you?" The bird's eyes closed with a slow, sad click. She sighed, looked again at the door to the block of flats. "You drew me here, so I suppose…"

She wrapped the Distracter in a handkerchief, stowed it in her suitcase and pushed through the door and into a narrow entranceway. Before she had a chance to wonder where she was, another door clicked open from somewhere above. She peered up at the spiraling metal staircase to see Bill leaning dangerously over the balustrade from the fourth floor.

"Dammit, Bill!" she panted, upon reaching his side. "What's going on? What are you doing here? I was worried sick."

Footsteps sounded from the entrance hall below.

Bill pressed a finger to his lips, then guided Marion down a short, ill-lit corridor, left down another and finally into a cramped one-bedroom flat that overlooked the street, much like his own bedsit. He locked and bolted the door behind him, took a breath.

Marion drew out the lifeless Distracter, placed it on the coffee table. "This was you, I presume?"

He nodded. "Sorry for the theatrics, but I needed a way to get your attention, and I couldn't risk coming out to get you."

She peeled off her sweater, rolled up her blouse sleeves. "Someone broke into your flat, didn't they? I saw the scuff marks on the lock."

He gestured to a threadbare couch near the window and settled down. "I'm not sure if they actually got inside, though. It was like that when I got there. Either way, I reckoned waiting here for Darc was a better option."

"Any idea who it was?"

"The person after Darc, I'd guess. If they've been doing a good job of tailing her, they'd know she stayed there last night."

Marion nodded, set herself down next to Bill. The couch springs groaned under their combined weight, and a plume of fine dust lifted into the stuffy air.

"Did anyone follow you here?" he asked, twisting his hands together, eyeing the Distracter on the coffee table.

"No, of course not. I was careful." She glanced around the flat, with its single bed, simple kitchenette and dusty, grimy living room furniture that looked as though it hadn't been cleaned in months. "Whose place is this anyway? And how did you get in?"

"My neighbor's. He's away for the week. Left me with the key so I could feed Hattie, which is a lucky coincidence I guess." He nodded at a wingback chair near the door and the purring lump of ginger fur curled up on top. "I thought it was better to wait here, since I have a good view of my flat and the bus stop Darc usually gets off at."

"Right, yes," Marion said uncertainly. "And I'm guessing you haven't heard from her again?"

He shook his head, ran his hands up and down his thighs. "I telephoned the boardinghouse. *Again*. But no one's seen her. Or at least they're not willing to tell me if they have. I hate waiting around like this, but I don't know what else to do. Something really bad's happened, Mari. I just know it."

Marion felt the cool turn of dread in her stomach. Yes, maybe something bad *had* happened, worse even than Bill could imagine.

She got up and started pacing the room. She closed her eyes and allowed her mind to do what she'd resisted for nearly a decade, to take her back to the weeks that changed her life forever, the weeks that had led to the death of her beloved mother, Alice. It was a story she'd only half told Bill, and few others, not because she'd wanted to keep any of it a secret, but because she'd wanted to forget and put the whole thing behind her for good. And, up until this morning, she was rather certain she had.

But now, as though it were happening all over again, she saw the look of terror on her mother's face as she picked up the stained paper package lying outside their front door nine years ago, tangled in bloodied yellow twine and knotted feathers. She heard her mother's breath quicken, saw her hands shake so violently that she dropped the package to the floor, where it landed with an awful wet thud.

"What is it?" Bill asked, drawing meaning from her silence.

She put a hand on the windowsill, feeling the need to steady herself. "You left the agency this morning, just before I saw it.

Something was sent to us, to *me*, I think, through a receiver box at the Filing Department. A dead raven."

"A *what*?"

"I don't know. Maybe I'm wrong. Maybe it wasn't for me. I guess… I guess it could've been a coincidence." She paused, shook her head. "Actually, no. It can't be."

Bill leaned forward, his posture stiff. "I don't understand. A dead raven was delivered to the agency. And…you think it was meant for *you*?"

"The yellow twine," she said breathlessly. "It was the same, I know it was. And the raven, of course. Oh, God. I can't believe this is happening again."

Bill raised his hands as though she were pointing a gun at him. "Okay, hold on. Just slow down, Mari, you're not making any sense. What is happening again? What yellow twine?"

She nodded, drew a long breath in through her nose, then exhaled the air slowly through her mouth, repeating the pattern until her pulse had slowed and the dizziness diminished.

"I told you my mother committed suicide when I was sixteen," she said, "but I never really told you why."

Bill nodded, clearly as confused as ever.

"We were living together at Willow Street, as you know, and in the weeks before her death, something odd started to happen. Mother had just been fired from her job at the textile factory, which of course meant that soon enough we'd have no money, no food, no way to pay the rent or utilities. I tried to convince her we'd be all right. She could find other work and if necessary, I could leave school and get a job myself. There was more to it, though, something else that was bothering her. She was tense and agitated, worse than I'd ever seen before. She'd sit by the kitchen window all day on her rocking chair, staring at the street outside through a gap in the curtains, as though she was expecting someone. Every time the doorbell rang, she'd scream at me not to open it. She'd pull the curtains closed, turn off the lights and keep quiet until the visitor, whoever they were, gave up and left."

Bill turned to look at the door, then the flat keys dangling from his fingers. If he wasn't terrified now, he would be soon.

"I kept asking mother what was wrong," Marion said. "But she only fobbed me off. And when she did speak, it was hard to make any sense of what she was saying. I can't recall what she mumbled all the time, something about selling the house, moving, leaving London, running away. Someone was 'coming for her' she said, and then, one day, I came home from school and found..." She trailed off, turned to Bill, suspecting he might already know. "Something on our doorstep, wrapped in yellow twine."

The faint blush in Bill's cheeks drained to white. "A raven?"

"It shocked me, of course, and I thought it strange, but that was that. You know our part of London well enough. The East End is always filled with grime and death. I presumed the bird was just some local kid playing a prank, or maybe it was something more serious but delivered to the wrong house. I didn't even tell mother, mostly because I thought it would upset her and she clearly didn't need any more upsetting."

The ginger cat, which had been sleeping soundly until then, lifted its head, stretched, leapt off the chair and stalked across the room, hair raised along its spine. Upon spotting the Distracter perched on the coffee table, it froze, hissed and backed away.

"But, soon enough, it happened again," Marion continued. "I went out for an evening walk and when I came back, there was another one on our front door, wrapped in yellow twine, just the same as the first." She paused then, remembering the day, no longer living at the back of her memory but vivid and clear as though it'd happened only hours ago. Stomach acid rose in her throat, searing.

"Every week from then on it happened again, over and over. Sometimes even twice a week. I was always the one to collect the ravens, always the one who had to get rid of them. Mother was a mess. She wouldn't tell me what was going on, except to say that the ravens were a threat from someone she knew, someone she had 'done wrong.' I asked why she thought so, and who this *someone* was, but instead of answering, she pointed to the yellow twine bracelet on her wrist and—"

"Yellow twine," Bill repeated, furrows deepening on his forehead.

Marion nodded quickly. "Yes. The very same stuff the ravens were entangled with—" She broke off, hopeful they'd spark a connection in Bill's mind, as they'd done in hers that morning. But he said nothing, forcing her to continue. "From then on, mother insisted I lock myself up in my bedroom, keep the curtains drawn and not leave the house for anything. Not for school. Not to go to the shops or to see my friends. She even made me promise never to use the telephone. I did as she asked, though I was growing more terrified and confused every day. I felt so alone. Even though, of course, I wasn't."

"What about the police? She didn't want to involve them?"

"No. And I didn't ask why. She wouldn't tell me anything anyway." She took another measured breath, though it sounded more like a hitching sigh. "One night, a few weeks after the last raven had been dropped off, the doorbell rang. This time, though, mother rushed to answer it. I waited in my room, listening. I couldn't make out what was being said, but it sounded like an argument that went on and on for ages."

"But you didn't see who she was talking to?"

"It was a man, that much I'm certain of. And I think mother knew him."

She watched as Bill turned his gaze to the middle distance, trying to put together the pieces of the puzzle.

"That was the end," she said. "After that night, everything ended. We never had another raven delivered."

"Alice never told you anything else? Like who had visited, or who had sent the ravens?"

She shook her head.

"And why a raven? I guess she didn't tell you that either."

"No. Never."

Bill thought for a moment. "But it was him, right? The man who came to your house was the man who'd been sending the ravens. Must have been. Which probably means he got what he wanted in the end, and so the threats, the ravens, stopped."

Marion shrugged. "It's the best theory I've got. But whatever my mother had to do or say to make the threats stop… it killed her. I thought, *hoped*, things would go back to normal after the last raven was delivered. I was wrong. Actually, I think mother was worse, more agitated and unsettled *after* the ravens stopped coming. She couldn't sleep. Didn't want to eat. Then, one month later, as you know, she killed herself."

Bill came to her side. With his hands in his pockets, he followed her gaze out through the window, to the sky, which had blackened with a coming storm. It wasn't long before a gale whipped up from nowhere, and brought with it a pelting rain.

"I'm so sorry, Mari," he said gently, turning to her. "I can't imagine anything so horrible. But… I still don't understand. You think the raven sent to the agency this morning is connected to the ones sent to your mother all those years ago. Maybe, okay, but how does Darc fit in with all this?"

"You don't remember? The bracelet made of yellow twine?"

Bill cocked his head, pupils narrowed. Then it hit him. "Your mum had one," he blurted, raising a hand to his forehead. "And Darc has one too!"

"I saw her wearing it when we met at the Mayflower on Friday," Marion said, nodding. "It caught my attention, but I couldn't pinpoint why at the time, not until I saw the raven in the receiver box this morning. It can't be a coincidence, Bill. The more I think about it, the more certain I am: Darcy and my mother are connected in some way to whoever sent those ravens."

Bill was silent for a beat. "But if that's the case, then so are you."

THE VISITOR

MARION STOOD AT THE WINDOW WHILE BILL paced frantically behind her, muttering to himself—*"Can't be, no way, she wouldn't lie."* It was now obvious to Marion that if Darcy and Alice had known each other, then the odds that Darcy had met Bill at the pictures by chance were minuscule. Had it been a setup on Darcy's part? And if so, why? She considered asking this question out loud, but was Bill ready to answer it?

The rain had stopped, though the sky remained gray and threatening. A knot of young men dressed in shabby suits and tartan caps were lingering on the pavement outside, chattering, occasionally peering up at the block of flats, as though waiting for someone. Farther off, closer to the bus stop, a beige Morris Minor was parked on the side of the road, one wheel propped up on the pavement, engine running. A man was sitting in the driver's seat, his face obscured behind the sun visor.

It was early afternoon, many hours since Marion had reunited with Bill and many hours since the raven had been delivered to *Miss Brickett's*. Still, there was no sign of Darcy. Which meant...what? She was gone for good? In hiding? Kidnapped? Dead?

"That's it," Bill said abruptly, coming to Marion's side. "I can't just wait around anymore. I have to do something. If Darc was coming back, she'd be here by now. I have to find her."

Marion kept her eyes fixed on the Morris as she answered. Truthfully, the last thing she wanted to do now was leave the flat and dash through the city on a wild-goose chase. But Bill was right. There wasn't much point sitting around any longer, and if she wanted to understand the connection between her mother, Darcy and the ravens, this was her only lead. The reality was—even though she'd tried for so long to forget— she wanted answers. No, she *needed* answers. Now, with the memory of her mother's final days exhumed, she knew she'd never be able move on without knowing the truth, however painful it would turn out to be.

"All right," she said, steeling herself. "So, let's think. Where could Darcy have gone?"

"Not to the police, that's for sure," Bill said immediately. "And not to the boardinghouse."

"What about family? She has a sister nearby, doesn't she? Maybe she's waiting this out someplace safe."

Bill shook his head. "She has five sisters, but none of them are in London. Besides, if she wanted safety, she'd be with me."

Marion had the tact not to mention that Darcy had originally intended to keep Bill in the dark regarding her troubles, and had it not been for Marion, he still would be. But it had been the same with her mother who, despite the terror she'd faced in those final weeks of her life, had been reluctant to involve even her own daughter. Clearly, whoever wielded the ominous yellow twine had a hold over their victims that was far stronger than she or Bill could imagine.

"I'm not sure it's quite as simple as that," she answered vaguely.

Bill ignored her, followed her gaze through the window to the Morris parked on the pavement. "Who is that?"

The man in the driver's seat, as if hearing his name, pulled the visor farther down, making it impossible to see anything but his hands on the steering wheel.

"Don't know. But he's been there a while."

"What's a while?"

Marion looked at her watch. "Eight minutes maybe." She wiped the window with the back of her sleeve, clearing a circle through the gathering condensation. "And he's had the engine running the whole time." She shifted left, drew the curtains.

Bill followed her to the coffee table, picked up the Distracter, threw it in his bag along with his coat, a notebook and a mauve scarf that Marion presumed belonged to Darcy. He handed Marion her suitcase and sweater, speaking quickly as he hurried to gather the last of his things.

"The man who visited your mother at the end, The Raven—he's the key to all this." He lifted his head, looked at the curtained window. "If we find Darcy, we find him and if we find him, we get answers."

If only it were that simple. "I don't know who he is," she said. "If that's what you're going to ask. I never got to see his face."

Or had she? Nine years was a long time, long enough to scramble memories and muddy thoughts. Was it possible she'd actually seen more of The Raven—as Bill had now christened him—than she recalled? He'd been standing directly in front of her mother, just beyond the threshold. He was taller than her, at least by a head, which meant Marion must have seen some part of his face. But it was nighttime and, on account of Alice's paranoia, all the lights had been extinguished.

She screwed her eyes shut, picking through the flotsam and jetsam drifting across her mind. Had she seen his eyes? His nose? His hair? She was beginning to think she had.

She started.

A knock at the door.

The floorboards in the corridor creaked.

Quiet, Bill mouthed.

Hattie, the cat, crawled out from under the couch, crept across the room toward the window. She leapt onto the sill, rubbed herself against the glass, purring loudly, oblivious.

Another knock, louder.

Marion flicked off the safety catch on her Spinner Knife, shuffled to the door, ignoring Bill's protests. She peered through the peephole, surprised to see an elderly, bespectacled woman standing in the corridor.

"Keys," Marion said, holding out her hand.

Bill nudged her aside, peered through the hole. When satisfied the visitor was not a threat, he unlocked the door.

The woman glowered suspiciously at the pair of them. "Where's Weston?"

Bill smiled meekly, extended a hand. "I'm Bill, Weston's neighbor. And friend."

"Where is he?" she repeated, refusing his hand.

"On holiday. He gave me the keys. To feed Hattie."

On cue, the cat bounded from the window, darted across the room and wrapped itself around Bill's ankles.

The woman bent over, rubbed Hattie affectionately between the ears. "Hello, dear. Yes, is that nice?" The cat meowed longingly, but scampered back under the couch when the woman straightened and dusted the fur from her hands. Marginally appeased, she fixed Bill with a softer look.

"There's a man outside," she explained. "Friend of Weston's, I think. Said he wants to speak to 'number forty-five.'" She jabbed an arthritic finger at the chipped gold lettering in the center of the door: *45*.

"Did he give a name?" Marion asked, running a thumb over her Spinner Knife.

The woman shook her head. "Not sure I liked the look of him, to be honest. But he said it's 'about the girl.'"

Marion looked at Bill, who was already twitching with angst and rage. *"The Raven,"* he hissed.

Marion reached for his arm, tried to pull him back, but he was already through the door and halfway down the corridor.

"Wait!" She lurched after him, leaving the elderly lady bewildered and alone. "What are you doing! Bill! He could be armed."

No sooner had she said it than a figure, dressed all in black, burst into the entrance hall at the base of the stairwell.

Bill skidded to a halt on the landing.

Clang.

A bullet hit the balustrade, ricocheted into the wall at his feet.

Marion raced to Bill's side, grabbed his arm and pulled him back into the corridor, out of sight.

Footsteps thumped up the stairwell.

"Now what?" Marion snapped. "Is there another way out?"

"Not unless we jump out the window. Just stay behind me."

Marion tried to shove him out of the way. "How about *you* stay behind *me*?" But somehow, despite Bill's willow-thin frame, he was unmovable.

Thud-thud-thud.

Silence.

Marion held her breath. Bill was shaking with rage in front of her.

"What's going on?" the elderly woman asked, peeking her head around the bend in the corridor.

"Get inside the flat and lock the door," Marion said to her urgently. "Now!"

The woman nodded, turned, disappeared back down the corridor just as a young man from a neighboring flat appeared at his door, pale faced and trembling.

"I heard a gunshot," he croaked, glancing up and down the corridor.

"You want to hear another one?" The intruder appeared at the other end of the corridor, a revolver hanging loosely at his hip. He raised an eyebrow at the neighbor. "Well?"

The neighbor didn't hesitate, happy to mind his own business now that he'd seen the gun. He slammed the door, leaving Marion, Bill and the intruder alone in the corridor.

"Who are you?" Bill asked, shuffling forward.

"You can call me Alan, but never mind the pleasantries," he said coolly. He was tall and lean with a defined jawline, clear brown eyes and glossy dark hair down to his shoulders. With his free hand, he produced a cigarette from behind his ear, slipped it between his lips. He nodded at the stairwell while lighting up. "Let's go for a walk."

Bill shifted left, lining up in front of Marion, blocking the way. "Where's Darcy?"

"I've got a gun, you fool," Alan reminded him with a sneer. "And I won't ask again. Now *move*."

Marion felt the muscles in Bill's arms turn rigid. "Just play along," she urged in his ear.

"You mad?" Bill whispered back.

"Please, Bill. We need to hear what he has to say at least. It'll be all right." She nudged him forward and, keeping one eye on Alan, led the way down the corridor, down the stairs and into the entrance hall. Bill followed quickly.

They paused near the exit and turned to see Alan descending the stairwell several strides behind them, the gun still loose in his grip and a cigarette clamped between his lips.

He halted at the base of the stairwell, set his eyes on Bill. "Outside," he ordered. "Gentlemen first."

Bill's stance was wide, protective. "Where's Darcy?" he persisted.

Alan raised the revolver, aimed it at Marion's head. He cocked the gun. "I really hate repeating myself."

"*Go,*" Marion said to Bill. "If he wanted us dead, he'd have pulled the trigger long ago."

It was flimsy logic, and Bill knew it. He shifted, everything in his posture screaming with fury. "Mari..."

"Just go!" she repeated, desperate now. Whatever Alan— The Raven—wanted, she was sure he wanted it from her alone, which made Bill nothing but collateral. *"Please."*

Reluctantly, Bill pushed his way through the exit, onto the pavement, clearly expecting Marion and Alan to follow. But Alan slipped past Marion before she could take a step. He slammed the door shut and slid the security bolt into place.

Silence, then an almighty racket as Bill threw himself against the door, fists pounding against the frame, rattling it so hard it wouldn't have been a surprise if the entire thing was ripped from its hinges.

"Sorry about that," Alan said amid the battering, his tone smooth and unperturbed. "But best we keep this conversation between us for now. You'll probably thank me for it." He lowered the revolver, took a step back toward the base of the stairwell. Here, under the bold fluorescent light of the entrance hall, Marion was better able to study his posture, his expression. He was impassive, she decided, and very much in control, which gave her no choice but to listen. She forced her shoulders to sink and took a breath.

"Where's Darcy?" She waited. No reply. "What have you done to her?"

Alan waved his free hand nonchalantly through the air. "She's safe and sound, you have my word. At least for now."

"Then why are you here?" Marion asked, speaking over Bill's incessant thumping. "What do you want?"

He spun the pistol carelessly around his finger. Once. Twice. It wasn't lost on her that the gun was Darcy's, the exact same Smith & Wesson she'd shown Marion last night. "Heard of The Raven, by any chance?"

Marion couldn't disguise the wheeze that escaped her.

"Aye, thought so," he said, speaking through the plume of smoke he'd just exhaled. "Now, your dearest friend, Miss Gibson, has gone and gotten herself into a fix and unfortunately for you, she seems to think you're the only one who can help her out of it." He paused, flicked the ash from the end of his cigarette. "But in order to do that, you're going to have to pay up. Greenbacks, cash, moola. Whatever you'd like to call it, I need four thousand pounds by tomorrow afternoon or you and your pal Darcy will find yourselves six feet under, got it?"

Marion held her breath.

A door creaked open on a floor somewhere above them. Footsteps.

Alan raised the revolver, fired a warning shot into the ceiling. "If I see your face," he snapped at the eavesdropper, "I'll put a hole in it."

There was a gasp. Quick footsteps. A door clanged shut.

Alan nodded as he turned his attention back to Marion. "We're running out of time here, love. Someone's going to call the pigs, and I've a feeling you'd like that even less than I would. So, I want four thousand pounds by tomorrow, noon. Do we have a deal?"

Marion dug her fingernails into her palm. "Of course we

don't. Are you mad? How am I supposed to come up with that sort of money by—"

"All right, let's make it five thousand, then." He cast his cigarette to the floor and ground it out with his heel. "Any objections?"

Marion opened her mouth again, though dared not say a word.

"Aye, quick learner, I thought you might be. Five thousand pounds by noon tomorrow or my heavies will be stopping by for a little visit." He thrust a hand under his coat and pulled out a brown paper envelope. "And if you think they won't be able to find you, or your chums—" he dropped the envelope to the floor and kicked it toward her "—think again."

She paused, but only for a second. Crouching, she picked up the envelope and pulled out a stack of photographs from inside. Jaw tight, heart hammering, she flipped through each in horror.

The snaps had been taken over the course of days, if not weeks. Some were clear and at close range. Others were hazy, shot from a distance. There were photographs of her entering the bookshop, getting on the bus, at the park, at Willow Street, at the Mayflower. Worst of all, though, there were also photographs of her with Kenny, with Bill, with Jessica.

She shoved them back inside the envelope and forced herself to meet Alan's gaze. "I'll get you the money." she said, cautiously, fighting the urge to ask the thousand questions dancing on her tongue: Why money? What for? How did you find me? Instead, though, she nodded, giving nothing away. "Five thousand. By tomorrow, noon."

"Good. I'll let you know the drop-off location when I've decided on one. But, word to the wise, if you try any funny business before then, any police, any double cross, any fancy plan, you'll regret it, I swear to God you will. And so will the lovely Miss Gibson. This stays between us, eh?"

THE RANSOM

"BASTARD!" BILL PANTED AS MARION OPENED the door and collided into him. "You all right?" He squinted over her shoulder, into the gloom of the entrance hall and the spiraling staircase above it. But like a wisp of smoke, Alan was gone. "What did he say?"

Marion didn't answer. She kept walking, desperate to put some distance between her and Alan and all the memories waking. Her legs carried her onward, as if directed by something deeper than her conscious will, a mechanism of survival. A sour taste filled her mouth as she tried to piece together what had happened. Yellow twine. Darcy. Alice. The Raven. A ransom. How did they all fit together?

"Mari, please." Bill reached her side, pulled her to a halt, his eyes darting from her face and back to the entrance hall. "Tell me what happened in there. What did Alan say?"

"He just—"

"Did he mention Darcy? Where is she?" His hand dropped

from her shoulder, and under the blazing streetlights, his skin was paper white. "Mari?"

"He didn't say where she is."

"So then why—"

This stays between us. Could she risk telling Bill the truth about the ransom? If she did, he'd try to help. He'd help her get the money, then come with her to deliver it, no matter the risk to himself. But if she didn't tell him, she could fix this problem on her own and keep him safe.

"You were right. He was looking for her," she lied quickly. "He thought we knew where she was."

It was approaching dusk now, and lights glimmered like jewels in the windows of Weston's flat while shapes moved behind the curtains. They were indistinct—perhaps the cat, perhaps the elderly lady. Or maybe Alan.

There was silence for a moment, as if the whole city was holding its breath, listening.

Marion shivered with impatience and shapeless fear—for Darcy. For Bill. For herself. "But please," she said, "with all those bullets fired, someone would've called the police by now and we can't risk the exposure. We have to leave."

An hour later, they found themselves in the cul-de-sac outside the bookshop. Marion, still dazed by her encounter with Alan, fumbled uselessly for her keys, aware of a presence trailing behind them, like a breeze touching the skin at the back of her neck.

"I got it," Bill said, nudging her gently aside. He slipped his own silver key into the door. The key turned clockwise, counterclockwise, then it spat itself out. Next, he inserted a larger brass key. Click. Clank, and the handle turned of its own accord. He pulled down the lever disguised as a lamp-post, and the door clicked open at last.

Bill ushered Marion inside and locked the door behind them, checking three times that he had. They stepped into the dimly lit shop, weaving their way through the warped, leaning bookshelves, around the butler's desk and down through the trapdoor. They stepped inside the lift; the doors clanged shut. Marion took a short breath of relief as the lift started to move, transporting them deep below the city streets. To safety. To *Miss Brickett's*. Back home.

"This is bad, very bad," Bill murmured, mostly to himself. Now that they were secure within the walls of the agency, he fell once again into his dread. He turned to Marion, his eyes dark and as narrow as slits. "He's The Raven and he's after Darcy. What if he finds her? We shouldn't have let him leave. Bloody hell, Mari. We had him right there, and we didn't even put a tracker on him!"

The lift jerked and groaned as it reached the bottom floor and the doors split open.

"I'm going back," he said, wedging himself between the doors, preventing them from closing.

"Don't be ridiculous. He's long gone." Marion stepped out and waited for Bill to follow.

"Maybe. But I can ask the neighbors in which direction he went. It's the closest we've been to him and—"

"No," Marion interrupted. "You can't go back there now. No way." She didn't know what else to say to keep Bill from leaving. Who knew how closely Alan was watching them, and what he might do if he (or his "heavies") spotted Bill now. After all, he'd made it rather clear that any "fancy plan" would earn Darcy a bullet to the head. But there was another reason she had to keep the truth from Bill, a more selfish reason. If she could get her hands on the ransom money and meet with Alan alone, maybe, just maybe—after he'd handed over Darcy— Marion would have a moment to ask him about her mother.

"I have a better idea," she said quickly.

Bill faltered a moment more, then nodded solemnly and followed Marion out of the lift.

They stepped into the Grand Corridor, lined by large stone statues, winged men—the sentinels. Their swiveling eyes turned, landing on Marion and Bill, and a mechanical whine sounded as their eyes—which housed hidden cameras—began to focus. The statues, as though satisfied with what they'd seen, extended their white marble arms and with them, a silvery light flickered on, illuminating the way ahead.

Marion wasn't sure what time it was, but the night-lights burned low in the surrounding passageways and a hush lingered, disturbed only by the odd patter of feet as the agency's evening staff plodded to their stations, weary-eyed and irritable.

"So what's this plan of yours, then?" Bill asked impatiently as they marched past a group of junior Inquirers, who, by the look of things, had only just completed their duties for the day and were heading to the library bar for a customary nightcap.

Marion strode onward, head down, her stomach in knots. She needed to find Bill a palatable distraction just as much as she needed to find herself a five thousand pound miracle.

Fortuitously, the former appeared as they reached the common room.

"Well, well, well. Look what the cat's dragged in at last," Jessica said, appearing at the threshold, arms crossed. "You've caused quite the fiasco with your little vanishing act, I hope you know." She eyed Marion severely, then softened her gaze, sensing something awry. "Where in heaven's name were you two today?"

Marion looked past Jessica, to the common room beyond. A few apprentices were huddled in groups around the hearth, enshrouded by a comforting fug of woodsmoke and tobacco.

A picnic blanket had been set out on top of the hearthrug and was scattered with hot cross buns, toffees and half-empty biscuit tins. With a bottle of scotch beside them, third-year apprentices Preston and David were battling over a game of backgammon while Maud stoked the fire and the second-years—Ambrosia Quinn and Thomas Proctor—amused themselves with a set of mechanical butterflies, leftovers from the Easter celebrations. Marion would've given anything to join them, and for one crazed moment she actually considered setting herself down on the hearthrug, taking a sip of scotch and pretending everything was perfectly normal.

"Frank's been worried sick, wondering where you were," Jessica continued, putting a swift end to Marion's wistful musings. "I'm guessing he's concerned the raven debacle had something to do with your disappearance." She swatted away a technicolored butterfly, which had escaped Proctor's grasp and was gunning for the door. "You heard about that, I presume? The thing Nancy pulled from a receiver box this morning. Heavens, it was awful. Truly, I wish I hadn't seen it. I'll have nightmares for months!"

Bill looked at Marion, but neither said a word.

"I'll take that as a yes," Jessica added, lips pursed. "Anyway, Frank's called Kenny back from Manchester and since the pair of them are about five minutes away from sending out a search party, I'd suggest you make an appearance in the Intelligence Department. *ASAP.*"

"I'm not involving Frank," Bill snapped in Marion's ear. "Or Kenny—" He stopped, cleared his throat awkwardly. "Oh, well, too late now I suppose."

Marion and Bill turned to see Kenny striding down the corridor, a red sweater slung over his shoulder, a satchel at his side and a coil of Twister Rope slithering up dangerously close to his neck. His hair was ruffled, rather than sleek, and his usually golden skin seemed to have taken on a dull, almost gray tone.

As he approached, he dropped the satchel, flicked off the Twister Rope and seized Marion by the shoulders. "Where have you been? I heard about the raven. Frank called but he didn't explain anything, just said you were in danger and had disappeared." He shook his head, drew her into his chest and whispered in her ear, his voice shaking. "Don't do that to me again, Lane! I really thought you were..." He trailed off, turned to Bill. For a moment Marion thought he looked furious, but then his expression eased, and he put a hand on his shoulder. "You okay, bud? Is it Darc? What's happened?"

"I'd like to know, too," Jessica said, circling Marion and coming to Kenny's side.

Marion looked at the common room door, through which a rumble of furtive chatter and the faint crackle of the fire could still be heard. "We'll tell you everything. Just not here."

Kenny nodded. "I'll let Frank know you're back, then meet you all in Intelligence. Deal?"

The foursome reconvened in the deserted Intelligence Department less than fifteen minutes later. Marion sunk into the first seat she found, dropped her head into her hands. She wished Bill would do the talking but he seemed reluctant, or incapable, of saying anything now.

"Could I have a drink?" she said, looking up to find Jessica at her side, clutching the chair arm worriedly while Bill sat motionless next to her.

"What would you like, love?" Jessica asked.

Despite Marion's request for wine, Kenny poured everyone a measure of rum. "All I got, sorry," he said, handing over the drinks.

"Darcy went missing last night," Marion began, clutching

her glass in both hands. "We were out looking for her. Unfortunately, someone else was too." She explained, briefly, what had happened with Alan at the flat, coating the tale with the same half-truths she'd fed to Bill.

"So this Alan fellow is after Darcy but we don't know why?" Jessica repeated somewhat incredulously. She took a sniff of rum, then pushed it aside and poured herself a glass of water instead.

Marion shook her head.

Kenny drew a cigarette from his desk drawer, lit up and studied Marion with a look that made her think he knew she was omitting something.

"What about the raven that was posted to us?" he asked. "It's connected to all this, correct?"

Again Marion looked at Bill, and again he ignored her completely. "It seems so, yes."

Kenny inhaled a drag. "Seems so, or is?"

"I don't know, he just—"

"Lane, come on." He ground out his cigarette, looped his fingers through hers and squeezed tight. "Tell us so we can figure this out together. We want to help."

"He's right, darling," Jessica said. "In it together, like always."

Marion nodded, making up her mind. She would tell them what had happened, but she wouldn't tell them what she was going to do about it.

"It started nine years ago," she began, "just before my mother died…"

When she finished, the department's central light—a dusty glass chandelier—flickered. She blinked at the twinkling light orb (a round, crank-powered torch) lying on the filing cabinet in front of her, alongside the slowly spinning wheels of a

Wire Catcher. It was one of life's cruel jokes, she supposed, that she was surrounded by gadgets that could burst into light, fly, crawl and slither, gadgets that altered sound, tricked the mind and defied gravity. And yet…nothing that could turn back time.

"Oh, darling," Jessica said eventually, pulling Marion into a one-armed hug. "I'm so sorry. I can't imagine how terrible it must be for you to relive all this." She turned to Bill but didn't seem to know what to say to comfort him.

"Frank knew your mother at the time, didn't he?" Kenny asked. "And I'm guessing he knows this story too? Which explains why he was so worried after the raven was delivered and you disappeared."

"I suppose he must," Marion answered. "Though I've never spoken about it to him, or anyone else. It was a horrible time and all I wanted to do was forget."

"Of course," Jessica said in sympathy, pushing her untouched shot of rum into Marion's hand.

"I need to find Darcy," Bill piped up, speaking for the first time in nearly an hour. "If that Alan bastard finds her first—"

"There's just something I don't understand about all this," Jessica interrupted, her eyes searching Bill's face as if she were seeing something there no one else could. "You met Darcy at the pictures and fell for her right away. And now we find out she already knew Marion's mother, or was at least connected to her in some way. I'm sorry, Bill. I love serendipity as much as the next girl but that just doesn't sit right."

Marion was relieved someone had finally said it, and even more relieved it hadn't been her.

"I know," Bill said flatly. "It doesn't make sense. But it doesn't matter, either. Not now, anyway. Darcy's in trouble and we have to find her. We can figure out the rest later."

"All right, then it's a good thing I was already packed for a tracking operation," Kenny said, throwing his satchel on the table and getting to his feet with an air of determination. He squeezed Bill's shoulder. "We'll find her, bud, I promise." He then turned to Marion and added, "I'll clue in Frank, and we'll get going right away. The sooner the better with these types of things."

"No, wait, wait!" Marion blurted, a little more vociferously than she'd intended. "We...we can't."

The last thing she needed was Frank or, heaven forbid, the Inquirers out searching for Darcy while Alan and his heavies lurked in the shadows, ready for an excuse to pummel the life out of any one of them. As much as she loved Jessica's and Kenny's reassurance that this was a problem they could all solve together, it wasn't. The Raven was Marion's demon to face. Alone.

"Alan knows who we are," she explained hesitantly, careful to pepper her lies with just enough truth to frighten Bill and Kenny into doing what she needed them to do. Which was precisely...nothing. "He's watching us. And if we go after Darcy now, he'll just follow us right to her."

Jessica cocked her head. "Watching us?"

Marion opened her suitcase, pulled out the envelope of photographs Alan had given her. She slid them across the desk. "He has been for ages, it seems. I didn't realize until—" She broke off, thinking back to Friday night, and the peculiar white light she'd seen at the end of the cul-de-sac outside the bookshop. The flash of a camera?

Jessica gasped as Kenny and Bill flipped through the pictures in appalled silence.

"Christ," Bill said, dropping his head into his hands. "And I'm guessing he's got the originals?"

"I'd imagine so."

Jessica squinted at a hazy photograph of her and Marion,

wrapped in scarves and trench coats, crossing Eel Brook Common arm in arm. "I remember this. We'd taken a half-day's leave and were on our way to lunch. It was in early March. That means this has been going on for over a month!"

Kenny threw the stack onto the table and started to pace. "Sneaky son of a bitch. He's set us up real good."

Pipes creaked menacingly in the ceiling, the sound reverberating through the department in a way that made it seem as though they were locked inside the belly of a ship at sea. A sinking ship, that is.

Marion got to her feet, stretched out the kinks in her neck and back.

Bill drew himself upright, looked at her. "You said you had a plan..."

Marion opened her mouth, closed it. Again, what she needed now was a delay, enough time for her to get her hands on that five thousand pounds (how, though, she had no idea) and bring Darcy to safety before Bill or anyone else blew her fragile plan to smithereens. However, a delay wasn't likely to sit well under the circumstances. Unless...

"Not so much a plan as an idea," she said, making her decision. "You're right, of course. We *do* need to find Darcy before Alan does. But with his eyes on us, we'll have to do it incognito."

Jessica drummed her bright red nails against the desk. "In disguise? You mean, in night coats?"

"That won't be enough," Marion said. "But Bal's got some new prototypes in Gadgetry. They might work."

Jessica clapped her hands together. "Oh, yes, I heard about those! Brilliant, darling. A couple of muscles pads and a chin reshaper and we'll be good to go."

"Thing is," Marion cautioned, "they won't be easy to get ahold of. Bal hasn't released them as official designs yet, since they're still in the testing phase. They'll be locked up in his office for sure." She paused for effect. It wasn't a lie—the curious things she'd seen Frank wearing yesterday evening *were* prototypes and therefore almost certainly locked away in Professor Bal's office. The caveat was, she had a key. "I'll have to wait for my shift in Gadgetry tomorrow and see what I can do."

Bill looked troubled by the proposed delay, but seemed to stop himself from saying as much.

"What about Frank?" Jessica asked after an interval of thoughtful silence. "And Nancy. I know you want to keep them out of this," she added when Bill shot her a stern look. "And I agree that's probably best. But it's going to be tricky. Tomorrow's a Tuesday. A working day. Us third-years have a five-hour shift in HR, remember, which will be a nightmare to get out of. Especially for me, since Gillroth's off sick and I'm deputy head of the department. And anyway, if we all take leave on the same day, especially after the raven debacle, Nancy *will* ask questions and Frank *will* send the troops out searching."

"Unless they know exactly where we are," Marion said, turning to Kenny. "You're an Inquirer, which means you can get a project request signed off. Correct?"

Kenny frowned suspiciously. "I suppose so but—"

"Good. Then make it something important, but also time-consuming. And make sure it starts at around 10:00 a.m. That'll give me enough time to get some disguises together. And you can't go home tonight," she added quickly, addressing Bill. "Alan will be watching your flat and the neighbor's and Lord knows the police will be swarming the area."

He nodded dully in reply. "I wasn't planning to. Anyway, I'm going up to the bar to think this through."

"I'll join you," Kenny said.

"And I'll get us some coffees," Jessica added.

There was a click at the top of the short staircase that led down into the neighboring Filing Department. Seconds later, Mr. Zimmerman appeared, dressed in a glossy green nightgown and puffy slippers.

Unaware of (or perhaps unconcerned about) the presence of the foursome next door, he paused in front of the wall of receiver boxes, staring up at the expansive network of pneumatic pipes in apparent awe.

"He's *still* here?" Bill asked.

"Will be for at least another week," Jessica answered.

Bill's eyes narrowed. "What does he do all day?"

Jessica flicked her wrist dismissively, while Zimmerman drew a notepad and pen from underneath his nightgown. "This sort of thing, I suppose. Oh, by the way, I wouldn't take the corridor to the senior staff room any time soon. Not unless you've an affection for arachnids." She shivered, then went on to explain. "Zimmerman's staying somewhere around there and has set up a… I don't even know what to call it…a *cluster* of those ghastly spiders of his to guard the place."

"Guard it?" Marion asked. "What for?"

Jessica shrugged, one eye on Zimmerman as he tucked away his notepad and pen and made for the staircase.

Marion cocked her head as something occurred to her. She got to her feet, picked up her suitcase.

"Mari? You *will* be joining us in the library bar, won't you?" Jessica asked, clearly expecting the answer to be yes.

"Ah, no. You go ahead though," Marion mumbled, starting for the staircase. "There's something I need to do. I'll see you tomorrow."

By the time she'd reached the library floor, Zimmerman had vanished. She scanned the tight paths between the bookshelves, the reading nooks, everywhere.

"Looking for something?" said a soft, singsong voice, belonging to Barbara Simpkins, the agency's librarian, who was seated in a rocking chair behind the reference desk, a glass of wine in hand (as usual).

"Zimmerman," Marion answered. "He was here just moments ago."

Simpkins fluttered her fingers, seemingly distracted by something to her left. Marion followed her gaze to the wall of shelves that lined the northern wing of the library. Zimmerman was standing, facing the tallest shelf, his hands in his pockets. He maneuvered left, around the shelf and was gone.

Marion turned to Simpkins. "And again! You saw that, didn't you? He just...vanished."

The librarian rocked gently on her chair. "I'm not blind," she answered cryptically.

"But...where did he go?"

Simpkins looked down at her now empty wineglass and sighed. "To his room, I suspect," she said. "Where else?"

Marion clicked her tongue irritably, walked over to the bookshelf where Zimmerman had been standing. She peered around the back, but found only a solid wall. She shuffled backward, retracing her steps. As she reached the bookshelf, she heard a clang, footsteps and a familiar voice.

"Marion," Frank said, slightly out of breath, appearing from behind the bookshelf. "I was just coming down to see you. Hugo said you were at Bill's flat today." He took a step back, as though to examine her. "What were you doing there? Are you all right?"

"Fine, yes," she answered swiftly. "We were working on an assignment. I'm sorry, it took longer than I'd planned." She peered over his shoulder at the wall, bewildered. "I might be going mad, but I swear I just saw Zimmerman walk through that wall. And now you as well?"

Frank guided her across the library in silence. Only once they'd passed through the large oak doors did he reply. "The secret corridors and thoroughfares in this establishment are innumerable, aren't they? I only discovered this one last week." He paused, then added, "A shortcut to the senior staff room."

She nodded, her mind working, a theory rising, the last pieces of her plan falling into place. "I see."

"I know you heard about the raven that was delivered to us." He studied her for a moment, wringing his hands. "I imagine the news must have terrified you because of, well because of—"

"My mother?" Marion asked.

He nodded sadly. "I don't understand it yet, what it means. I fear there's something—"

"I've had a rough day," she interrupted curtly. "I'm sorry, Frank, but I can't bear the thought of something else to worry about right now. Would you mind if we talk this through another time?"

"Yes, I mean no. Of course not, my dear. And there's nothing to worry about, really." He didn't sound the least bit sure of himself, but Marion didn't have time to concern herself with why. "You just leave it to me to investigate, all right? In the meantime, may I ask that you remain here at the agency, just to be safe?"

"Of course," she agreed, giving him a reassuring nod. She wasn't proud of it, but after so much practice, she'd become awfully good at lying.

THE LYING GAME

MARION WOKE IN HER CHAMBER IN THE STAFF quarters at six the following morning. She groaned as she curled up into the crook of Kenny's arm. What she would've given to stay there and forget everything, to burrow her head under his chin and pretend things were back to how they'd been just one week ago. Simple. Easy. Safe.

Instead, she pulled herself upright, her weary eyes tracing the room: the pine work desk in the corner, covered with tools, a grease-stained handkerchief and the disassembled parts of what might one day be a Price Watch—a new design she and Professor Bal had been working on, a device that could hold the passwords and secret codes to every door in the agency. Behind the desk was an old chest of drawers, and on top of that, Kenny's ragged metallic rose, a glossy copy of Professor Bal's new *Gadgetry Manual* (given to her on her twenty-fifth birthday last year), a makeup case and several framed photographs. Her eyes fixed on the one she'd had the longest, the one of her and her mother.

Last night, just after she'd left Frank in the corridor outside the library, Marion had been alerted by a member of the cleaning staff that a telephone call had come through for her in the bookshop. It was Alan, as expected, who gave her the address of their forthcoming meeting and reminded her that if she didn't show up with five thousand pounds in her pocket, Darcy would pay with her life.

But Marion didn't need the reminder, or any further motivation. Giving The Raven what he wanted and bringing Darcy to safety was not the simple act of selfless bravery it appeared to be. Yes, Marion was committed to saving Darcy's life. Yes, she would've done the same for anybody (with one or two exceptions). But her sheer determination, and decision to do this alone, was an act of redemption and closure more than anything else. And it was about her mother, as much as it was about Darcy. Nine years ago, she had watched her mother wither and die in fear of something she never understood. She had watched, but done nothing. Too young, weak and naive to help.

Things were very different now.

"You were out late last night," Kenny said, pulling himself upright to look at her. "What happened?"

New day, new lies. "I got waylaid."

He cocked his head.

"The first-years," she explained. "They spotted me in the library and asked for my help with a gadgetry…thing." She leaned against the headboard and pulled the sheets up to her chin. It wouldn't be long until the first stage of her plan fell into place. Less than half an hour, in fact. But fooling both Kenny *and* Bill—the two people in the world who knew her best—was going to require a certain degree of creativity. She didn't want to think about how furious they'd be when they realized they'd been hoodwinked, but, as the saying goes: easier to ask for forgiveness than permission.

"I got a project request signed off by Nancy, like you asked," Kenny said. "She came down to Intelligence just as we were leaving."

Perfect. So, if anyone wondered where Bill, Marion and Kenny were all day, they'd simply have to examine the work roster pinned to the noticeboard at the end of the Grand Corridor to see that the trio was engaged in a complex but completely false transmitter-testing assignment in chamber 573, which was half a mile down a dingy and ill-maintained passageway north of the auditorium that no one traversed unless absolutely necessary.

"And Jess?"

He stretched his hands behind his head. "Nope. She can't get out of her shift in HR, since she's supposed to be in charge. She won't be joining us."

Even more perfect. "Right, probably best anyway." She shoved the sheets aside and unfurled herself from his arms. "The fewer of us there are traipsing around aboveground, the lower our chances of a slipup."

Kenny nodded unenthusiastically.

"Now, about those disguises I promised," Marion added. "Bal's on leave this morning, which is perfect." She wriggled into a pair of high-waisted trousers and a gray rayon blouse, pulled on her steel-capped work boots (just in case) and a light sweater. She glanced briefly at the disassembled Price Watch on her chest of drawers, wondering if the passwords and secret codes Professor Bal had already programmed into the memory circuit included the one she needed now. But she didn't have time to check. And more to the point, the gadget was a dismantled prototype.

"Where you going now?" Kenny asked.

"Gadgetry."

"It's 6:00 a.m."

She sighed. This whole thing would've been a lot simpler if she was the only one involved. Now that she was forced to juggle Kenny, Bill, Jessica *and* Frank, it was becoming rather tricky.

"I *can* tell the time, thank you," she replied stiffly. "Like I said, Bal's on leave until lunchtime. This might be my only chance to nick the disguises before he returns."

Kenny got out of bed, marched to the mirror, his bare skin glistening under the light of the gas lamp, muscles flexing. He eyed her through the mirror as he applied a lick of wax to his hair, styling his trademark wave. He finished, dowsed himself in cologne, put on a pair of jeans and a golf shirt.

"You're not telling me something," he said suddenly, turning to face her, his shirt riding up, exposing a strip of golden skin above his belt. "What is it?"

She opened her mouth, closed it.

"Is it about us?"

"What? No. Why would you say that? We're fine."

Kenny put his hands behind his head, puffed out a gust of breath. "Then it's about Bill."

"Bill?"

"You're worried about him. I saw the way you watched him last night in Intelligence. You think he's going to run off looking for Darcy on his own."

She frowned at him, amazed. That was exactly what she'd been worried about last night—among several other things.

"Yes," she said uneasily. "It's just…he's so desperate to help, but I don't think he understands what we're dealing with. Alan and his friends are dangerous. They *will* kill him if he interferes. And I couldn't bear it, Kenny. If something happened to him…out of everyone, he's the one I—" She stopped short, realizing she'd just made it sound like she cared about Bill's safety more than anyone else's. Though in some sense, this was true.

Kenny watched her, unblinking, then nodded slowly, as if he'd come to some decision.

Marion looked at her watch, muffled a gasp. The first stage of her plan was about to commence, and the thought sent a jolt of adrenaline through her limbs.

"What?" Kenny asked. But before Marion could answer, there was a rapping at the door.

They both flinched. Someone was knocking so urgently the lintel rattled.

Kenny gave Marion a questioning look, then opened the door.

Bill was standing in the corridor, hair tousled, trousers and shirt creased, as though he'd slept in them. Not particularly off-character, but still. Something was wrong.

"Hobb," Kenny said, concerned. "You all right?"

Bill looked from Marion to Kenny like he was trying to figure out if he'd just interrupted something important. "Here—" he handed Kenny a sheet of paper "—I found it slipped under the bookshop door about five minutes ago. It's from Darcy, apparently."

Marion read the typewritten note over Kenny's shoulder.

The Mayflower. Today. 11:30 a.m
I'll explain everything. Don't come with Marion. Just trust me.
Darc

"It's a trap, got to be," Bill announced, taking back the letter. "If it really was from her, she'd have written it by hand. She doesn't even own a typewriter."

"I agree," Marion said. "But if it's not from her, then it's got to be from Alan. Or one of his cronies. Either way…"

Bill nodded vehemently. "I've got to go. It's my only lead. I'll just be prepared. For anything."

Marion whipped a headscarf and a pair of shoes from her wardrobe. "I'll organize the disguises, just in case."

"Yeah, thanks, but I don't think you should come, Mari," Bill added, right on cue. "Whether this is from Darcy or Alan, there's got to be a reason they didn't want you there."

"I don't care," she said, realizing that at least some objection was necessary to seal the deal. "I won't let you go alone. It's far too risky." Kenny was staring at her, so she averted her eyes, just in case he really could read her mind.

Kenny nodded, breaking his focus at last. "I'm coming with you, Hobb. Lane, you get us those disguises. Deal?"

Marion swallowed, hard. "Deal."

She waited until Bill and Kenny were down the corridor and out of sight before doubling back to collect the haversack she'd packed last night. She laid out its contents on the bed— the disguises she'd already pilfered from Professor Bal's office late last night. Clearly, she wasn't only learning the art of lie-telling, but of stealing too. Overriding the stab of shame she felt for everyone she was about to deceive and mislead, however, was a sense of burning determination.

So, with unwavering focus, she sifted through the items: a box of silicone facial enhancers, two pairs of contact lenses and light-distorting spectacles—a set each for Kenny and Bill. Because, while they'd soon discover that their forthcoming trip to the Mayflower was nothing but a wild-goose chase, they'd still be better off getting there incognito.

Satisfied, she wrapped the disguises in a pillowcase and placed them in Kenny's wardrobe, on top of the suitcase she was certain he'd take with him on the mission.

"Right," she muttered, getting to her feet. "Now for the hard part."

From a small brass box she kept hidden beneath her bed, she retrieved a tatty piece of yellowed paper and an odd looking monocle, complete with head strap and several lenses of varying shape and size. Carefully, she unrolled the parchment—the only comprehensive map of *Miss Brickett's*, which showed every passageway, every room and every secret corridor (albeit in invisible ink). The map, which had been in Marion's possession since she started at the agency, had passed through the hands of several other employees over the years—including Bill—and was one of the most bizarre, yet useful, items she owned.

She fitted the Gray Ink monocle to her eye and selected the lens through which the map's ink would become decipherable. As though by magic, the parchment transformed from a useless piece of paper lined with strange, silvery furrows, to a treasure trove of information. And there it was—the secret corridor Frank had emerged from, which bypassed the passageway filled with Zimmerman's clockwork spiders and led to the senior staff room.

Better still, just as she'd hoped, the map provided a simple instruction as to how to enter the bypass: *Five paces left from the gas lamp. Knee height. Counterclockwise 2, pull 3.*

Freshly mopped, the library's marble floors glistened with a sheen of moisture, while the scent of bleach and furniture polish suggested it was merely minutes since the cleaning staff had completed their morning shift. It was ten thirty, which meant the senior Inquirers would be enjoying their midmorning tea break in the Intelligence Department, while the first- and second-year apprentices would be neck-deep in gadgetry training and the third-years (barring Bill, of course) would be boring themselves to sleep in the HR Department. Thus, Marion only had the odd straggler and the agency librarian— Miss Simpkins—to contend with.

After spotting Simpkins asleep (or blind drunk) at her desk, Marion made her way toward the bookshelf that obscured the secret corridor. She scanned the wall behind the shelf, located the gas lamp the map had indicated, then measured five paces to the left.

"Knee height," she mumbled to herself, drawing out a penlight. Though she had no idea who had used their knees for this particular measurement, it was sensible to assume they were taller than Marion—because, frankly, everyone was. Thus, she guided the penlight beam in a generous line up and down until she found the furrow of a subtle joint and next to it, a nearly invisible latch that lay flush with the wall.

Just as the map had instructed, she turned the latch twice counterclockwise, then gave it three quick tugs.

A door creaked open, and she stepped into the plush, red-carpeted corridor beyond.

She drew a light orb from her bag and shuffled silently onward, around a gentle bend, then another. The corridor was longer than she'd imagined, and as it snaked its way around what must have been the southern boundary of the auditorium, chatter and muffled laughter filled the silence. At last, she came to the end of the corridor, marked by a wall and a circular door, beyond which (according to her map) lay the senior staff room. She stepped through the door, coming out into yet another passageway and, to her right, a door with a brand-new copper plaque displaying the name, *Mr. L. R. Zimmerman.*

She rapped against the door, just in case. But no one answered. She waited, counted to ten, then extracted a Skeleton Key from her bag and slipped it into the keyhole. The gadget twirled and spun, hissing and clicking until the door sprang open.

Zimmerman's makeshift accommodation was compact but comfortable, furnished with a single bed, nightstand, dresser and antique rolltop desk. She stood in the center of the room, surveying everything around her, trying to imagine where a man like Zimmerman would hide his recently acquired ten thousand pound cash prize. The worst-case scenario was that he carried the money with him wherever he went, but if that was so, then why had he bothered filling the corridor with security spiders?

"So where, then?" she muttered, pacing the room. She checked under the mattress, in the nightstand, the dresser.

Nothing.

Finally, she turned to the rolltop desk, noticing for the first time a strange clacking sound coming from within. She hooked her fingers under the edge of the roller shutter and pulled upward, revealing a set of ten small drawers with embossed brass knobs on either side of a larger (and sleeker) chrome chest. And perched on top of the chest was a similarly sleek and polished mechanical spider.

Eureka.

Bending over the chest, she brought a hand to its surface. Immediately, the spider's pincers began to clack threateningly. She hesitated for a minute, listening to the low buzz of Zimmerman's peculiar safe. It wasn't anything like the contraptions she was used to—Bal's dainty designs—but still, she'd cracked safes and deciphered codes so many times before. She would figure out how to disarm the spider, she just had to think.

She paced back and forth in front of the rolltop, eyeing the device from every angle. It was only when she paused that the memory sparked.

If I'd known we were going to play dirty like that, I'd have added a little heat to that arachnid's fancy-pants alkaline battery.

Moving quickly, and muttering to herself as she did, she pulled a Time Lighter from her bag, turned the dial five times clockwise.

"Little bugger, you're afraid of heat, aren't you?"

A brilliant amber flame sprang from the lighter's fuse.

The spider's many eyes began to spin, as though in terror. Marion slid the lighter across the desk and stepped backward. The spider shot left, then right, trying to avoid the rising heat. But it was a futile act, and soon the creature began to stagger and slow, at last collapsing into a mound of silent metal.

Marion waited a minute, then flicked the spider out of the way and clicked open the chrome chest. Her heart rate doubled as she dipped her fingers into the stacks of cash, drew out exactly five thousand pounds, then scribbled a note and placed it inside.

The best she could hope for was that by the time the missing money was discovered, it would already be in Alan's hands. What would happen then was up for debate, but she'd cross that bridge when she got to it.

THE RAVEN

MARION ARRIVED AT BENTHAL GREEN IN HACK-
ney at 11:45 a.m., just as a light rain started to fall.

She wiped the wetness from her eyes and squinted at the address she'd written down during her call with Alan last night.
She was in the right place (and on time), of that she was certain, but it didn't make her feel any less restless. By now, Kenny
and Bill would be at the Mayflower—in full disguise—waiting
for Darcy or her captors. It wouldn't take long for them to realize that the rendezvous had been a bluff. But how long until
they understood the bluff had been orchestrated by Marion
herself, right down to "Darcy's" letter, which she'd slipped
under the bookshop door at four that morning?

Her shoulders tensed, muscles twitching at the thought of
their disappointment, anger and sense of betrayal. But…*but*…
nothing she'd done had been without reason. Sending Kenny
and Bill off to the Mayflower had bought her just enough
time to borrow (not steal) the money from Zimmerman's

safe. And if things went according to plan, she'd return to the agency within the hour, Darcy on her arm and a tracker fitted to Alan's newly acquired loot. This would provide her with an opportunity to later locate and return the cash to its rightful owner. And if she was cunning enough, she might even manage to drop Alan off at the police station while she was at it. Surely, then, by anyone's standards, it would be fair to say that her lies and deceit had been worth it.

Emboldened by imaginings of her perfect plan (and ignoring the many ways it could derail), she took a long breath, pushed back her shoulders and surveyed the street ahead of her.

The area was as impoverished as she'd expected: gray, grimy, fetid. Several buildings stood in perpetual ruin. The alleyway on which Alan had suggested they meet was just off Lark Row, a slum street that hugged the gentle curves of Regent's Canal. One side of the street was lined with public housing units in disrepair, windows greased and fractured, the other with a tall chain link fence.

The street was mostly deserted, thanks to the swiftly worsening weather, but in the near distance, a clot of barefoot, soaked children in grubby attire played an exuberant game of football, slipping, splashing, thrashing, oblivious to their misfortune and the pelting rain.

"Number five," she whispered, scanning the line of housing units until she found what appeared to be a garage door, nestled between two unsightly redbrick walls, bearing a large, tarnished copper 5.

She checked the Spinner Knife on her wrist, concealed just under her blouse sleeve. Next, she drew out a tracking stone—a tiny chrome disk about the size of a pea—and secured it under the strap of the bag containing the money.

"Right," she said, rapping the garage door. "Showtime."

Several minutes ticked by. Marion shifted on her feet, turning to look over her shoulder every few seconds, rolling the Spinner Knife around her wrist. She told herself she was prepared for a setup, or even an ambush. But was it true?

She wavered as the door began to lift, rolling itself into the ceiling. There was a good chance Alan wouldn't let her and Darcy leave, even after she'd handed over the money. And if he'd brought his heavies to the rendezvous, a single Spinner Knife would be of no use whatsoever.

Perhaps she shouldn't have come alone after all…

The door clunked to a stop in the ceiling. Alan appeared in the entranceway, dressed as he'd been the last time they'd met—in a long black coat and matching shirt and trousers, his hands concealed behind his back. The steel handle of what looked very much like a knife was peeking out from under his belt.

She fought back the maelstrom of emotions churning inside her at the sight of him—anger, hatred, regret, fear. She would not let him get to her.

He inclined his head in greeting and gestured for Marion to come inside.

"Where's Darcy?" she asked, pulling her coat lapels closer across her body as she followed him through the door.

"On her way."

"What do you mean, 'on her way'? Either she's here or I'm leaving."

Alan brought his hands to his front. "She's inside. There. Upstairs."

She shrugged off her coat and folded it over her arm. Glancing around the garage, she noticed the space was crammed with cardboard boxes, a car's dismantled bumper and several broken, rotting pieces of furniture. On the other side of the garage was a single door, which stood wide open. She craned her neck to see where it led, catching sight of a small room beyond and, farther on, a short, narrow staircase.

Alan caught her gaze, pulled the door closed and locked it.

She fiddled with her coat, still hanging over her arm. Alan was mute.

"I have the money," she said, keeping her voice level. "Five thousand in cash. Exactly what you asked for." She tapped the bag slung over her shoulder. "So, let's just get this over with, shall we?"

Alan glanced behind him, at the door, now locked. "Thanks for the money, but that's not really what this is about. A ransom was the only way we figured we'd get you here alone."

We?

He moved closer. "Darcy was sure you'd come if you knew she'd been taken hostage. I suppose she was right. So, tell me who it is."

"What?"

"The Raven," he said, through gritted teeth, moving his hands to the blade tucked under his belt. "Darcy said you'd know who it is. Tell me, so I can slit their throat."

Marion felt her pulse pound in her neck, in her head, everywhere. She didn't understand what was happening. "But… you—" she drew a sharp breath "—I thought *you* were The Raven."

"Me? You thought I killed my own brother, then?" He laughed, stopped, cocked his head.

"Oscar Biggar is your brother?"

He leaned to his right, pressed a large black button on the wall. A grating sound filled the garage, like a large metal object being pulled across the ceiling.

Marion spun around to see the garage door unfurl. The muscles in her legs twitched, urging her to escape while she still had the chance. Somehow, though, she found her feet fixed to the floor. Rolling up her sleeve, she exposed the Spinner Knife. She pulled the gadget over her wrist and spun the catch. A three-inch blade flicked upward.

In response, Alan pulled his own knife from under his belt, raising it like a sword as he repeated, "Tell me who it is. And quickly. I'm not a very patient man."

"I just said, I thought *you* were The Raven!" Marion snapped back.

Without warning, Alan sprung forward, pushing her against the wall with a tooth-rattling thud. He seized the bag of money slung across her shoulder and yanked it so hard it split down the middle, sending notes flying across the garage like confetti. Marion ignored the throbbing pain behind her eyes and the lump forming at the back of her head. She whipped the Spinner Knife sharply upward, nicking Alan in the armpit. He winced, and blood trickled down his side, but instead of flinching or backing away, he wrapped his fingers around her wrist and bent it backward.

Pop. Crack.

She screamed at the lightning pain surging up her arm, into her neck. Her grip loosened reflexively and the Spinner Knife clanged to the floor.

Alan kicked the weapon away and recoiled just enough to reposition his own blade to her stomach. "One more chance, or I cut you to ribbons. Who is The Raven?"

She felt cold metal tear through her blouse, touch her skin. "The Inquirers know where I am," she said. "They'll track you down. You'll never get away with it."

He dug his fingers harder into her neck, compressing her windpipe. She wanted to gag, but stopped herself, terrified that the movement would send Alan's blade right through her stomach.

"Just…take…the money," she sputtered. "And…go. You don't want blood on…your…hands."

Alan sniggered. "You're about twenty years too late for that line, I'm afraid."

Her vision began to tunnel. Her limbs became like rubber.

The seconds ticked by. She started to gargle, to squirm desperately. But the harder she struggled, the faster her energy waned. She thought of Kenny. Bill. Jessica. Frank. Her mother. She thought of Professor Bal and the Gadgetry Department, the world she'd loved so much. She wanted so desperately to fight for her life. But there was nothing left to give.

She grew limp. Her body folded.

Alan released her. She fell to the ground, gasping for breath, clutching her throat.

Seconds passed in darkness, then minutes. She couldn't tell if she was dying or coming back to life. Her heart was hammering in her chest—that was a good sign at least. Slowly, she forced her eyes open.

The blackened air smelled of urine, mold, car fumes. Her vision was hazy, her mind slow. Why had Alan backed away? Why was he over there, getting to his knees, hands above his head? Why was she alive?

She blinked, sucked in a lungful of air, then another and another until her body began to tingle and her mind to clear. Her eyes adjusted to the dark, and the shadows beyond the wall of cardboard boxes took shape. Someone else was inside the garage. Suddenly, she realized who.

"All right, enough theatrics. The show's over, kids," cooed a voice from a few feet away. "On your feet, Marion. Quick sticks."

The fluorescent light fizzed on, and the garage was cast in a blood-orange glow.

Darcy stood in the center of the space, her gloved hands

clutching her Smith & Wesson. She wore a neat, gray-blue coat dress, and a silk scarf was tied around her neck.

Marion's head was spinning, trying to make sense of what was happening. She got to her feet, moved over to the nearest wall, leaned against it, steadying herself. Her Spinner Knife was lying a foot away. But could she reach it in time?

"I'm sorry, sweet," Darcy said, addressing Alan, who was seated on the floor and no longer armed. "You look knack-ered. It's tough, ain't it, trying to kill us girls? Poor thing, you just never seem to get it right."

Alan looked up at her with an expression so vile it turned Marion's stomach. He opened his mouth, his lips twitching, though no words came out.

"Oh, don't look so hard done by. You enjoyed that a little bit, you dirty bastard. Killing's your game, we both know it." She kicked him in the back. "Sorry I didn't let you finish the job, but that's not why we're here."

Alan coughed, then snarled, *"Bitch."*

"Shut it!" Darcy snapped. "You'll speak when spoken to. Understand? I'm the one with the revolver."

"Wh-what are you doing?" Marion stumbled forward, one eye on the revolver, which was aimed somewhere between her chest and Alan's head.

"What does it look like?" Darcy said. "I'm saving your life."

"Then put down the gun, dammit." She waited, but Darcy was unrelenting. "We've got to get out of here. Come on!"

Darcy didn't flinch, instead she raised the gun an inch higher so that the barrel was level with Marion's forehead.

"Darcy? What's going on? What are you doing?"

"It's a long story," she answered vaguely. "I'll get to it in a moment."

Marion rubbed the hot, bruised skin on her neck then gin-gerly touched her aching wrist. She was restless, and her fluttering pulse suggested she wouldn't be able to hold her frayed nerves together for very much longer.

"Let's hear it then," Marion said.

"*Don't* rush me!" Darcy shrieked, curling her shoulders inward. "It's taken me forever and a day to plan this bleeding thing, and I'm not going to mess it up now." She pushed back a lock of hair, took several long breaths.

In front of her, Alan gave Marion a pleading look, then a subtle shake of his head. Was he trying to say something? To warn her?

"You lured me here," Marion said, thinking out loud. "Didn't you? Alan wasn't holding you hostage. So what is this about then?" She realized, just as she said it, that she probably already knew the answer. If Alan wasn't The Raven, then...

"You knew Alice," Marion went on, unable to stop herself as the opportunity arose. "I saw the twine bracelet you wore at the Mayflower. My mother had one just the same." She looked from Alan to Darcy and back again. "What happened all those years ago?"

Darcy fell silent, staring into the middle distance. As she emerged from her reverie, she ran her tongue over her teeth, her expression transforming with menace. "Alice never told you? Not a thing?" Her perfectly plucked eyebrows twitched with incredulity.

"She never got the chance."

Darcy smiled, though no emotion reached her eyes. "Actually, I'm not surprised she kept it to herself. It wasn't like we were proud of what we did for the bastards." Once again, she kicked Alan in the back, hard. He groaned and folded forward, arms wrapped around himself. "But when life gives you lemons, as they say, you ain't got no choice but to strap a bag of crack to your thighs and get on with it." Darcy stopped, frowned a little. Could she read the sheer bewilderment—or shock—on Marion's face? "Oh, so you really meant it, eh? She didn't tell you a bleeding thing about us. Well, let me put it to you like this—Alice and me were best friends. That's where the bracelets come in. I made one for her, one for me, and I suppose you can guess what she gave me in return." Marion couldn't guess, and Darcy didn't bother to explain. "We were family, far as I was concerned. We had each other's backs, you know. At least, that was until the day she scampered off and left me to the mercy of this nasty piece of filth." She stared at Alan, and it seemed as though she was caught in some sort of momentary daze.

Alan squirmed, breathing heavily, hands twisting while Marion shuffled one step to the left, closer to her Spinner Knife. She picked it up. Darcy didn't seem to notice.

Electricity pumped through Marion's fingers, every muscle primed. She lifted one foot off the ground, ready. Carefully, Alan rose to his knees.

But Darcy snapped back into focus before either could do anything further.

There was a brief interlude of silence as Alan slumped back onto the floor, defeated, and Marion dropped her shoulders. The moment had passed, and with it, their opportunity for escape.

Darcy resumed her monologue. "Your mother betrayed me, even though she'd promised—" She broke off, started again. "Her and that lousy Cheevers left me to rot without so much as a goodbye. I warned her. I told her I'd never forget, that one day I'd get my revenge." She came closer, the revolver now trembling in her grip. "Pity I never got the chance because, like the coward she was, she strung a rope around her neck and pissed off to the Pearly Gates."

Marion pressed a hand against the wall, the room spinning. It was as though, at the mention of her mother's suicide, a veil had fallen, cutting out all the light. She had no control over her limbs as they propelled her forward. She reached out for Darcy, swiped the Spinner Knife through the air. But Darcy was swifter, and had seen it coming.

Marion tripped over a piece of furniture, tumbled to her knees, and it was only when her breathing had calmed that she realized the revolver was pressed to her temple.

"Don't test me, sweet!" Darcy snarled in her ear. "I didn't come here to kill you, Marion Lane, but *by God*, I will if I have to. And spare me the blubbering," she added as Marion's eyes pricked with tears. "If anyone should be crying, it's me. And if anyone's to blame, apart from this idiot and your cowardly mother—" she glanced at Alan "—it's Phillip Cheevers."

Marion shook her head, exhausted now. *Phillip Cheevers.* The name spun through her memory, but made no connections. *Who the hell is Phillip Cheevers?*

Darcy let out a quick breath, regaining her composure. She pouted, stepped away from Marion while keeping the gun aimed at her head.

"Bill…" Marion croaked. "You used him, just to get to me."

Darcy shook her head and, for the first time, looked uncomfortable.

"You've been following me everywhere, all the times I went over to Bill's flat," Marion went on. "Then you followed him to the pictures that night a few weeks ago, pretended to meet him there by fate. You made him fall for you because you knew that if he did, I'd do whatever you asked of me."

"Let's not get all soppy about it," Darcy said. "I did what I had to. Wasn't anything personal." She passed Alan a quick glance.

He met her gaze, barely, shook his head. "It's all a game to you, isn't it?"

"Not a game. I don't play games."

Alan made a sound that was somewhere between a cackle

and a groan. "Don't play games? Except this time, eh?" He tried again to lift himself onto his knees but what damage Darcy had done to his back prevented him from remaining in the position for longer than a second. He collapsed, panting hard. "It was you all along," he said, "wasn't it? *You're* The Raven. You killed Oscar. You—"

"I need you to bring him to me," Darcy said, calmly, ignoring Alan.

Marion felt something writhe in her belly. She ignored it. "Who?"

"Who do you think? Phillip Cheevers! I know you know where he is, and I know you can convince him to meet with me."

Marion opened her mouth, the words she wanted to speak nearly slipping out. *I don't know who Phillip Cheevers is.* But something stopped her. Instinct. Intuition. She balled her fists, ignoring the pain of ripped tendons and split skin. "And then what?"

Darcy shut her eyes, jutted her jaw. "And then everything will be better. Your mother, that stupid lying silly little bitch ruined my life. It's about time we reset the scales of justice. This is how we do that. Everyone who was involved in sending me to the slammer needs to say sorry, innit?" Her eyes flickered back to Alan. "Well? Go on, sweet. Oscar said his sorries and can rest in peace. Now it's your turn."

There was a short, strained silence.

"Say it," she hissed.

At last, through clenched teeth, Alan growled, "Sorry." He couldn't have sounded less sorry if he tried.

All the same, Darcy nodded and turned back to Marion. "See? Easy. That's all I want from Cheevers too. I'll send a note through the mail slots to let you know when and where you're to drop him off. It might be tomorrow. It might be in a week. You'll just have to be ready."

"And how am I supposed to find him?"

"*Don't* treat me like a fool!" Darcy shrieked. "I find it very rude, and rude people get—" She stopped, eyes darted left.

Alan, in one last piteous attempt, was swaying on his feet, listing to the left as he reached for Darcy's revolver.

Pop.

Darcy pulled the trigger, felling him instantly.

Marion placed a hand over her mouth as Alan's legs twitched with the last sparks of life.

"You bring me Cheevers," Darcy went on, casually, as though nothing had happened. "Or I'll pass on your whereabouts to the police." She plucked an envelope from her pocket, held it upside down and gave it a shake. Several photographs fluttered to the floor, copies of the ones Alan had given Marion at the flat.

Marion nodded. So, she was right. It was Darcy who'd been following her, not Alan.

Darcy smiled. "I'm sure the police will be very interested in seeing some of them, don't you? Especially since one of the people in these photographs will be wanted for murder before long." She rolled up her sleeves, dusted her gloved hands on her dress and assessed the scene—Alan's limp body splayed out on the garage floor, blood gathering in a pool around his head.

"Murder? But…but," Marion spluttered dumbly. "*You* killed him. I don't understand."

Darcy fluttered her gloves fingers and laughed. "Yeah, but it ain't my prints on the weapon, sweet. Just Alan's and…"

Marion remembered then—she'd touched the gun on Sunday night with her bare hands.

Darcy nodded, reading her mind, then said in a bizarrely reasonable tone, "Look, I'll do what I can to set this up like a suicide, though I don't think them Scotland Yard specials are going to fall for it," she added. "Not when we've got two brothers dead within the month. But it'll buy you time at least, which is the best anyone could ask for under the circumstances." She took a step forward, the revolver perfectly in line with Marion's chest. "Now, I suggest you hightail it before the neighbors come knocking."

She pressed a button on the wall, and the garage door started to groan as it rolled upward into the ceiling.

Marion backed away into the street, where she stood, breath shallow in her chest, limbs numb, the rain coming down thick and fast.

PHILLIP CHEEVERS

THE SECOND CORRIDOR SOUTH OF THE FIELD
office, with its feeble lighting and tight bends, was as familiar to Marion as the back of her hand. Its warped stone ceiling was garnished with sprigs of festive gold tinsel and dotted
with tiny whirring clocks that Professor Bal had installed last
Christmas Eve but never removed. It led to Frank's office, a
place she'd spent much of her apprenticeship—chewing over
case theories and future plans, discussing the past, her life,
Willow Street, Alice. It was home, as much as anywhere had
ever been. Tonight, however, the evening following her terrifying ordeal at Benthal Green, Marion walked the corridor,
heavy with dread and foreboding.

Just five hours prior, she'd stumbled back to the bookshop,
splattered with blood and sweat, clutching her damaged wrist,
every muscle in her body tight and stiff and throbbing. The last
thing in the world she wanted was to run into Kenny, Bill or
(heaven forbid) the agency's head of security—Mr. Nicholas—

to whom she'd probably have to explain where she'd been and why there was a disfigured clockwork spider in Zimmerman's room and five thousand pounds missing from his safe. Unfortunately, she came across all three, and in that order exactly.

"Bloody hell, woman! Where have you been?" Bill fumed, joining Kenny moments after he'd encountered Marion in the Grand Corridor.

"I'm sorry," she mumbled. "I just…"

"Darcy wasn't at the Mayflower, neither was Alan," Bill went on regardless. "But I get the feeling you already knew that."

"I'm sorry," she said again. "I had to distract you and buy myself time, and that was the only convincing way I could think to do it." She winced as she touched her wrist.

"Buy yourself time for what?" Bill snapped uncharacteristically. "What the hell is going on here, Mari?"

"Easy, Hobb," Kenny said, his eyes assessing Marion's attire and general state of misery. "What happened? Are you hurt?" When she didn't answer, he pulled her into his chest, slipped his fingers under her hair and felt the tender lump that had formed there. "Darn it, Lane, what have you done to yourself this time?"

She tried to harden herself against it, but she was exhausted and in pain and, frankly, still in shock over everything that had happened. She broke down in a fit of heaving sobs so forceful they took her breath away.

After she'd cried herself dry, Kenny peeled himself away from her, his hands on her shoulders. "I'll take a flier and say whatever happened didn't go according to plan?"

"I thought I was saving Darcy from The Raven," she muttered miserably. "I thought I could do it myself but… I've messed everything up all over again and I don't know what to do to fix it."

"No, Mari, don't say that. It'll be all right," Bill said, suddenly sympathetic, though it was clear he—along with Kenny—still had no clue what had happened or why Marion was so upset.

She looked up at Bill, wondering for a moment if there was some other way to do this. Could she avoid telling him the truth? Could she think up some elaborate lie to explain what had happened at Benthal Green that had nothing to do with Darcy? Then she remembered a promise they'd made to each other in their first year—to tell each other everything, even when it's hard. Well, this definitely counted as hard.

"It's Darcy," she began carefully.

Bill stared at her, not blinking, his face expressionless.

"She killed Oscar in Petticoat Lane. And she killed his brother, Alan, right in front of me. It was all a setup. She was the one who sent Alice the ravens nine years ago. She was the one who sent *me* the raven through the receiver box. Everything. *Everything* was her. Darcy's been The Raven all along."

Bill continued to stare at her—blankly—for several more seconds. Then he stammered, "N-no way, can't be. I mean... *can't be.* She didn't, she wasn't even—"

"I'm sorry, Bill," Marion repeated for the umpteenth time, cutting him off. "I can hardly believe it myself but it's the truth. I promise you." She reached for his hand, but drew back with a wince when her injured wrist flexed uncomfortably and a stab of electric pain surged up her arm. "I can explain everything later," she added on a defeated sigh, "when I understand it myself. First, I really need to speak with Frank."

"But I don't understand what you mean," Bill said, almost irritably. "Darcy isn't a killer, for Christ's sake! She must've been framed or something. Alan must have—" He broke off, interrupted by a booming voice that made Marion's stomach sink.

"Aha!" said Mr. Nicholas, wagging a finger at Marion and grinning like a Cheshire cat. "Just the person I was looking for." He approached, twirling a pocket watch in his hand (though no accompanying spy snake was in sight, thankfully). His scarred eyebrow twitched as he scrutinized Marion's sullied, miserable appearance. But if he noticed the blood on her blouse, he decided to ignore it. "So, tell me. Where were you at exactly 10:55 this morning, Miss Lane?"

Marion closed her eyes and took a long breath, stopping herself from saying something rude.

"She was with me," Kenny said, pointing at the roster on the noticeboard behind them, which listed the details of their faux transmitter assignment. "And Hobb. It says so right there."

Nicholas wasn't a terribly bright chap but even he wasn't *that* easy to fool. "Oh, yes, how convenient. You were locked away in a chamber no one ever visits at the exact time my security system registered an intruder in the, well, in a place they shouldn't have been."

Marion, Kenny and Bill stared at him but said nothing.

"Well?" Nicholas pressed. "Explain!"

"Oh," Marion said at last, feigning confusion. "So you're saying the intruder was *me*?" She was exhausted and harried and desperate to speak with Frank, but knowing from experience there was only one way to effectively deal with Mr. Nicholas (especially when he was in *this* mood), she kept her manner unperturbed.

He dropped his watch into his blazer pocket. "As a matter of fact, that is *precisely* what I'm saying."

"So you must have proof, then? A photograph of me in this undisclosed location at exactly 10:55, perhaps? Or maybe you have a witness?"

Nicholas sucked in his cheeks. "I have a report of missing property," he said, a little frazzled now. "*Substantial* property.

And there's only one person in this entire establishment who could possibly have bypassed the security system, as far as I'm concerned."

"Well, give them my congratulations," Marion snapped, no longer able to contain her irritation and impatience. "Now, if you'll excuse me."

Nicholas grabbed her by the arm and spat out a string of insults. Unfortunately for him, however, Kenny and Bill were in an equally foul mood. Kenny seized Nicholas's right arm while Bill took his left. They dragged him backward like a rag doll and pinned him up against the wall.

"Let me go! I'll have you sacked, you fools! I'll have you sacked right this second!"

"Go," Kenny said to Marion over Nicholas's maniacal hissing, which had already drawn a small crowd from the neighboring chambers and corridors.

Bill nodded, adding, "We'll sort this idiot out. Just go!"

Now, standing at Frank's office door, Marion drew out the key he'd provided her with last year and stepped inside. As she'd expected, the room was deserted and dark, lit only by a single, guttering lamp. She checked her watch—it was ten minutes to nine. According to the work roster, Frank would be in the Intelligence Department until nine fifteen, after which he'd more than likely return here for a scotch and cigar and a bit of light reading. That gave her just enough time to settle down and gather her thoughts.

She slipped around the back of the large wardrobe at the other end of the office and up the corkscrew stairwell to the second floor, the Games Room. Even before she'd entered, she could smell the woodsmoke, the rich scent of coffee and tobacco. But as she stepped inside, she paused, her senses detecting something else as well. Something that didn't belong.

Nancy was sitting in Frank's favorite wingback chair by a crackling fire, a glass of water resting in her lap, fingers curled around it a little too tightly. Her unyielding posture, paper white complexion and severe features were as threatening as ever. Or maybe a fraction more than usual.

Beside her was a small oval stool and on it, an opened envelope. A letter peeked out from inside. It was a curious thing, luminous silver ink printed on charcoal paper. Marion tried to read the handwriting but caught only a single sentence before Nancy tucked it into her pocket:...*twelve months at our facility should do.*

Nancy gestured for Marion to take the seat opposite her. "You weren't expecting me, of course," she said. "But considering recent events, I thought I'd pop in to see how you are."

Marion settled down, crossed her legs. "I'm fine, thank you."

"Really?" Her eyes traveled to the bruise on Marion's wrist, the ruby ring around her neck, the tapestry of bloodstains on her blouse.

Marion pulled a cushion onto her lap, curled her arms around it like a shield. Clearly, Nancy knew something was amiss. She always did, somehow.

"Frank will be in momentarily. You know that, I presume, though I believe he's under the impression that you are currently embroiled in a transmitter-testing project with Hugo and Hobb in chamber number—" she flicked her wrist irritably "—whatever. But I suppose that was a ruse of some sort?" Nancy watched her intently for several long and intolerable seconds, expressionless. "Mr. Zimmerman and I had a rather difficult conversation earlier today. He appears to have lost some money from his safe. Apparently, the thief was thoughtful enough to leave behind a note, assuring him they would pay back the sum in full." She took a sip of water, cleared her throat. "So? How are you planning to do that, exactly?"

Marion stalled, gulped in a mouthful of air.

"Might I remind you," Nancy continued, impervious to Marion's reaction, "that you were supposed to become an Inquirer this year. But I'm afraid thieves and liars do not generally make my list of worthy candidates for the badge."

"You don't understand," Marion spat out. "I didn't steal it for fun. I had no choice! I can explain everything, I promise."

"And indeed you shall. But for now, I must consult with the High Council, who will decide, collectively, whether this is a transgression we can overlook or not."

Marion closed her eyes, tried to stem the dread that was threatening to overwhelm her now. Apart from being set up for murder, she could hardly imagine anything worse than losing her Inquirer badge before it was even pinned to her chest. No, that wasn't true. There *was* something worse. Much, much worse. Namely, being sent to the Holding Chambers—the agency's highly concealed in-house prison cells: deep, dark pits carved into the earth. Would the High Council decide that Marion should be sent there as punishment? Would she spend the rest of her life locked away in complete darkness and isolation? The terror of such a thought was tangible. She'd seen the chambers once before, she'd seen firsthand the grim fate of those unlucky enough to earn a sentence there. Indeed, no one had ever survived longer than a few months of imprisonment. But surely theft wasn't a crime worthy of the Holding Chambers. *Surely.*

"Frank told me about your mother," Nancy said, drawing Marion from her somber rumination, "and her connection to the raven that was delivered to us through the receiver box on Monday morning. He's gravely concerned about you, and I'm starting to see his point." She expelled a lungful of air, for once relaxing her posture. "I can see you're afraid, Miss Lane, and while I may not be the first person you think of to come to with your troubles, perhaps, for once, I should be. I care, more than you might expect. You're an apprentice at my institution, and therefore I will do anything to protect you. Whatever predicament you have gotten yourself into, I *will* solve it. Of that you can be certain." She reached out a hand. Her touch was cold and hard, yet strangely reassuring. "You must let me help you. You must tell me exactly what has happened."

Marion listened to the fire crackle, silver smoke curling up into the chimney. For the first time in her career, she saw a genuine softness in Nancy's eyes. Mixed, of course, with the fierceness she was known for.

"It's such a mess," she began, shaking her head. "I thought he was The Raven when all along…"

Nancy withdrew her hand, placed it in her lap instead. "Please, from the beginning, Miss Lane."

For a moment Marion felt like walking out. Or running out, preferably. Even with all Nancy's assurances that she was here to help, and was keen to listen, she still wasn't the easiest person to talk to. Especially not about something so personal. Because although the story involved Bill and Darcy, at its core, it was about Marion's mother.

"It started a few weeks ago," she said at last, and only because Nancy was staring at her with such intensity that walking out didn't seem like an option just then. "With Darcy Gibson, Bill's new girlfriend."

Nancy's face remained unmoved, but for the smallest shift in her eyes. The name meant something to her. "Are you saying Miss Gibson is *with* Mr. Hobb?" she asked with obvious disbelief. "You mean courting him? How on earth did that happen?"

"They met at the pictures. But Darcy's been following me for over a month, so that must be how she found out Bill and I were close, then she used him to manipulate me. Same thing she did with Alan. She planned it all so perfectly and no one suspected a thing." She paused, her mind began to spin uncontrollably, winding back to the very beginning, the afternoon she'd met Darcy at the Mayflower for the first time. What other piece of Darcy's plan had she missed? There *was* something, she was almost certain of it.

Nancy took another sip of water, placed the glass on the side table. "How much of this does Frank know?"

"Just what he's told you. About the ravens sent to my mother."

Nancy raised an eyebrow. "I see."

"I don't think he knows anything about Darcy?" Marion added, framing it as a question. "Or, if he does, he certainly doesn't know Bill's dating her."

There was a silence, broken only by the low hiss and pop of the fire, and the distant voices of the night shift workers drifting up from the corridor outside Frank's office. Briefly, Marion wondered what Kenny and Bill had done to Mr. Nicholas, or what Mr. Nicholas had done to them.

"You said she's 'planned it all so carefully'. Planned what, exactly?" Nancy asked, breaking the interlude.

Marion took a breath, lowered her eyes, and—somewhat reluctantly—told the story as best she could.

"She murdered Alan Biggar right in front of me," she concluded. "And yes, I took the money, the five thousand pounds from Zimmerman's safe. I wish I'd found another way, but Alan made me believe he'd kill Darcy unless I handed over the ransom. I had a plan… I had a plan to get it back but now…"

"There will be time enough to worry about the money," Nancy said coolly, "and the consequences of your actions. You *will* repay Zimmerman. One way or another. But let us not get into all that just yet."

Marion nodded, choosing to ignore Nancy's ominous subtext. "Darcy said she'll make Alan's murder look like suicide to 'buy me time.' Whatever that means. But how can I possibly trust anything she says now. Besides, my prints are all over the gun and she said she'll send the police my way unless—"

"Unless what?" Nancy interrupted impatiently.

"Unless I hand him over."

Nancy looked confused for the first time since the start of their conversation. *"Him?"*

"Someone my mother knew, apparently. Darcy says she wants to talk to him, get him to say sorry for what he did to her. But I'm quite sure she actually wants to kill him. Like Oscar. Like Alan."

"His name?" Nancy pressed.

"Phillip Cheevers. Frank will know him. I hope. That's why I need to speak with him. Urgently. We can't let—" She stopped, Nancy's face was no longer blank and unreadable. She was, very obviously, shocked. "What? You know him? Who is he?"

Nancy got to her feet, wandered over to the drinks cabinet, poured two fingers of scotch into a tumbler and handed it to Marion.

"Miss Gibson has the bookshop address, I presume?" Nancy asked. Marion nodded in reply. "And of course, she knows your Willow Street residence. You understand the implications of this, I hope."

"I understand that I'm done for, yes."

"Not just you, Miss Lane."

Marion opened her mouth, then closed it as she heard something: footsteps—brisk and heavy—coming up the spiral staircase.

"Sorry I'm late, Nancy, it seems we've had a development

in the—" Frank appeared at the threshold, out of breath. He glanced at Nancy, then Marion, eyes widening. "Ah, Marion, you're here too. I, eh, I just bumped into Mr. Nicholas. He was absolutely furious—" He broke off again, took a seat beside her, touched her gently on the hand, where he noticed the web of fresh bruises on her wrist. She'd forgotten, up until then, how badly it was throbbing. "My dear, what on earth's happened?"

Marion passed Nancy a sidelong glance, she nodded, and Marion preceded to repeat the tale of her encounter with Darcy, Alan's murder and string of events that had led up to it.

"Darcy and *Bill*?" Frank said, even more shocked than Nancy had been. "My God, if only I'd known." He began to fidget, to twirl a pen through his fingers, to touch his chin, his mustache. Occasionally he threw a glance at Nancy, though she seemed to be ignoring him completely. "I'd heard Darcy had been released from prison but I didn't think…" He trailed off.

Marion realized then that Darcy had already mentioned she'd been sent to prison. But for what, she wondered?

"Hmm, yes, yes," Frank went on elusively. "She was released just four months ago. I expected her to cause some trouble. But this…"

"Darcy is looking for Phillip Cheevers," Nancy explained.

Frank turned his eyes to the wall. His skin was pallid, as though he'd seen a ghost.

"She said she'd send the police after me for Alan's murder if I don't hand him over," Marion added. "I'd like to think she's bluffing, but going on experience, I doubt it. She has my home address. She knows where I work." Why did she get the feeling she was teetering on the edge of a cliff, a swift breeze sweeping in from behind? She pressed her hands together in her lap and asked the question she wasn't actually sure she wanted to know the answer to. "I suppose you know who Phillip Cheevers is?"

Frank made a sound, something between a gasp and a sigh.

"It was Frank's alias," Nancy answered, as Frank continued to stare blankly ahead, "when I hired him in the early forties, just after he freed your mother from the Biggar Brothers' enterprise. The brothers were London's most infamous gang leaders, known for their East End cocaine operation in the forties and fifties...among other things. Your mother and Darcy worked for them for several years, I believe."

Frank put down his glass, blinked at last. "I'm sorry, Marion, I really am, but Alice didn't want you to know about that part of her life. She was afraid you'd be ashamed of her."

Marion was so stunned by what Nancy had just said that she found she couldn't speak.

"Perhaps I should start at the beginning, yes?" He waited for Marion's shoulders to drop before continuing. "As you know, I met your mother when she was just fifteen and I was seventeen. You've guessed this already, of course, and I suppose I haven't ever really denied it, but your mother and I were very much in love, even then when we were just kids. But how can you know yourself at such a young age? How can you know what you want? I didn't understand what I was feeling, and I couldn't possibly have considered settling down to marry then.

"Of course, I lost my chance, just as I deserved. Alice found someone else." He blinked at Marion, and her chest ached at the regret so evident on his face. "She married your father at eighteen, and you were born just a year later. I wanted to be happy for her. I wanted to convince myself that we'd never have worked, that we were destined only to be friends. But it wasn't true. I couldn't stand the thought of her with anyone else, never mind Devon, your father. So, as you know, I left London for Dorset, thinking the distance would heal my wounds. I joined the force and tried to forget Alice altogether. We wrote to each other occasionally, though neither of us were ever truly honest about how we felt." He swished the scotch around in his glass, then took a long sip. "In fact, it was only after your father died in '42, that things changed between us."

Marion picked at the memories of her father's death. She was only eight when it happened, but she remembered the shift in her mother that came afterward. Not sadness, not even pain, but rather cynicism, or a recognition of the impermanence of life. Alice had lost both her father and her only sister all before she was twelve. And while she'd tried to make the most of her life, her scars, like cracks in a mirror, forever changed how she saw herself.

"She wrote to me afterward," Frank continued, "and admitted how much she missed me. She hinted that perhaps there was a chance for us to try again, and asked if I might return to London. I considered it, certainly, but I wasn't ready. I knew she was distraught over Devon's death, even though others said she was in some ways freed by it. But you can't lose so much at such a young age and remain unchanged."

Marion nodded absentmindedly. She could recall very little of her father, other than the fact that he was loud, a drunk and seldom affectionate. She knew Alice had loved him, in some sense, though—as marriage was for so many women in those days—the union had been one of convenience and financial security more than anything else.

Frank caught Marion's eye as she looked up. "So, I decided to give her time, three years, in fact. In the interim, we corresponded as usual, though Alice's letters became more infrequent and…distant, as time went on. I began to worry and decided to return to London immediately." He paused to take a breath. Or steel himself. "I found Alice had changed, even

more than I'd expected. She'd withered, withdrawn into herself. You were only ten or eleven at the time but even then,
you saw it too, I think."

Marion glanced at the hearth, her eyes blurred by the dancing amber flames. She saw her mother's face flicker in her
memories, rarely smiling, seldom spirited, burdened by all the
pain she kept to herself. But it was true, Marion *had* known,
even at a young age, that her father's death had been Alice's
point of no return.

"She told me she'd found a job in a textile factory," Frank
went on. "But I knew it was a lie. She was exhausted, battered,
and I sensed she was ensnared by something. Or someone."
He wrung his hands, hesitating again. "I wish this were easier to say, but the truth, your mother's truth, will be hard to
hear, Marion. Upon returning to London, I heard through the
grapevine about a protection racket up in the East End, run
by two young men known as the Biggar Brothers. Oscar and
Alan, both of whom had avoided military service by receiving
an exception thanks to their 'Steel Works Factory', which was
regarded as a key industry at the time. After some inquiries,
I also discovered that the brothers were using young women,
sometimes even girls, to smuggle cocaine and other narcotics
into England during and after the war. They cajoled women
from the streets, desperate, hopeless souls who had nowhere
else to go and no other means of earning money.

"The worst part, however," he went on, "was that in between smuggling cocaine, the women were 'encouraged' to
work in the brothers' brothel. The brothers' insisted that the
women were never physically forced into prostitution, but
they might as well have been. They all knew that as soon
as they'd embarked on their first expedition as a drug mule,
they were trapped. They'd done something illegal. They were
criminals, and there was little chance of them going to the

police or making money any other way. They were, in all respects, imprisoned for life." He allowed Marion to take a sip of scotch, then another. "After your father passed, your mother had nothing. No money. No prospects. No education. She had you to look after and rent to pay. In essence, she was the Biggar Brothers' perfect catch."

"No," Marion cut in, throwing back the last of her drink, feeling the burn as it filtered down her gullet. She knew what Frank was going to say next, and she didn't want to hear it. "My mother worked in a textile factory, just like she told you. Just like she told me. She went there every morning, *every* morning. She came back and we cooked dinner together. She would never have lied. Not like that. Not for so long. Not to me—"

Nancy gave her a pitying look, or perhaps it was supposed to be a kind one.

Frank placed a hand on her shoulder. "I'm sorry, Marion. She and Darcy worked for the Biggar Brothers for many years. Darcy was just sixteen when she joined, and even more desperate than your mother. Alice took her under her wing, so to speak, and tried to protect her from the worst of the brothers' malice. And when your mother eventually decided to tell me the truth about her work, and begged me to help her escape the ring, she insisted that she wouldn't leave unless I found a way to help Darcy escape too. She felt responsible for Darcy's fate, and it made her sick with worry to think about what would happen to her if she was no longer around as protection.

"I mulled it over for months, trying to think of a way to get the two of them out of there safely. It was hard because both Alice and Darcy had committed a number of criminal offenses in their time with the brothers, smuggling drugs and…" He shook his head, twirled his thumbs. "In the end, I had to make a choice. Somehow, the brothers heard about my aspirations, that I was coming for two of their 'girls' and in response, they contacted me with an ultimatum. I learned then that there was something the brothers disliked more than anything else, and that was being undermined. It was never really about Alice or Darcy, but about power. They didn't want a copper like me to think I had the upper hand." He paused, dipped his head as though he couldn't bear to look Marion in the eye any longer. "They offered me Alice, for a price. And if I refused the bribe, they'd kill her, along with Darcy. Of course, I offered double the sum for both of them, but the brothers refused outright. Alan, as I later learned, had a 'relationship' with Darcy at the time and was determined to keep her under his thumb.

"As I said, it was about power, and they knew they had it all. I had no choice," he added softly. "I had no choice but to leave Darcy behind. Alice was distraught, utterly ridden with guilt, and although we negotiated with the brothers for weeks, it amounted to nothing. They wouldn't let Darcy go under any circumstances or for any amount of money. I knew there was only one tool left in my arsenal—the legal route. So, I approached some colleagues at the Met—a Detective Inspector and a Chief Inspector. I gave them Darcy's name and address, suggesting they arrest the brothers, close down the operation and offer Darcy clemency if she agreed to testify against them." He sighed, knocked his head back and looked at the ceiling. "Unbeknownst to me, the brothers already had several members of the Met in their back pocket, ready to do their bidding for some dosh. And The Chief Inspector was one of them. He tipped them off and within days, the brothers closed down their operation and vanished."

"And Darcy was arrested?" Marion guessed.

He nodded sadly. "It took them a while to find her, but yes. And in the interim, she put two and two together and realized who had sent the police after her, which set her off on this…path of revenge, shall we call it."

Marion stared at the flames, dancing, licking the grate. "Why a raven though?" she asked, moments later.

Frank walked over to a cabinet near the fireplace. From inside a locked drawer, he drew out something made of tarnished, mismatched metal. A bird. No, a raven.

"Have you ever wondered where you get your knack for fixing things?" he asked, placing the creature in Marion's lap. "Your mother was similar, though for her it was *making* things. She made this as a gift for Darcy, but found it returned to her several nights before the…*other* ravens were delivered."

Marion ran her fingers down the bird's wings, claws, long, sharp beak. It was made with rusted, dull scraps of brass and copper, but it was still a masterpiece. Clean joint lines, perfectly proportioned, intricate and robust. On the back of its neck, Marion noticed an engraving: *To my dearest Darcy, with love.*

"A little oil and some care, and the wings and beak will open," Frank said. "It doesn't fly, like our Distracters can, but indeed it was our first prototype for the gadget."

"Which is why I once considered offering Alice a position here," Nancy explained to Marion's further disbelief. "Of course, she died before I could get around to it."

Marion stared at the bird in a stunned, numb silence. Her mother had always been adept at sewing curtains and patching up leaks in their roof. But this wasn't the work of an above-average housewife. This was art. She searched her recollections, trying to remember what she might've missed. And maybe, through the fog of an old memory, she could see Alice sitting at the kitchen table with a pair of pliers and a small hammer, a sheet of tin laid out in front of her.

Was it just a coincidence then, Marion wondered, that the Distracter had always been her favorite gadget?

Without permission, she placed the raven in her bag and looked up. "You've had this for nine years," she said, weary now, "and never thought to tell me about it?"

Nancy's expression was blank, but Frank looked regretful.

"It seems unkind of me, I know," he said. "But it was a part of Alice's past, which she made me promise not to reveal to anyone, and *especially* not to you." He shrugged sadly. "And because of the engraving, it would've been impossible to give you the raven without explaining who Darcy was."

Marion only sighed, too exhausted to be angry. "The night the last raven was sent to our house, someone came to visit. Yesterday, I was convinced it was Alan but now I think…"

Frank nodded. "I came to tell Alice that Darcy had been arrested, which is when she finally told me about the ravens and how Darcy had been threatening her." He broke off, turned his eyes to the floor. Marion noticed they were glistening. "In the end, Darcy pleaded guilty to drug trafficking and prostitution to avoid a trial. It cost her eight years in prison. And, of course, the brothers got away scot-free."

Marion trailed a finger around the rim of her glass as she watched the flames in the hearth shrink and die, the room darkening, growing colder. She still couldn't accept what Frank had said about her mother, the lie she'd lived for Marion's entire life. Nor could she begin to untangle the web of secrets Alice, Darcy and Frank had spun together.

"My mother's guilt about Darcy's arrest was the reason she killed herself," she said softly. Frank didn't answer. But really, he didn't need to. They both knew it was true. "So why didn't you fight for her, for Darcy, I mean? After my mother died, it was the least you could've done, surely? Instead, you let her go to prison for eight years." She wasn't exactly angry with Frank for leaving Darcy in prison—how could she be after what Darcy had done—but still, some part of her could understand how betrayed and alone Darcy must have felt for all those years behind bars.

"There was nothing I could do," he said flatly. "Darcy *was* guilty of the crimes she went to prison for, and after she was arrested, my Chief Inspector 'friend' put a word in with my boss in Dorset and had me fired for 'obstructing the ends of justice.' But also—" He stopped abruptly, and Marion waited patiently. "The other reason I didn't try to get her out after Alice died was because I was afraid of exactly, well, exactly *this*. You see, I tried to visit her in prison. I wanted to explain what had happened, to make her see the truth. But she refused to see me, or listen to what I had to say. She was utterly convinced Alice and I had betrayed her and because of that, I knew she was dangerous."

"That's why you gave me the Spinner Knife," Marion said, thinking out loud. "And made me take those extra evasion classes."

Frank nodded. "I knew she'd been released from prison and, while I hoped her time behind bars had softened her, I still feared she'd one day seek revenge by coming after me. Or worse, by coming after the one thing Alice had loved more than everything else."

Marion pushed her hair from her face, stretched out her neck. Things made sense now, but that didn't mean she felt any better. In fact, she might've felt worse.

"Okay…so what are we going to do?" she asked several minutes later. "We can't ignore Darcy's ultimatum, and we can't hand you over."

Frank got up to stoke the fire, his gaze distant and thoughtful.

"I've considered speaking to Constable Redding," he said, referring to *Miss Brickett's* long-time Scotland Yard liaison, with whom they occasionally shared information on London's crimes and criminals and who in exchange—albeit reluctantly—turned a blind eye to some of the agency's unlawful affairs. "But I'm incredibly wary of such a strategy. I just don't know who we can trust anymore. Especially considering the fact that the brothers have reinvented themselves since their drug trafficking days."

Marion nodded, recalling the word the newspapers had used to describe Oscar Biggar: *philanthropist*.

"Apparently they were running some sort of clothing business," Frank added. "And although we suspect there's money laundering going on behind the scenes, it's all been very well hidden. I am certain that what the public will see is simply the brutal murders of two hardworking business owners who have continuously donated large portions of their profits to charities in and around London. Even in Scotland Yard there are very few who know about the brothers' past, and if they do, they're not going to admit it. For obvious reasons."

"I am glad to hear you say that, Frank," Nancy said predictably, stiffening in her seat. It was well-known to everyone who worked at *Miss Brickett's* that Nancy had never trusted the police, even Constable Redding who—as far as Marion was concerned—was not so much untrustworthy as he was utterly incompetent. "There is absolutely no chance I will agree to involve Redding," Nancy went on, "or any of his useless friends. And not just because of our troubled history with the police. In case either of you have forgotten, there is a dead body waiting to be discovered in Benthal Green with Miss Lane's prints all over it, which I'm afraid to say is a problem even Redding will not overlook."

"Okay," Marion said, "so we keep the police out of it. I'm happy with that. But then what? There must be another way to put an end to this."

"There might be," Frank said thoughtfully, "but we'll need time. Darcy is frightfully sharp. And desperate. If we're going to outwit her, we'll need to be clever about it."

"Of course, only… I don't know if we *have* time," Marion said. "Darcy made it clear she'll be in contact soon, but she didn't say when. It could be in a week, or tomorrow, or even tonight."

Frank looked ready to add something more, but instead wandered across the room in silence. Marion watched him shifting like a wraith in the shadows, his shoulders hunched, his arms tight at his sides. It was almost as if she was seeing him for the first time, like a stranger, cold and distant. Frank Stone or Phillip Cheevers. Who was he, really?

13

MURDER WEAPON, MISSING

"WHERE DID THIS HAPPEN?" NANCY SNAPPED AS Rupert Nicholas guided a bruised and bleeding senior Inquirer through the Grand Corridor, which was now crawling with chattering staff members—everyone keen to get a first row seat to whatever new drama was unfolding at the agency.

"Near...Benthal," the Inquirer spluttered, wiping a trail of blood from his lips while clutching his side. "Came out of nowhere. The...whole mob."

It was Thursday morning, two days after her meeting with Frank and Nancy, and Marion stood, like everyone else, at the end of the Grand Corridor. Unlike her colleagues, though, she only wished to collect her work roster from the notice-board, find out where she was on duty for the day and bury herself in one mind-numbing task after the other for as long as was humanly possible.

"Did anyone follow you back here?" Nancy asked next, her

tone devoid of sympathy. "McMurray! Answer me. Yes or no. Did anyone follow you here?"

The injured Inquirer shook his head noncommittally, but by the time he actually answered, he, Nancy and Mr. Nicholas had turned toward the infirmary and were out of earshot.

Marion examined her work roster blankly, doing her best to ignore the announcement that had been posted alongside it on the noticeboard. She picked her nails—fully aware her old habit was back with a vengeance but in no state to care—and turned toward the chamber she would be stationed at for the morning. But as she reached the corridor mouth, she was stopped by another senior Inquirer—Aida Rakes—who was holding out a reel of Twister Rope and a small brass device disguised as a pen but which, when triggered, would send an emergency alert to any other pen-wielding Inquirers within six miles.

"Keep the rope demagnetized and on you at all times," Rakes said without preamble. "And trigger the pen whenever you're unsure of someone aboveground. Of course, you won't be going aboveground any time soon, but you get what I'm saying."

Marion looked up at her and groaned. "Frank's idea, I guess?" she said, assuming he'd instructed Rakes to track Marion down and provide her with yet another piece of self-defense equipment.

"No. Nancy's," Rakes explained sharply. "New protocol, on account of what happened to McMurray and the others."

"Oh…yes, I saw him being carried in. What happened?"

"He was attacked by the mob. Poor sucker got it pretty bad, though not nearly as bad as the other three last night. And they weren't even one of us. If it gets any worse—" she shook her head despondently "—well, let's just pray for some luck."

Marion had no idea who "the mob" was, or the three others who'd been attacked, or even what Rakes meant by them not being "one of us." She decided not to ask, though, certain she'd find out soon enough. She nodded, shoved the Twister Rope and emergency pen into her haversack and marched on into the gloom.

She arrived at a dreary teaching chamber west of the infirmary to find the rest of her fellow third-year apprentices already present, each bent over a variation of a complex puzzle lock they were meant to be solving—an assignment they'd been tasked with for the morning.

The cavernous room had an almost sinister feel that made Marion suspect it had previously been used by the defamed alchemists who'd once called the labyrinth home. The floor was carpeted in a faded red-and-gold Persian and surrounded on all sides by decrepit bookshelves, some of which were so old and termite-ridden that they appeared to have caved in entirely. A large gas fire—enriched by Professor Bal's trademark 'living flames'—burned silently in the center of the chamber, around which the apprentices' work desks had been arranged. But despite this, the air was uncomfortably chilled and everyone—except Maud, who seemed impervious to extreme temperatures on either end of the spectrum—was wrapped in blankets, coats and scarves.

The group paused as Marion entered. They looked up, their expressions bleak, their hands hovering over a curious array of half-assembled locks of every shape and sort. The purpose of the assignment—to open one's lock without setting off any of its internal alarms—seemed obsolete under the circumstances.

"You've seen this?" Jessica asked, holding up a copy of the announcement Marion had seen posted to the noticeboard at the end of the Grand Corridor. "The Induction Ceremony has been postponed. Indefinitely. *And* we've been ordered to remain underground until further notice."

There was a loud clamor from somewhere beyond the chamber. Arguing, someone yelling, a door slamming.

"Complete shambles," Jessica went on, pulling a large woolen shawl around her shoulders with a shiver. "I mean, everything!"

David Eston—an ill-natured third-year whom Marion had tried very hard to like but never succeeded—was the second to speak as she approached the fire. In his typically callous manner, he gestured to the unoccupied desk to his left, which was covered in dust and crawling mites. "So, Lane. You're going to tell us the facts? Or are we just supposed to guess, as usual?"

Marion settled down. Using her left hand (the other now bandaged and still throbbing from Alan's assault), she drew out her own puzzle—a large bronze pyramid with seven circular hatches, which had to be opened simultaneously in order to prevent the emission of an ear-splitting alarm. She gave Bill a sidelong glance as she set about examining the contraption. Following her conversation with Nancy and Frank in the Games Room, she'd met with Bill, Kenny and Jessica in the common room, where she'd told them everything over a bottle of wine.

But had Bill or Jessica spilled the awful news to anyone else? Had they mentioned anything about Darcy and what she'd plotted? Or Frank's alias? Or the fact that Marion had recently witnessed a cold-blooded murder for which she might very well be the prime suspect? The thought consumed her with shame and regret. Everything that had unfolded in recent days seemed to be her fault. If only she hadn't come up with the grand plan to hoodwink Kenny and Bill, steal five thousand pounds from Zimmerman and mosey on over to Benthal Green, none of this would've happened.

"Word is," David went on unperturbed by her reluctance to answer, "Zimmerman was the one who suggested the agency go on lockdown. That true?"

She frowned, shook her head, ready to toss the rumor aside. Then she remembered the letter Nancy had been reading in the Games Room the night of the Benthal Green disaster. Luminous silver ink on charcoal paper. Weren't those the colors of *Der Schatten*?

"Why would *Zimmerman* make that call?" Preston asked, grinding out a cigarette with one hand while twirling a screwdriver inattentively with the other. His miniature disk-shaped puzzle seemed to shiver at the mere sight of the tool.

"Who knows," David said, his small dark eyes fixed squarely on Marion and burning with suspicion. "Maybe because it was *his* money that was stolen. You want to tell us more about that, Lane? And while you're at it, why don't you tell us how you got that bandage."

"Oh, for goodness' sake, David!" Jessica piped up, flashing Marion an empathetic look and David a scowl. "Why do you insist on being so insensitive? You're never going to be a decent Inquirer carrying on like that. If Marion wants to tell you, she'll do so in her own time."

David shrugged, pulled a cigarette from Preston's pack without asking and lit up. He exhaled a plume of ghostly smoke into the air, knocked back his head. In front of him was a half-assembled lock that looked like a simple shoebox but which, Marion recalled from a past assignment, could only be opened by solving a complex number riddle. "Look, I'm not trying to be an arse or anything—" David went on.

"Try a bit harder, mate," Bill snorted protectively.

"—I'm just repeating what Lane said last year. At Christmas, at Willow Street, remember?" He took another long drag, and this time exhaled the smoke right into Marion's face. She did remember, unfortunately, about the Christmas celebration she'd hosted for the apprentices at Willow Street last year, the first they'd had since Amanda's death. "You said we should always stick together, yeah, help each other out because we're all each other's got. Well, if you really meant it, then let us help." He looked around him, at the others, and for once he wasn't wearing a scowl. "Something's up, chaps. You see it, all of you, I know you do."

"There's always 'something up' in this place," Preston stated sensibly. "Doesn't call for panic, if you're asking me."

"I wasn't asking you," David shot back. "And no. This is different. When in *Miss Brickett's* history has the Induction Ceremony been canceled and the entire place shut down 'for safety concerns'? Not even Michelle White's murder in our first year, or Amanda's murder last year, was enough to cause this level of disruption. And now they're handing out Twister Rope and emergency pens? Nah, there's something rotten going on, and I've a feeling Lane knows exactly what it is."

Marion replaced her screwdriver with a set of tweezers and began plucking at her puzzle's ridiculously tiny bolts, trying to distract herself from the cold ache in her chest. She didn't want to look David in the eye. Because he was right.

"I don't know anything about Zimmerman getting in-volved," she muttered while Jessica and Bill turned uncom-fortably in their seats. "That's the truth. But…yes, I did take money from his safe. It was for a good reason," she added quickly. "And I had, I *have*, every intention of paying him back. As soon as I've figured out…well, as soon as things have settled down." She laid the tweezers on the desk and pulled her fingers through her hair. The full, sordid tale would surely be dispensed through the rumor mill soon enough. She might as well get to it before anyone else did. "It's just that things have become a little more complicated than I expected." She took a long breath. "And it now appears as though I've been entrapped."

"Entrapped? For what?" Maud asked, fidgeting.

"Murder. Among other things."

There was a short, stunned silence, the only sound Preston's puzzle, which was giving off a concerning mechanical groan and emitting puffs of black, sweet-smelling smoke.

"By whom?" Maud asked next, her hands suspended over the puzzle in front of her, a complex-looking contraption with five interconnected keyholes.

"Darcy," Bill answered dully.

"*What?*" David said, glancing at the others as though he expected to find them laughing, like this was some sort of horrid joke. "Darcy? Your girl Darcy?"

"Who else?" Bill said with a groan.

Maud shook her head, and, absentmindedly, inserted a Skeleton Key into one of her puzzle's outermost keyholes.

There was a loud click, causing everyone to look over.

Marion flinched, recognizing the mistake, but before she could say anything, the lock cracked open and a colony of tiny clockwork fire ants scurried out from within.

"Oh, crap!" Maud said, throwing both lock and key into the air and jumping to her feet.

Jessica gasped as the ants spread out across the chamber floor, some disappearing under the Persian rug, some aiming for the door and some heading directly for the apprentices. She lifted her feet onto her chair, turned to Marion and said, in a pleading voice, "Mari! Do something, quick!"

Casually, as though this sort of thing happened on a regular basis, Marion slammed the heel of her boot onto what appeared to be the largest of the ants, which immobilized the entire colony instantly.

"Next time, disarm the code before you try the key," she warned Maud, sitting back down with a huff.

A thick silence descended as the apprentices caught their breath and stared, unfocused, at the motionless mechanical ants scattered like flecks of ash across the chamber floor. No one seemed to be able to process what Bill had just admitted. Or what it meant. And, as if feeding off the gathering energy of the group's panic, the flames of the gas fire blazed ever brighter.

"I don't understand," David said at last, turning to Bill, twisting his beefy, calloused hands together in a rare display of angst. "Darcy's framed Marion for murder because, what? She's jealous?"

"Jealous?" Maud repeated with a confused smile.

David gestured discourteously at Marion and Bill. "Christ, I don't need to spell it out, do I? Three's a crowd, yeah?"

"David! What did we just discuss about sensitivity?" Jessica snapped. "Besides, that's a ridiculous thing to say. Marion and Bill are not, well, they're not—" She paused, blinked slowly at Marion as though she suddenly wasn't quite so sure of her conviction, then mouthed, *Are you?*

"No. We're not, obviously," Marion said quickly, choosing to ignore David's smirk. "And this isn't about Bill at all. It's about my mother. And a man named Phillip Cheevers." The grin on David's face vanished swiftly, replaced by a look of confusion. "Though we know him as Frank."

By the time Marion had finished filling in the others on Frank and Alice's past and how it related to Darcy and everything else, the gas fire had mostly petered out, turning the chamber into a frigid chasm. Fingers numb with cold and minds thoroughly distracted, the apprentices abandoned their puzzle locks and rearranged themselves into a tighter circle.

Jessica handed out the cups of tea and coffee she'd made in the kitchenette next door, along with a plate of biscuits.

"Phillip Cheevers," she mused, repeating the name thoughtfully, her breath lifting like silver smoke to the ceiling. "It's funny, isn't it, that we're surprised he's been keeping so much about himself a secret. But why wouldn't he? Why wouldn't everyone who works here?" She blew onto her mug of tea, took a sip. "We're Inquirers, and if you think about it, we're supposed to live like ghosts, aren't we?"

Marion agreed, though she didn't like to think that the closest thing she had to a family—Frank, and everyone in this room—might not be exactly who they were pretending to be. She wrapped her good hand around her mug and shivered.

"What about McMurray?" David asked abruptly. "I heard he was beaten up near Benthal Green. What was that about, then?"

"I heard Nancy sent him to 'clean up' a crime scene," Preston supplied. "Guess we now know what crime that was."

Marion was beginning to feel sick.

"It was a mob who attacked him," Maud said nonchalantly. "Group of civilians hanging around near the crime scene, apparently. No idea why they'd go after one of us though."

"I think *I* do," came a high-pitched voice from just outside the chamber. Ambrosia Quinn—the freckled, red-haired second-year apprentice—appeared at the threshold, holding an armful of freshly printed copies of *The Daily Telegraph* and several other newspapers. Clearly, she'd been listening in for a while. She faltered, catching sight of Marion, a strange look coming over her face.

"What?" Marion snapped, craning her neck to see the paper, her pulse already beating hard in her ears.

"Oh... I didn't think you'd be here," Quinn said.

"Where else would I be?"

"And why does it matter?" asked Bill.

Quinn glanced down at the stack of papers. She couldn't have looked more discomposed if she'd tried. "Just don't know if you'd want to see this—"

"Hand the bloody thing over, mate," Bill commanded, putting his mug on the floor beside him and getting to his feet.

Quinn shrugged, then threw out copies of *The Daily Telegraph* to anyone in reach.

Marion caught a copy, smoothed it out on her lap as Jessica, Bill, Maud and Preston leaned over her shoulder, all of them reading the headline with bated breath:

FAMILY TRAGEDY, OR VICIOUS DOUBLE MURDER?
London Philanthropist Brothers Die Days Apart. Murder Weapon Missing.

The body of local businessman and co-owner of Biggar Clothing Chain, *Alan Michael Biggar (45), was discovered two nights ago in a storage facility in Benthal Green, Hackney. This comes less than two weeks after the mysterious death of his older brother and business partner, Oscar Biggar (50), at Petticoat Lane market on Sunday, April 10. While at first glance, Alan Biggar's death appeared to be suicide (a .22 Smith & Wesson revolver was discovered in his hand and a bullet lodged in his temple), further investigation of the crime scene has revealed what Scotland Yard now calls "suspicious elements" that "suggest the scene was staged." Namely, fingerprints that did not match the victim's were discovered on the revolver, as well as on an empty and bloodstained duffel bag. Most curiously, however, was the item concealed within the bag: a "bizarre tracking device" that officers claim is "not like anything we've seen before."*

Furthermore, it has recently emerged from a declassified coroner's report that Oscar Biggar's death was caused by strangu-

lation with an object that left a "vague but distinctive mark on the victim's neck." Police were reluctant to provide further details on the matter, but did state that they are currently on the hunt for what they now believe is the murder weapon.

Detective Inspector Donald Knead of Scotland Yard, who is leading the investigation, has this to say: "We are most perplexed by this bizarre and multifaceted case and are still trying to put together the pieces of the puzzle. However, after consultation with MI5, we now firmly believe that the tracking device found in the bag at the scene of Alan Biggar's 'suicide' almost certainly belongs to, and is operated by, The Inquirers. These underground frauds have, in my opinion, haunted London's streets with their unsavory investigations and unnatural gizmos for far too long."

Detective Inspector Knead went on to say: "We've been aware of the Inquirers' existence for over a decade, and in that time we have let them exist in the shadows without objection. In the past, I'm ashamed to admit that we have occasionally overlooked their transgressions, only because we believed that the benefits of their service to the citizens of London outweighed the risks of their illegitimate enterprise. But this is simply too much. We cannot continue to condone such vigilante nonsense. Enough is enough. Thus, we urge the citizens of London to report any sightings of Inquirers and for anyone who knows someone who they believe to be an Inquirer, to come forth immediately. It is indeed time to bring the Inquirers to justice."

Alan Biggar leaves behind a wife. Oscar Biggar, leaves behind a wife and two children (10 and 6).

Information pamphlets were handed out by Scotland Yard yesterday morning to all residents of the London boroughs: Hackney, Islington, Newham and Waltham Forest. If you did not receive yours, please contact the number below.

Marion lifted her eyes from the article. She dropped the newspaper on her desk as a queasiness bloomed in her gut. She'd expected a repercussion, of course, from Alan's murder. She'd expected the reality of her fate to trickle in through the coming days, bit by awful bit. But this was so much worse than she could ever have prepared for.

"And, um," Quinn mumbled, handing Marion another piece of paper—the Scotland Yard pamphlet. "You might want to see this too, I guess."

Marion perused the pamphlet for five seconds—*Ten Ways to Identify an Inquirer and What to Do If You See One*—then scrunched it up and tossed it across the room.

"They have your fingerprints," Jessica croaked.

"They have *some* fingerprints," Bill said, though his tone was unconvincing. "They don't know they're *Mari's*. Not yet."

"And our tracking stone!" Maud supplied, staring at Marion with unmasked horror.

"So… Oscar Biggar…" Jessica went on, voice thin and quivering, "that was…did Darcy?"

Marion nodded. "I don't have any proof but yes, it must have been her. She's out for revenge on everyone who wronged her. Oscar, Alan, Frank and…well, my mother."

"Oscar was murdered on Sunday the tenth," Bill muttered, pressing his fingers into the side of his head as though he was trying to stem a migraine. "We were already together then. She stayed at my place that night. Jesus."

Marion touched him gently on the hand. She wanted to say something comforting, but she was about one minute away from imploding herself. Or whatever happened when one's entire world fell apart. She couldn't feel her limbs, and while she was desperate to get to her feet and pace, run, just *move*, she knew her legs couldn't carry her.

Preston picked up the newspaper and reread the article

under his breath. "What's this about a missing murder weapon, you reckon?" he asked, offering Marion a drag of his cigarette. And although she didn't smoke, she inhaled, coughed and inhaled again. "They say Oscar Biggar was strangled with something that left a distinctive mark on his neck. I'm guessing that's got to be some kind of—"

"That's a problem for another day," Maud interrupted quickly. "It's the tracking stone we should be worrying about now."

"Or maybe not," Jessica said with such pathetic hopefulness that it actually made Marion squirm. "The police can't *prove* the tracking stone is ours. It's just a theory."

"Who else would it belong to?" David said irritably. "James Bond?"

Jessica threw him a glowering look. "What I mean is, they can't prove it in a court of law. They assume it's ours just because MI5 said it's not theirs. And maybe because it's a little bizarre looking...or something like that."

"Doesn't matter, though," David said. "The fact is—" he ripped the newspaper from Preston and jabbed a finger at the article "—it's out there now, yeah? The *assumption* that we're behind the murder has been put out there and that's all the public needs, because assumption *is* reality. And I'm pretty sure that if they think one of us killed Alan Biggar, they'll think we killed his brother too. The police might need proof, but the public doesn't. Just ask McMurray."

"Does Darcy know about the bookshop?" Maud asked, looking from Bill to Marion. "Christ, she does, doesn't she?"

Feeling suddenly chilled to the bone, Marion retrieved a coat from her bag and draped it over her shoulders, then pulled a blanket up to her chin. She curled up in her seat, hands under her thighs, staring at the newspaper on her desk and the puzzle lock in pieces beside it. Her eyes traveled to Bill, who was running a finger absently along his chin. Then to David and Jessica and Preston, who were staring at *The Daily Telegraph* in silence while Maud tossed a pair of pliers from hand to hand.

The Inquirers had always played a balancing act with the law, swaying precariously on a tightwire far too lax for the weight of their secrets. They had remained upright all these years, mostly by luck, partly by good management. But that was changing now, thanks to Marion's carelessness.

The chamber door split open, snapping her back to the present.

Nancy's slim, stiff silhouette loomed in the threshold. Behind her stood Rupert Nicholas, and slithering at his ankles, a clockwork serpent.

RECEIVER BOX THIRTY-ONE

NANCY STEPPED INSIDE, EYED THE NEWSPAPERS strewn throughout the chamber, the apprentices huddled around the remains of the gas fire. Behind her in the corridor, eagerly awaiting further instruction, was Mr. Nicholas and his dreaded spy snake.

"I see," Nancy said, pushing her cat's-eye spectacles farther up her nose and gesturing to the pile of newspapers. "The news has spread already. I might have guessed."

Everyone shifted nervously, as they always did in Nancy's presence.

Through the slit in the doorway, metallic scales glittered like cut glass, and a soft hiss echoed through the chamber.

Nancy moved farther inside, her hands clasped at her waist, while Nicholas paced impatiently in the corridor, muttering under his breath and throwing Marion the occasional dirty look. Although the issue of Zimmerman's missing cash was no longer any of his business, he clearly felt otherwise.

"This might not come as a surprise to you, but as a result of this report, we are now facing some very dire complications," Nancy said, tapping the nearest newspaper with the toe of her shoe. "The police and the public believe we are, in some capacity at least, involved in the Biggar Brothers' murders." She paused. No one moved, save Nicholas, who shuffled over the threshold, turning a pocket watch over in his hand.

He pressed something on the watch. The snake followed. *Clink-Schlik, Schlik—Clink-Schlik, Schlik.*

"And I'm afraid Senior Inquirer, Dicky McMurray, has now had firsthand experience of the consequences of these assumptions," Nancy continued. "He was attacked just this morning on his way to Benthal Green. I sent him there to remove evidence from the scene of Alan Biggar's murder. He arrived to find a mob waiting and had he not been armed with a Distracter..." She trailed off. "Fortunately, or perhaps *unfortunately* for some, Scotland Yard's identification pamphlets are rather vague, which means the mob isn't entirely sure who are Inquirers and who are not. For example, two young men and one woman, supposedly dressed like Inquirers, were attacked last night. One of the victims was beaten mercilessly. I'm told the mob was trying to get him to reveal the location of our headquarters. Of course, he couldn't and he is currently in hospital with severe injuries, including several broken bones and a potentially life-altering head wound."

"Good God," Marion muttered, placing a hand on the edge of her chair. Really, could it get any worse?

"Now," Nancy added, "while we have always had discretion and disguise on our side, I am afraid this incident clearly demonstrates that it is no longer safe for any of us, no matter how inconspicuous or careful we are, to venture aboveground for any reason other than an emergency. If there are family or friends you would like to inform about your forthcoming absence, please speak to Mr. Perry in the Filing Department, who will arrange a discreet letter, or preferably, a telephone call. I am afraid that is all I can offer you for the time being."

David cursed under his breath, his gruff features already twitching with the first signs of an unbridled temper. "Are you ordering us to stay underground? Or are you asking us to?"

"I am *ordering* it, of course, Mr. Eston. If you work under my name, you work under my rules. I am responsible for your safety and whether you agree or not, this is the only way I can ensure your protection and anonymity." She flicked her wrist, a secret signal.

Behind her, Nicholas fiddled hastily with his signature pocket watch and, in response, the snake at his feet slithered across the chamber, its yellow eyes—cameras—swiveling in its head, settling on each of the apprentices in turn.

David seemed to shrink in his seat as the creature slithered closer, its tongue tasting the air for movement.

"Now, just so you're aware, this snake will be patrolling the Grand Corridor, day and night," Nancy announced through tight lips, "protecting us from…unwelcome guests." She clicked her fingers and, reluctantly, Nicholas turned a dial on his pocket watch, calling the snake back to his feet. Marion let out a breath, and David let out a grumble. "I would prefer a timely warning," Nancy added, as if to further explain the need for the snake, "should our security be breached. We must assume the public or police will eventually unmask one of us and, of course, if they do, they will discover that the bookshop is a ruse."

"But still," Jessica said, voice shrill with disbelief. "They'd never get in, right? Through the trapdoor. Through the lift. They'd never figure it all out."

No one seemed to argue with this, though Marion doubted they agreed with such a proclamation. Maybe finding the trapdoor concealed between the floorboards behind the butler's desk would take hours, if not days. And yes, the lift that delivered its passengers from the bookshop to the tunnels beneath the streets was fitted with a multitude of security features that made it nearly impossible for anyone who was not a *Miss Brickett's* employee to use. *Nearly.*

Nancy touched the bridge of her spectacles and repeated, "The snake and Rupert will be on patrol until I have come up with a better solution. I am sorry if that is unsettling, or an inconvenience, but I am quite certain you would prefer it to having our premises raided by the police, or a bloodthirsty mob." She nodded at Nicholas, who slinked away, followed by a slither of metal and scales. She then set her eyes on Marion. "Miss Lane. May I speak with you for a moment? Privately."

"Miss Gibson has chosen a time and place," Nancy explained minutes later as they marched from the chamber, down the icy corridor and past a line of deserted offices. "The Filing Department received her letter less than an hour ago." Next, they passed the infirmary, in which Marion heard an undertone of nervous chatter. It was likely that the entire workforce already knew about Darcy Gibson's ultimatum, the entrapment and absolutely everything else. *Wonderful.*

"We can't hand Frank over to her," Marion said. "She'll ask him to apologize and then she'll kill him."

Reaching the towering doors that guarded the library, Nancy stopped, forcing Marion to do the same. "I know that, Miss Lane, and it leaves us with only one alternative." She touched her throat, and the thin gold chain that hung there.

"Agreed," Marion said hastily, thinking on her feet. "We ambush her at the rendezvous point. Which is where, by the way?"

Nancy looked at her as though she were a child who'd just

said something absolutely idiotic and which was hardly worth correcting. Obviously, intercepting Darcy wasn't the "alternative" Nancy was thinking about. "And what would you suggest we do after we've managed to 'ambush her,' as you put it?"

"Well, then we…we… I don't know," Marion said dumbly. "We just need to keep her under our watch so she can't talk to the police. Or harm Frank, obviously."

"Brilliant, thank you," Nancy said. "I hadn't thought of it like that." Again, she touched the chain at her throat, which Marion now noticed held a tiny locket, engraved with the agency's emblem—a half-formed circle, encasing the letter *I*. No further proof was needed that *Miss Brickett's* was the closest thing to her heart. If she had one, that is. "And by 'keep her under our watch,' do you perhaps mean lock her in the Holding Chambers?"

Marion swallowed. That was exactly what she'd meant, even though the idea made her shudder. "Maybe just until, I don't know, we can think of something else."

"I see. Well, unfortunately that's not an option. After last year's…fiasco, the High Council and I decided to have the Holding Chambers closed down. Permanently."

By "fiasco," she knew Nancy was talking about the time Marion and Bill had *almost* aided the escape of the Holding Chambers' last remaining prisoner, ex-Inquirer and Michelle White's murderer—Edgar Swindlehurst. And while he had died during the botched getaway, his near escape served as a warning that the chambers weren't quite as secure as everyone had once assumed.

"Okay," Marion said slowly, digesting this new piece of information and trying to decide how she felt about it. Part of her was relieved the Holding Chambers had been closed down (especially since she was still waiting to hear what her punishment for stealing Zimmerman's cash would be). Part of her, though, was troubled by the news. If they couldn't lock Darcy up at the agency then what *could* they do with her?

"We incapacitate her," Nancy said simply, as if Marion had asked this question out loud.

Something, or someone, rustled behind the nearest book-shelf. The lights flickered. Marion's heartbeat pounded in her temples.

"Incapacitate?" Marion echoed, her voice slightly shrill with disbelief. "You mean...*kill*?"

Nancy gave her a look that was as unreadable as ever. "You need not worry about the details, Miss Lane. Leave it to me."

It wasn't something Nancy had ever said out loud, so plainly. But it was something everyone, in some sense, already knew. Nancy would protect the agency at all costs. She would do anything to secure their secrets. Even this. Even *murder*.

This was the first time Marion had been here—privy to a *Miss Brickett's* whitewash, witnessing the deception from within. Had similar conversations been held between Nancy and the High Council when Michelle White was murdered two years ago? And after Amanda Shirley's murder last year? And the mysterious vanishing of Ned Ashbry several years before that? What sort of cover-ups and cleanups had been undertaken for those incidents? she wondered now.

It felt wrong, like a betrayal, for Marion not to object to what she'd just heard. But while she couldn't accept the injustice of it, for the first time in her career, she truly understood: *Miss Brickett's* was built and sustained on secrets. Rightly or wrongly, Nancy had chosen to form her organization under-ground, concealed from the world and the long arm of the law. And that was where it would have to remain. Forever.

They arrived at the Filing Department moments later. Though starkly lit, it felt distinctly eerie under the circumstances.

Kenny and Frank were standing solemnly and in silence,

staring at the colossal wall of pneumatic tubes and connected receiver boxes, one of which had been pulled open to reveal a single piece of paper with a single line of script.

Kenny touched Marion's hand as she came to his side. For once, he actually looked as exhausted as she knew he was. His shirt was untucked and creased, and he was dressed in the same pair of jeans he'd been wearing for the past three days. Nothing wrong with that, unless you were Kenny Hugo. Even his hair, though still (miraculously) styled into its customary side wave, seemed to have lost some of its sheen.

"It came through about an hour ago," Frank said gravely, nodding at receiver box thirty-one.

Marion leaned closer and read the note. *"Bring me Cheevers, Saturday, 6:00 a.m. Knightsbridge station. P.S. In case you're planning something clever, just know I have an insurance policy."*

She looked up at Frank, but his expression was obscure. She turned to Nancy, thinking of the conversation they'd just had in the library.

"Obviously," Nancy said, "we need to find out what this 'insurance policy' is before we finalize our plans for Saturday."

Marion was about to ask if by this she meant they couldn't go ahead with a plan to "incapacitate" Darcy until they'd found out what her insurance policy was, and whether it was something that could derail an execution.

But instead she turned to the sound of footsteps tumbling down the staircase. The door to the department burst open and Bill appeared, flustered and out of breath, at the threshold.

He eyed the foursome cagily, then the receiver box and the note inside. "Is it from her?" he asked, wiping a lick of sweat from his neck. "I heard something had come through. I'm guessing it's not good news."

"Depends, I suppose. Darcy's set a day and time," Kenny explained. "This Saturday morning at Knightsbridge station."

"What time?"

"Six."

"So what are we going to do?" Bill asked.

"Well, there's something else," Kenny said, after Nancy gave him an approving nod. "We received another letter this morning. A tip-off from someone who calls herself Pearl."

"Darcy's roommate at the boardinghouse," Bill confirmed. "I know her. I gave her my telephone number and the location of our nearest letter case, should she hear anything about, well—" he shook his head and sighed "—you know."

Kenny put a hand on his shoulder. "Yeah, she addressed the letter to you. She says she has some information we'll find interesting. About Darcy's plan. She left a telephone number. We tried to call right away, but no one answered. Eventually we got through to someone, but they hung up when we said who we were looking for. Either she got spooked and changed her mind, or she's been silenced."

Bill started to pace, hands in his pockets, shoulders hunched. "Could be either, really," he muttered. "I mean, Darcy wouldn't be happy if she found out, would she? But Pearl *did* seem like the type who'd get the willies. I tried to get something out of her when I was looking for Darcy. It was like drawing blood from a stone. I had a feeling she knew something, though, else she wouldn't have been so guarded."

"But since the letter was addressed to you," said Frank slowly, nodding at Bill, "it might be best if *you* tried to get in contact with her instead. Unfortunately, since our last attempt, the telephone line has been engaged."

Bill stopped pacing, drew his hands from his pockets and clasped them together behind his back. "Then I'll go to the boardinghouse. I can't promise she'll be forthcoming, but I guess it's all we've got."

"No!" Marion said hastily, an awful dread growing in the

pit of her stomach as she relived her rendezvous in Benthal Green. "What if it's a trap? Something Darcy's set up. We should expect it, after everything."

"Doubt it," Kenny countered. "And even if it is, what choice do we have? It's this or we go in blind, let Frank meet Darcy at the station on Saturday without any idea what she's plotting. Which is a death sentence, if you're asking me."

"I know but…it's just too convenient," Marion insisted, her cheeks reddening as her voice raised. "Pearl reaching out all of a sudden, then not answering the telephone so that Bill's forced to meet her at the boardinghouse. Come on! You've got to see how amiss this looks."

Bill shrugged. "I do. But like Kenny said, what choice do we have?"

Nancy looked at her watch. "Well put, Mr. Hobb. Now, does that mean you're agreeing to pay Pearl a visit?"

Bill nodded but said nothing.

"Good," Nancy said. "I will have Professor Bal organize a traveling kit immediately and ask Mr. Nicholas to ensure the Grand Corridor and exit are cleared for you."

"This is madness!" Marion snapped, glaring at Nancy, then Frank. "You just told us how dangerous it is for Inquirers to venture aboveground and now you're—"

"Mari, relax," Bill soothed. "I'll be fine. Besides, like everyone always says, I don't look like an Inquirer. No one will suspect me."

It was supposed to be a joke, of course, but it only made Marion more furious. She grit her teeth and, with Nancy and Frank engaged in a private discussion, she pulled Bill and Kenny aside. "Let me go instead. Please."

"Are you crazy?" Kenny said. "You're a wanted murderer in Scotland Yard's eyes."

"Rubbish. The police have nothing but some mystery finger-prints. No one knows my face." *Yet*, she thought but didn't say.

"No one but Darcy," Bill piped up. "Please, Mari, don't argue. There's no chance any of us will let you do this."

"Just think for a moment. *Think*," Marion said. "If this is a trap, and I'm the one who falls into it, there isn't much Darcy can do to me. She thinks she needs me alive in order to bring her Cheevers on Saturday. That's all she cares about. But it's a very different story for you, Bill. You're just leverage to her." She immediately regretted her choice of words, which forced Bill to confront—once again—the fact that Darcy hadn't ever really loved him. She softened her tone and added, "Darcy knows us, she knows how much I care about you, and what I'd do to protect you. That's why she used you to get to me in the first place."

Bill nodded, then rubbed the back of his neck in frustration. "Mari, I know all that but…you don't understand, Pearl won't speak to anyone else." He gestured to Nancy and Frank, who were now done with their conversation and had rejoined the trio. "They've already tried. It has to be me."

Kenny looked at Marion, and for a moment it seemed as though he wanted to say something. His lips moved, he shook his head, turned to Bill instead. "You're right, bud. About everything. But so is Lane. It's dangerous, and it could be a setup. So… I'm coming with you."

Marion dug her nails into her palms. This was absolutely *not* what she'd had in mind, but before she could object, Kenny took her hand and said under his breath, "I promise you, Lane, I won't let anything happen to him." And when she huffed, he repeated, *"I promise."*

"Then it's settled," Nancy announced. "Hobb, Hugo, be ready at dusk."

INSURANCE POLICY

MARION PADDED QUIETLY DOWN THE GRAND Corridor, slipping between the marble columns, careful not to be seen as she trailed Kenny and Bill. Bedecked with Professor Bal's unique disguises, it took her a moment to realize who was who. Kenny wore spectacles and contact lenses that made his large brown eyes look more like pinpricks. His normally coiffed hair was slick against his scalp and parted down the middle, and something very strange had been done to his jawline, though Marion couldn't quite figure out what. Bill was similarly transformed by a blond wig, false mustache, chin enhancers and a waistband that widened his girth considerably.

Marion shuffled around a winged statue at the end of the corridor, catching sight of Mr. Nicholas, who was hovering near the lift, a spy snake curled at his feet. He yanked at a lever fitted to the wall, retracting a set of trip wires stretched across the floor, allowing Kenny and Bill (and, unbeknownst to everyone, Marion) to pass through.

"How long will you be?" Nicholas asked impatiently, ushering the men into the lift while Marion crouched behind the nearest column, listening in.

"Not less than two hours," Kenny answered, giving the snake a sidelong glance. "It'll take us at least that long to drive there and back, never mind everything else."

Nicholas tapped what appeared to be some sort of timer fitted to the lift door. "Then I'll set this to unlock again in three hours. You won't be able to use the lift before then. Understood?"

Marion waited until the doors had closed and the gears clanked into motion. She counted to sixty, just about enough time for the lift to reach the bookshop, drop off its passengers and begin its descent.

Nicholas reached for the timer as the lift clunked and jerked, now less than two seconds from reaching its starting point.

"Fifty-nine, sixty..." She drew an unlit light orb from her haversack and lobbed it down the corridor.

Immediately, the snake at Nicholas's feet unfurled, awoken by the rapid motion. Its eyes flicked on, its silvery scales glinted. Nicholas frowned at the orb, gathering speed across the smooth marble floor, but before he could decide where it had come from, or whether to investigate the matter, his snake darted out from under his feet. He faltered for a moment, then marched after the serpent and its prey in a huff, giving Marion a split second to step inside the lift.

Moments later, she opened the bookshop door, stepped out into the cul-de-sac. She paused, tilted her head, listening. The purr of Kenny's car engine. The quick rap of her heart. But was there something else? Another heartbeat, not quite in sync with her own. She glanced over her shoulder, at the bookshop behind her. A warm orange glow was pulsing from its window, as though calling her back to safety. But it was just an illusion. Nowhere was safe now.

At the other end of the cul-de-sac, Kenny's beloved Hudson sedan appeared from the shadows, its engine purring gently, headlights winking.

The passenger door strung open, and Bill climbed inside.

"What the blazes!" Kenny said from the driver's side, winding down his window as he spotted Marion marching toward the car.

"Ah, bloody hell," Bill grumbled. "What are you doing here?"

"I already told you." She tried the back door, but it was locked. "We're all in this position because of me so I'm coming with you, like it or not." She tried the door again, still locked. "Now let me in!"

"How did you get out?" Bill asked, clearly baffled and also slightly impressed. He rubbed his false belly and shook his head. "Nicholas...the snakes..."

"There's no time to explain. Point is, our dear Nicholas has set the lift to unlock in only three hours, which means I can't go back. So, either you leave me alone in the bookshop, which is really quite dangerous all things considered, or you let me come with you." She crossed her arms. "Well? What will it be?"

Kenny dropped his head onto the steering wheel and groaned while Bill reached behind him and unlocked the back door.

"You can't argue with her when she's like this, mate," Bill said to Kenny. "Trust me."

Kenny slipped a cigarette between his lips, struck a match and lit up. He was still miraculously handsome, despite his ghastly hairstyle, pinprick eyes and peculiar jawline. "Fine, Lane. Get inside. But let's beat feet. We're already late." He took a drag as she climbed inside, then stamped on the accelerator and pulled away at breakneck speed, tires screeching on the tarmac.

"Um, might be a better idea to drive like a normal person, since we're trying to avoid suspicion," Marion pointed out, one hand gripping the edge of her seat, the other the door handle.

Kenny took a sharp left at the end of the cul-de-sac, then veered right down New Kings Road, the smoldering cigarette drooping from the side of his mouth.

"He's *not* normal, so that's impossible," Bill chipped in, similarly clinging on to whatever he could.

Kenny tapped the brakes aggressively as they arrived at a stop street. "Quit complaining, both of you," he said with a grin. "You wanna get there or not?"

"Alive, yes." Marion gasped a little as the car accelerated once more, then swerved recklessly around a man on a bicycle (who threw up his hands and cursed in response).

After some further encouragement, Kenny brought the car back down to a reasonable speed, allowing Marion to watch the glittering lights of London zip past her window. It almost felt like any other night, and for a moment she allowed herself to imagine that the three of them were off to the pictures, or dinner at a pub.

"You both look ridiculous, by the way," she added frivolously. "But completely unrecognizable, which I suppose is the point." She sniffed the air, frowned. "And is one of you wearing perfume? What *is* that smell?"

"Definitely not me," Bill said, running his fingers through his wig.

"It's called cologne, babe," Kenny said. "Heard of it?"

"No, not *that* smell," Marion said. "There's something else, something—"

"Yeah," Bill piped up, "yeah, you're right, Mari. I smell

it too. Actually, I think—" He opened the glove compartment, scratched around. "Ha! Knew it!" He held up a large purple bottle of hairspray. "'*Aqua Net*, extra strong hold,'" he announced triumphantly, causing Kenny to flinch and the car to swerve slightly to the right. "What's this about, then?"

Kenny shrugged. "How'd you think I get *the wave* so perfect every time? You're welcome to borrow some, by the way."

Marion snorted as Bill chucked the bottle to the side and started laughing. "Ah, blimey, this is brilliant. I bloody well knew it! Mum used the stuff every day. I'll never forget the smell."

"Yeah, yeah," Kenny mumbled. "Cut the gas, Hobb."

"*Aqua Net.*" Bill continued to chuckle under his breath. "Brilliant!" He spasmed with fits of laughter, and Marion found herself smiling for the first in what seemed like ages. God, all she wanted was for this to be over, for them to turn the car around, drive back to the bookshop and pretend everything was normal again. But what *was* normal these days? Chaos and disaster seemed to follow her everywhere, ever since her first months at *Miss Brickett's*, and Michelle White's murder. Would there ever be a time when she could simply concentrate on her job, and enjoy the company of the people she loved most, the people in this car? She put her hands in her lap and stared blankly through the windscreen in front of her, feeling the unease crawl like mites in her stomach.

The car slowed as they neared their destination, the boardinghouse in Peckham. While London central had been loud and bustling, here, south of the Thames, the streets and alleyways seemed subdued, even desolate.

"Take the next right," Bill instructed, pointing at the street ahead while consulting the map he'd brought along.

They drew up alongside what had probably once been a lavish manor house but which now looked more like a prison.

Its second and third floor windows were barred and dim, and its front door had been replaced with a security gate.

Kenny ground out his cigarette. "This it, Hobb? You sure."

"Yeah," Bill confirmed, peering out the window. "I'm sure."

The street on which the boardinghouse stood was lined with parked cars, rubbish bins and, unfortunately, several groups of pedestrians. Marion turned to the knot of young men loitering near a parked van a few feet off. They were chattering among themselves, backs turned to the street. But when Kenny searched for a place to park, two of the men turned around and glared unashamedly at the car.

"There's something I don't trust about this setup," Marion reiterated as Kenny pulled into a space just yards from the van.

"Neither do I," Kenny said, "which is exactly why you shouldn't have come." He pulled up the hand brake and turned off the ignition. "Now listen, both of you." He turned in his seat to give Marion a swift glare. "I'm the most experienced with this sort of thing, so you're going to do exactly what I tell you, or I'm turning us around and driving right back to the bookshop."

"Of course, Hugo. I always do as you say, don't I?" Marion chirped sarcastically as she drew out a pair of night-vision binoculars and scanned the street twice over. She was looking for Darcy, first and foremost, but she was also keen to make sure there wasn't anyone loitering near the boardinghouse who might've passed for a member of Scotland Yard. Because despite her earlier reassurances to Bill and Kenny, there was always a chance Darcy had already blown Marion's cover and revealed her identity to the police.

She checked the street a third time, then opened her door.

"Whoa!" Kenny said, pulling her back before she'd managed to set a foot on the tarmac. "It's definitely not going to be you going in there."

"Absolutely not," Bill agreed immediately, wedging his now widened frame into the space between the Hudson's two front seats.

"Do we really have to have this argument? *Again?*" Marion angled her body so that she was facing both Bill and Kenny. "There's no way I'm not—" Something cold wrapped around her wrists, and for a moment she was unsure what it was. Then she realized. "What on earth are you doing? Get it off me! Get it off me right this minute!"

Kenny looked at Bill, then the coil of Twister Rope he'd flung at Marion, which was tightening swiftly around her wrists. "She's not going to listen—" he extended a hand in Bill's direction "—so please, explain."

Bill looked Marion right in the eye, which she had to give him credit for because she imagined her stare was now one of particular fury. "Mari, look, if Frank finds out you're here and we just let you wander into the boardinghouse, he'll kill us."

"I don't care! Take this thing off me!"

"Darcy could be inside," Kenny said. "And you're the only one who's not in disguise. It's too dangerous."

"She's not going to harm *me*, bozos!" Marion snapped. "How many times do I have to say this—Darcy thinks I'm the only one who can hand over Frank. But she'll have no trouble killing either one of you, or taking you hostage. Bill, for heaven's sake, can't you see how vulnerable *you* are, especially?"

Marion might've been talking to the pavement for all the consideration she got.

Kenny turned to Bill, completely ignoring Marion as she writhed furiously within her bonds. "You got the hardware, Hobb? Let's get this over and done with."

"Spot on." Bill dug around in his bag, pulled out a second coil of Twister Rope. "I'll be back in a moment."

Kenny put a hand on the rope, forcing Bill to pause. "Not you, Hobb. I'll be the one going in."

"What?" Bill said irritably.

"Like I said, I've got the most experience with these things. Just trust me." Gently, he pried the rope from Bill's fingers.

"But Pearl won't—"

"I'll tell her you're here and bring her to the car. Easy." Kenny looked at Marion through the rearview mirror, gave her a small nod. "I won't be long," he added, exposing a flash of tanned skin as he slid the rope under his shirt. "Keep a look-out. I'll send a signal if anything interesting happens. Otherwise, hold tight till I get back with Pearl."

"What sort of signal?" Marion asked, her heart now thumping in her throat. It was a cool night, but sweat was already gathering at the back of her neck, and on her chest.

"I don't know, a gunshot, a flare, something like that." He flashed Marion a grin, though it seemed somewhat forced. "Kidding, Lane. Just cool it, I'll be fine. Take over here, Hobb," he added, tapping the steering wheel, "and make sure you're ready for a quick escape." He opened the door and stepped onto the pavement.

"Kenny, wait!" Marion said desperately as Bill climbed over into the driver's seat, placed his hands on the steering wheel. "Please...just." She sighed. "Be careful."

He tapped his head in a mock salute and started for the boardinghouse.

"Bill, take this bloody thing off me!" Marion snapped, holding her bound hands in the air.

Bill hesitated a beat, then, registering the fury on her face, set to work demagnetizing the rope.

"You know, we wouldn't have to resort to these sort of

things if you weren't always so stubborn." The Twister Rope slipped to the car floor with a soft thud. "Sometimes I think you actually *want* to get yourself killed."

She ignored him, grabbed the binoculars and pressed them to her eyes. Kenny had already reached the boardinghouse gate and was chatting to an elderly, haggard woman who'd just appeared from inside. Marion held her breath as he disappeared from sight and a silence fell upon the car.

Outside, a slice of moon appeared from behind a coat of gray clouds. The air was breathless, and Marion felt an urge to open a window and gulp down whatever oxygen came her way. Instead, she turned to Bill, who'd fallen into a reverie and was staring listlessly at the street ahead.

"You all right?" she asked as the minutes ticked by languidly.

He shrugged, ran a finger around the steering wheel. "Not really. I just can't make sense of it all. Why did Darcy use me like this? Why didn't she just go after you from the beginning?"

"She figured it'd be less suspicious, I suppose. I mean, how would she and I have become friends without you being involved? It would've been a bit strange for her to just walk up to me in the middle of the street and strike up a conversation."

"Yeah, guess so. I just can't believe I didn't see her for what she was." He blinked, shook his head. "I think I was infatuated with her more than anything else. But still, makes me feel like a proper idiot. And it hurts, too."

Marion kept her eyes on the boardinghouse, even when Bill's flickered in her direction.

"I mean, I hate her," he went on, "she makes me sick… everything she did to you, to Alice. It's just…" He removed his hands from the wheel, placed them in his lap instead. "It's strange, how you can't just turn it off, you know."

"Were you in love?"

He shrugged. "Like I said, it was infatuation more than anything else. I was an idiot, obviously, for not seeing through her, but you know how it is in the beginning." He paused and again his eyes flickered momentarily in Marion's direction. "But no. It wasn't love, not even close." He was silent for a long while. "Kenny, on the other hand. He really loves you, you know that, yeah?"

Marion shifted in her seat but said nothing.

"Those gadgets he's been working on," Bill added with a chuckle. "That rose, the singing Distracter. All because *you* love gadgets. It's so obvious it's almost a bit...ridiculous."

She laughed. "That rose is basically a deadly weapon. But I see your point."

"And this whole thing about protecting me, following me around like a bodyguard. It's not for me. It's for you, Mari." He reached back and squeezed her shoulder. "Like I said, he really loves you. So, if you love him back, let him know, yeah?"

Something twinged in her chest. "I don't know how. Or maybe I do. I'm just scared."

"The second one."

"It's because of Mum and Dad, I think. They had such a rubbish marriage. So sad, so tragic. But it wasn't like that in the beginning, you know. They were happy once, and then it all went so bad. How do I know that won't happen with me and Kenny?"

"You don't. That's just life. But if you love someone, it's worth the risk. Always."

Marion could think of nothing more to say, so checked the time and changed the subject. "Where is he? He's taking too long."

"It's been ten minutes."

"Yes, but how long does it take to walk inside, fetch Pearl and come back. He said he'd give us a signal if there was—"

"Look," Bill said, interrupting.

Kenny emerged from the boardinghouse at last, accompanied by a pale, willowlike figure wearing a faded floral nightdress and white puff slippers. Her hair was in rollers, and she held a lit cigarette between her lips. The pair made their way down the stairs, through the gate and onto the pavement.

"That's her, that's Pearl, right?" Marion asked.

Bill nodded. "And she looks about as forthcoming as she was last time I saw her. Great."

Voices lifted, Kenny's brisk and loud, Pearl's a high-pitched whine. Their exchange continued for several minutes, escalating as Kenny ripped the cigarette from Pearl's mouth and ground it out on the pavement.

Pearl, clearly furious, turned back to the boardinghouse. But before she'd taken a step, Kenny had her by the wrist. He nodded at the Hudson. Pearl tried to pull away. Their voices rose again, but eventually they seemed to reach some sort of resolution. Kenny pointed to the car once again, and this time Pearl followed him willingly across the street.

"Take it off," Marion said to Bill. "Your disguise. Quickly, or she won't talk to you."

Bill did as she suggested, ripping off his waistband and wig just as Kenny and Pearl reached the car and clambered into the back seat alongside Marion. Kenny closed and locked the doors, handed the Twister Rope over to Bill.

"Who the hell are *you* now?" Pearl asked, eyeing Marion.

Marion put on her best fake smile. "Lovely to meet you, too."

"I asked to speak to him," she replied, jabbing a finger at Bill. "No one else."

"And here I am," Bill said. "These are my colleagues. You can trust them. Promise."

Pearl shrunk back into her seat, folded her arms across her body. "If Darcy finds out I've spoken to any of you, she'll slit my throat."

"Likewise," Marion said. "So go on, please. The sooner we get this over with, the better for all of us."

Pearl turned her head to the window and the grim board-inghouse, looming above them. The streetlights twinkled in a rising smog, their strength slowly dwindling.

"They're here again—" She nodded at the group of men near the van, one of whom was staring directly at the Hudson. "They've been hanging around since last week. And don't ask, 'cause I don't know who they are."

"Take a guess," Kenny said impatiently.

Pearl swallowed, weaved the belt of her nightdress around her fingers. "Seems to me they work for that fella who came around and threatened me the night Darcy went missing."

Marion looked at Bill and Kenny, mouthing the name, *Alan*. Great. First a civilian mob out hunting the Inquirers and now a Biggar Brothers' mob out hunting Darcy.

"I reckon they're looking for her, like everyone else," Pearl explained. "But she ain't coming back here, that's for sure."

"Why do you think that?" Marion asked.

Pearl shrugged, but instead of providing an answer, she changed the subject. "I tried to be her friend, I did, but to be honest, I never trusted her. I mean, how could I, seeing as the cow came straight from prison?"

Bill moved in his seat, but said nothing in Darcy's defense.

"I told Mrs. T I didn't like it. Said I didn't want no shifty woman sleeping in my room, else I'll have to worry about her stealing my pantyhose in the middle of the night. Or worse. But who you get as a roommate in this hovel is just luck of the draw, ain't it? Anyway, a few weeks ago, I came home early from my night shift down at the club and found her sitting on the floor next to the bed, all shifty like. She nearly had a fit when she saw me, tried to pack it away."

"Pack what away?" Bill asked as Pearl paused, turning once again to stare wistfully out of the window.

"Well, I don't think she thought I'd seen anything, or she would've been more careful with her words. But she said it was something she might need if 'they try to kill' her, who-ever *they* are."

Marion, Kenny and Bill exchanged glances.

"Right," Marion said. "And what was this *thing*, exactly?"

"It looked more like a death wish, if you want the honest truth. You don't get nothing good from a pile of shells and nails and wires, do ya? Bullet shells, that is, cartridges. Loads of them, scattered everywhere. Then there was something that looked like part of a drain pipe, about this long—" She spread her hands apart to indicate a length of about six inches. "Now, I don't know much about anything, I'll admit, but I sure as hell know pipes and wires and bullets make a right mix of trouble."

Nails. Cartridges. Wires. Piping. *"Pipe bomb,"* Marion muttered to herself.

She turned back to Pearl, trying to decide whether she trusted those small, flitting eyes. Was it possible she was making this up? "How sure are you about what you saw?"

"You think I was hallucinating or something? Think I could've seen ribbons instead of wires and pebbles instead of bullets? I'm positive," Pearl said. "No doubt about it." She looked at Bill, her expression becoming almost piteous. "I'm sorry for what she's done to you. I figure you was just a pawn in her little game, same as the rest of us fools. But don't beat yourself up about it, all right, love? You couldn't have seen it coming. That Darcy's a first class liar—has been since the day she came to live here. She even charmed the socks off Mrs. T, which is some feat, I'll tell ya." She reached forward and touched Bill gingerly on the shoulder. "You're better off without her, love, trust me."

He nodded awkwardly, and rubbed his neck.

Out of the corner of her eye, Marion noticed Alan's heavies shift on their feet. One of them called out, though his words were lost to the hum of the city.

"We should go," she said, suddenly anxious. "We're too exposed here."

Kenny acknowledged her with a nod, turned to Pearl. "What do you know about Saturday morning?"

Pearl frowned. "What?"

"Saturday morning," Kenny repeated. "Knightsbridge station. Ring any bells?"

"No, it don't."

"And do you know where Darcy might've relocated to once she left the boardinghouse?" Marion asked hastily.

"You think she'd tell *me* that?"

Kenny looked at Marion, shrugged.

"Just let her go," Bill murmured despondently.

"He's right," Marion said, nodding at Bill. "Let's just get out of here."

Pearl opened the door, got out. But as she started for the boardinghouse stairs, she paused, looked over her shoulder.

Marion followed her line of sight. Three of Alan's heavies broke off from the group and began marching across the street.

Pearl's eyes flickered with terror.

"Kenny—" Marion breathed.

"Pass me a Twister Rope," he said. "Quick!"

Marion grabbed hers from the floor, lobbed it over. "I'm coming with you."

Kenny got out, the rope hanging loosely over his shoulder.

"Kenny, wait." She tried to move, but Bill held her back.

"Just hold on," he said, releasing her. He placed one hand on the key, dangling from the ignition, one on the gear stick. He waited a second longer, then started the engine.

Meanwhile, Pearl tried to run toward the car, but one of the men was already at her side. He grabbed her by the arm, threw her to the ground. From about a foot away, Kenny cast the Twister Rope at the attacker's legs. It coiled itself around his feet, and he tumbled awkwardly to the pavement.

"Run!" Kenny said, lifting Pearl upright. "To the car!"

She nodded, sped across the street, just as the other two men arrived at the scene. Leading the pack was a robust man, holding a long metal object that looked something like a fire poker.

Kenny tried to dash right, toward the Hudson, but the men cut in front of him. He was surrounded.

It happened so quickly that Marion didn't have time to react. Kenny was on the ground, the thugs looming over him. All she could see now was the rhythmic flash of the fire poker going up and down. All she could hear was Kenny's low groans, jagged breath.

Pearl reached the car and clambered in.

"Bill!" Marion screamed. "Do something!"

Bill applied the accelerator and the Hudson hurtled toward the mob, headlights on, glaring. They were less than half a foot away when the men finally noticed the car coming toward them.

Bill cursed under his breath, hands pressed to the steering wheel, foot to the brake. But it was a moment too late.

Thud. A body hit the Hudson's front bumper.

The car came to a halt in the center of the mob, though the circle was broken now. Marion flung open her door, knocking someone hard on the hip. She found Kenny, splayed out on the tarmac, his skin sticky with blood. She nudged him gently in the ribs, tears already pouring down her face.

"Kenny, please. Get up, please. We have to move!"

With a groan, he lifted his head and looked over her shoulder at the Hudson, Bill behind the wheel, Pearl in the back seat.

Smash.

A rock hit the windscreen, creating a spiderweb of fissures through the glass.

"Hurry up! Come on!" Bill pleaded, practically dancing in his seat with agitation.

With Marion's assistance, Kenny hauled himself into the back seat, Marion climbing in after him. Bill hit the accelerator even before the door was closed, and as they sped away, Marion noticed a body lying still on the pavement behind them.

SECOND CHANCES
Friday, April 22, 1960

DARCY ROLLED OVER, PULLED THE MUSTY SHEETS up to her chin, ignoring the stranger lying at her side. He meant nothing, just a way to fill the void. Unlike Bill, though, he hadn't succeeded.

The morning light, pale as honey, was streaming in through the bedsit's moth-eaten curtains, and for a moment Darcy was reminded of the carefree days of her childhood, and the cramped bedroom she'd shared with her five sisters in a flat above a sweet shop just a few blocks from here. Strange as it seemed now, as a young girl, Darcy was known for her perennial cheerfulness. Despite her circumstances—the rats that chewed at her shoes, the mites that gnawed at her scalp, despite all the squalor and rotten fortune surrounding her—Darcy had woken each day, rapturous for the opportunities that lay ahead.

A more realistic person might insist that in the backstreets of the East End, *opportunity* was a dangerous thing, especially for women. And they'd be right. But to young Darcy, who'd seen the world through rose-colored glasses, each day was its own thrilling adventure. Being the eldest of her sisters, it was a foregone conclusion that she'd spend her days assisting her mother in the sweet shop. But selling confectionary in a time of world wars and food rations was a futile venture, especially for someone as industrious as Darcy. So, while it took a fair bit of cajoling, she finally managed to bamboozle her mother into an agreement of sorts. Darcy could spend her days wandering the city—no rules, no questions—as long as she returned at dusk with more money than the shop had made in twelve hours (not including commission, which she pocketed before her mother had counted the profits).

Some days it was easy pickings. A watch here, a diamond ring there, pawned off to a shifty broker north of the river. Other days required a little more resolve, like the time she mistakenly lightened the pockets of the Seven Dials' most infamous hatchet man and was obliged to hand over her entire month's plunder in compensation. But there were worse things than hatchet men and dirty brokers lurking in London's shadows—crooked tricksters with their sugarcoated lures, disguised as princes. Opportunists, just like her. And by the time she realized that men like Oscar and Alan Biggar existed, it was too late. And slowly, brick by brick, a wall of distrust grew to obscure what had once been her hopeful, beautiful world. But of all the things Darcy had lost to the Biggars—her innocence, her freedom, her future—losing her joy was the worst.

Now, as she sat in bed, twirling the yellow twine bracelet around her wrist, Darcy was reminded of the last time she'd truly felt joy. It was a Sunday in the middle of summer, many years ago, and because both Oscar and Alan were out of town, Alice and Darcy (and the rest of the girls) had had the day off. They probably should've spent it planning a way to escape the ring without landing themselves in prison, but instead Alice had suggested a picnic in Hyde Park. Even now, Darcy could feel the sun's warmth on her cheeks as she lay next to Alice on the grass, staring up at a cloudless blue sky. It was hard to feel happy in those days, but somehow, whenever she was around Alice, she did.

"I made us something," Darcy said excitedly, presenting Alice with one of the matching yellow twine bracelets she'd spent all weekend trying to get right. "Now we really *are* sisters," she announced, and together they solemnly swore to never remove the bracelets as long as they lived.

"Sisters," Alice agreed, teary-eyed, then plucked out a gleaming brass bird from her handbag. "And guess what? I made something for you, too."

Darcy stared at the magnificent creature, stunned. She couldn't remember ever telling Alice that a raven was her favorite bird, or that birds were her favorite animals. Maybe that was just something sisters knew about each other, instinctually.

"One day," Alice said wistfully, as Darcy continued to stare at the metallic bird in wonder, "I'll make it fly. All the way up there—" she pointed at the vast expanse of sky above them "—and it'll be free."

Darcy squeezed her hand. "Like us?"

Alice squeezed back. "Like us."

Darcy blinked now, looked down at her wrist to find her bracelet snapped in two. She'd broken it without realizing. Or maybe on purpose.

The man sleeping beside her stirred. "Hey, you up?" he groaned.

Darcy ripped off the covers, got to her feet. "You should leave now."

The man picked up his trousers from the floor, pulled them on. "Why's that? You got another fella popping by?"

"More than one," she said cavalierly. It was true, in a way.

Not lovers, though, but the entirety of London's underground was out looking for her now. And she wasn't just talking about the Inquirers. She'd heard through the grapevine that a group of thugs had been loitering outside the boardinghouse for days, courtesy of Alan Biggar (may he rot in hell), which was partly why she'd relocated here, to an inconspicuous bedsit a few miles away. Having to keep her head down was nothing she hadn't expected though, especially after her plan took a detour the day she'd slung a belt around Oscar Biggar's neck.

It was Alan she'd sent the first raven to, hoping to lure him to the market that Sunday. Alan first—the smarter of the two—Oscar second. But when Oscar arrived at Petti-coat Lane instead, she had to pivot and reverse the order of the murders. Unfortunately, just as she'd predicted, Alan sus-pected her straightaway. He wasn't a witless idiot like his brother, and when he learned of Oscar's murder, he knew exactly who to blame. He tracked her down at the boarding-house, convinced of her guilt, ready to slit her throat. And he would have, had she not looked so innocent and scared, then coughed up that brilliant story about Marion Lane knowing who The Raven was. Problem was, even though she'd got rid of him now, she still had his heavies to deal with—men she knew from the old days, men who now worked to clean the brothers' cash through their shifty clothing chain enterprise. More than likely, Alan had warned his chums that if anything happened to him, Darcy was the one to blame. But she'd be damned if she let any one of those scum near her again. Those days were done.

"Same time tomorrow, love?" said the man now hovering over her, his belt still loose, shirt still untucked.

"No. I told you. This was a one-off."

"Moving on to better things?" he cackled.

"Something like that."

This time tomorrow, if all went according to plan, Darcy would finally be free of the one and only thing that had consumed her for eight years. She'd waited so long to get here, and now that it was near, she felt almost giddy with a kind of morbid excitement. Course, there were a few details she needed to finalize before the stage was set, one of which was turning out to be particularly tricky.

While sweet cheeks was gathering the rest of his clothes from the floor, Darcy glanced at the parcel wrapped in brown paper, sitting pretty on the chair beside the washstand. A coldness slithered down her spine as she worried, not for the first time, whether she'd done it right. Ironically (or maybe serendipitously) she'd learned the fine art of making pipe bombs from her old cellmate, who'd learned it from her brothers, who were esteemed members of the IRA. But it was one thing learning and another thing *doing*. And since gunpowder, pipes and nails were hard to come by in prison, this happened to be the first time Darcy had actually put one together.

The door of the bedsit slammed shut as sweet cheeks finally let himself out. *Good riddance.*

She gathered the five thousand pounds Marion Lane had so kindly delivered to her in Benthal Green and got dressed. The money was far more than she needed for the last stages of her plan, but after she'd suggested the ransom idea to Alan, he'd got a bit carried away, poor sucker, thinking *he'd* be the one walking off with the cash. Funny little world, ain't it?

Darcy marched across the courtyard and up to the monstrous doors of Holloway prison, the hairs rising at the nape of her neck. There weren't many places in London that she hated as much (though the boardinghouse was a close second) and the thought of returning here, even as a free woman, made her sick. Maybe that's because she wasn't free, and never would be. And yes, sometimes she wondered if all the anger she held on to was worth it. Maybe letting go would be easier. But how was she supposed to do that? How was she supposed to forgive Alan and Oscar and Phillip Cheevers for what they'd taken from her? How was she supposed to forgive Alice's betrayal? Anger and revenge wouldn't stop the pain, she knew that, but at least it was a distraction. And for now that was all she could hope for.

Catching sight of Darcy, a round-faced prison guard in a well-pressed uniform hauled herself from her chair and waddled over. "Well, I never! If it ain't my favorite little troublemaker, Miss Gibson herself."

Darcy pecked the guard lightly on the cheek, proud of herself for not recoiling at the familiar stench of old sweat and garlic that hit her in the face.

"What brings you?" the guard asked. Miss Ferg, as her charges knew her, was in her early fifties with thin, mousy brown hair, eyes the color of coal and skin the color of dishwater. Truly, she was as ugly as a toad. But she was also prone to the odd touch of bribery, which made her a firm favorite among the Holloway inmates who were looking to improve their circumstances. The rules were simple and always the same: do Miss Ferg a favor, and she'd do you one right back.

"Don't worry," Darcy chirped. "I ain't back for good behavior or nothing." She leaned up against the doorframe and grinned innocently.

"You missed me, then?"

"Course I did." Darcy fluttered her eyelashes and chewed her lip. Was it possible to miss anyone less? "In fact, I was just thinking about your birthday last year and how much fun we had celebrating. I could do it all over again, honest."

Miss Ferg's dishwater skin turned a shade grayer.

Darcy slipped her hands into her dress pockets, pulled out a wad of cash and waved it in Miss Ferg's face. "You remember how you used to bribe that old matron to let me out of my cell so I could do your hair in exchange for a Mickey Finn. One haircut for one Mickey, was how I remembered it."

Miss Ferg swallowed loudly. Of course she remembered.

"But, hold on," Darcy said, frowning, "didn't I cut your hair three weeks in a row without a single Mickey to show for it?" She sighed dramatically but kept her tone pleasant as she added, "Course, I understand, you had no choice. The chief officer was watching you, then, wasn't she? And you must have heard she came my way asking what I knew about all those corruption rumors that were doing the rounds. But I lied for you, didn't I, like the good friend I am." She licked her lips, twirled a tendril of hair around her finger. "You made a promise to me afterward, I think. Now, what was it?"

Miss Ferg recoiled slightly, shook her head, the loose skin beneath her chin flapping like a pair of fleshy wings. "Come on, love," she said with a nervous laugh, "don't be like that now. You wouldn't want to get me fired, would you? I know you wouldn't. Not after everything I've done for you."

Darcy made a conciliatory gesture and clicked her tongue. "Don't fret, Miss Ferg, I ain't going to tell no one. The truth stays between us, honest to goodness." She paused a moment. "Thing is, you did say that if I ever needed anything…"

Miss Ferg let out a sigh of relief and the color washed back into her face. "Yes, yes. I remember. So what is it you need, love?"

Darcy inclined her head and grinned triumphantly. Sometimes, it was just too easy. She gave Miss Ferg a sealed envelope, unmarked and with no return address. Obviously. "You've some copper friends in the Met, am I right?"

"Wouldn't call them friends, but I take your meaning."

"Good. Then you'll pass this letter on to the most senior

one for me tomorrow morning." She handed the woman the wad of cash. "And this is for your troubles."

Miss Ferg pocketed the cash but was less excited about the envelope. She cleared her throat nervously, eyes darting all over. She seemed properly anxious, which was odd. Had she given up her old ways? Was she a bit out of practice? "I don't know, love. Depends what's inside this envelope of yours."

Darcy flicked her wrist with an air of nonchalance. "Nothing too interesting. You can read it if you'd like. Just some information I'd like passed on."

Miss Ferg looked down at the envelope once more, considering the offer. If she refused, Darcy would have to knock the silly woman over the head and take back her cash. She really hoped it wouldn't come to that.

"You'll say it's from a friend of yours," Darcy went on encouragingly, her voice now dripping with charm. "You can make up a name—Tom, Henry, Michael, Lucy, Hannah. Anything but Darcy. Got it?"

"And, eh, then what?"

Darcy smiled victoriously and gave the old woman a wink. "And then, Miss Ferg, we'll call it even."

NANCY'S PLAN

THIRTY-SIX HOURS HAD PASSED SINCE MARION,
Bill and Kenny's trip to the boardinghouse. Kenny had been
admitted to the agency's infirmary for trivial wounds: a split
lip, a sprained ankle, a bruised skull and mild concussion.
Pearl, although unharmed in the assault, was too terrified
to remain in London and had asked to be dropped off at the
nearest train station, from where she traveled to her cousin's
house in Northampton.

Now, as Marion paced the corridor outside the ballroom
alone, her chest tight with anxiety, she recalled what Bill had
told her that very morning, about the chaos brewing aboveground. Much like the rumor mill at *Miss Brickett's*, whispers
had begun to spread through the city streets, mutating as they
grew. Only a handful of people had witnessed the altercation
between Kenny and the Biggars' heavies, but by nightfall,
the press had got hold of the story, and the headlines of every
newspaper in London glared with lies and embellishments.

Innocent Bystander Maimed. Suspect Believed to Be Undercover Inquirer!

Unprovoked Attack on Another Civilian!

Man with Bizarre Gadget Turns Violent in Vicious Civilian Attack!

Hit-and-Run. Victim in Critical Care. Suspect in Possession of Strange Gadget!

London—No Place for Vigilantes!

And perhaps worst of all was the article that had been printed in *The Daily Mail*, the headline of which read: "Murders, Cover-Ups and Soviet Spies: The Truth Behind London's Infamous Private Detectives." It was a five page, in-depth exposé into several of *Miss Brickett's* supposedly secret secrets, including the disposal of Michelle White's body into the Thames two years ago, the Workshop's collection of illegitimate surveillance gadgets and the agency's highly flawed screening process, which had led to them welcoming a Soviet spy into their apprenticeship program last year. Marion had a horrible feeling it was Constable Redding who'd leaked these calamitous tidbits to the papers. Maybe because he thought he was doing the right thing, probably because he was afraid—thanks to his ties to the agency—that he'd go down with them if he didn't jump ship.

And already, several of the agency's letter cases had been vandalized—smashed with hammers and fists or defiled with waste and rubble. Gnarled graffiti, depicting the Inquirers as hooded, grim-faced figures with sickles and swords had sprung up all across the city—in tube stations and bus stops and, most worryingly, outside Scotland Yard. An old butcher's shop in Fulham, just blocks from the bookshop, was apparently thought to be the Inquirer's headquarters and had been broken into overnight and ransacked. Every floorboard had been ripped up, every inch of wall prodded and poked. Another "suspect" establishment—an abandoned haberdashery in Chelsea—had been burned to the ground and a message, sprawled in red paint, left on the wall outside: *Justice for the Biggars!* Across the Thames, a group of protesters had gathered, waving their placards, calling for the Inquirers to be hunted down and charged with assault and murder and collaborating with the Soviets. According to the papers, five "suspected Inquirers" had already been arrested and were being questioned by the police. Though this, at least, Marion knew to be false. For now, the only piece of hope she held on to was that the identity of all the Inquirers remained a secret. But for how long? she wondered.

And if that wasn't enough to cause sleepless nights, pondering the information Pearl had delivered at the boardinghouse sure was. Several hours ago, Marion had met with Frank and Nancy and informed them about the piping, nails and wires: Darcy's insurance policy. Their reaction was much the same as Marion's had been. Shock and frustration. Darcy's plan was almost certainly to plant the pipe bomb at Knightsbridge station and set it off if Frank didn't arrive or if anyone tried to kill her. In other words, she was going to do whatever it took to get what she wanted.

Marion turned to the sound of footsteps approaching from the men's washroom.

Bill and Kenny emerged, Kenny dressed in a simple lemon button-down and gray jeans, hobbling on a pair of crutches, while Bill (clothed, as usual, in a nondescript ill-fitting shirt and trousers) trailed a foot behind.

"You look better," Marion said, curling gently into Kenny's arms. It wasn't entirely true, since the bruises on his face had turned a shade of deep purple, the cut across his lip was crusted and swollen and his ankle had doubled in size. Still, he was alive, and that was enough for her.

He wrapped himself around her and hugged tightly in reply.

She peeled herself from his chest and opened her mouth to say something more: *I'm so sorry this happened. Thank you. I love you.* Instead, the words caught in her throat, and she said nothing.

"How'd the meeting go?" Bill asked anxiously.

She shrugged. "As expected, I guess. They were alarmed to hear about the bomb."

Bill looked over Marion's shoulder at the entrance to the ballroom. The door was closed, but even so, a chorus of chatter was audible from within. Understandably, nothing at the agency had functioned as normal the past few days. The Filing Department and all the receiver boxes had been shut down, Gadgetry had been closed and no one seemed able to do anything but sit around and spread gossip.

"And now they seem adamant they have no choice but to agree to Darcy's ultimatum," Marion added, once Bill had turned his gaze back on her.

"So…what?" Kenny asked, frowning. "Frank's actually thinking of going to Knightsbridge to have a chat with a cold-blooded killer? What's he hoping for exactly? A reconciliation?"

"I don't know," Marion said with a desperate lilt. "I've been wondering the same thing for hours." And she had, almost incessantly. What on earth did Frank think Darcy was going to do when she saw him? Listen to his apology, shake his hand and walk off?

"Well… I'm sure they have *some* kind of plan," Bill said,

not sounding very sure at all. "I mean, Nancy will definitely be going with Frank to the station, right? And probably a few other senior Inquirers, too." He waited a minute, then repeated, *"Right?"*

Marion drew a long breath. "Frank seems to think so, yes," she said, recalling the uncertain smile Frank had given her before he'd said, "And, of course, Nancy will be there to back me up if anything goes awry." But would she, really? Marion wanted to believe so and yet, during her visit to the Department of Gadgetry just fifteen minutes ago, she'd discovered something that filled her with a cold, gnawing doubt.

For a while they just stood together, the three of them, staring at one another in a grave and thoughtful silence. There was so much to be discussed, so many paths down which they could let their minds travel. But at the same time, it felt as though they all knew that no matter what was said, the conclusion would remain the same. What happened tomorrow at Knightsbridge station would alter the course of *Miss Brickett's* future, and the future of everyone who worked there. One way or another, things were going to change, irrevocably.

"Anyway," Marion said with forced levity, trying to ignore the horrible sinking sensation in her chest. She gestured to the door behind her, which had been pushed open to reveal the vast, gleaming expanse of the ballroom. "I heard there's a party on. Shall we join?"

The ballroom, with its vaulted ceiling supported by shimmering marble columns, was once the most opulent room within the labyrinth. Now, on account of the High Council order instructing all employees to remain underground until further notice, it had been transformed into something of a dormitory. The floor was lined with mattresses, trunks, bags, mismatched crockery and cutlery and tubs of leftovers from the kitchens. Desks, couches and even a portable gas fire had been hauled in from the nearest offices and chambers. And everywhere Inquirers, apprentices and staff members were gathered in pockets, playing cards or board games, laughing and chittering as though oblivious to what was going on in the streets above them. Or what might happen tomorrow.

Marion, Bill and Kenny arrived at the gas fire, around which Jessica, David, Preston and Maud were already seated, playing a game of *Miss Brickett's Cluedo*.

"Join us," Jessica said, looking up. "We've just started." She shuffled to the side, making space while David and Preston poured the newcomers a glass each of sherry and offered around a bowl of salted nuts.

There was a stiff silence as Marion, Kenny and Bill sipped their drinks and the others watched them, unblinking. Despite the game set out in front of them, no one seemed to be in the mood to play.

"So…" David said, leaning back on his hands. "Tomorrow's the big day, yeah?"

"What's that supposed to mean?" Bill snapped.

"Well, either your girl Darcy gets Frank's head on a platter, or she cuts her losses and yaps to the police. Isn't that where we stand?"

He was staring directly at Marion when he said it, as if he expected *her* to reply. But she gave him nothing.

"And I know Frank's an okay bloke," David drawled on with a smug smile, "but I don't reckon he's going to sacrifice himself to save the agency, which means the police will be traipsing through our corridors by breakfast time tomorrow."

"That won't happen," Jessica said flatly. She waited, fiddling with the deck of cards in her hand, until everyone had turned to look at her. "Because there's a third option. I had breakfast with Patrick this morning and he told me about the—"

"As in Castle?" Maud interrupted with a wry grin. "The junior Inquirer slash agency joker?"

"Is there another Patrick I'm unaware of?" Jessica snapped. "Yes, Maud, Patrick Castle."

"Since when do you have breakfast with *Mr. Castle*, then?" Maud asked, still grinning.

A touch of red came to Jessica's cheeks but other than that, she completely ignored Maud's comment.

"He told me about an administrative procedure that the High Council call *The Fold*." She straightened the Cluedo deck in front of her and turned over the top card absently—a weapon, the poison dart. "As I understand it, in the event of an impending...calamity, where nothing further can be done to protect the agency and its employees, the High Council will launch the first stage of *The Fold*."

"Which is?" Maud asked impatiently.

Jessica turned over a second card from the deck, another weapon: the Herald Stethoscope. "They incinerate absolutely all our files," she said. "Employee records, case files, everything. Stage two is the evacuation, where everyone is given some sort of kit, containing money, false identity papers and further instructions on how to...well, vanish."

Marion tucked her trembling hands under her thighs. "Vanish?"

"I didn't fancy asking for the details," Jessica said. "But I think you can hazard a guess." She paused, sighed. "The final stage of the plan is permanently sealing the trapdoor in the bookshop. I don't know how, exactly, but apparently no one would ever be able to get in after that. Or out, of course."

As though to add to the finality, the grandfather clock near the door struck ten.

"And then what?" David asked, shifting in his seat, his smug smile long gone.

Jessica frowned. "What do you mean 'and then what'? And then nothing, David. It's over. Forever. That's why it's called *The Fold*."

Marion stared blankly ahead, her mind racing. Although shutting down *Miss Brickett's* was unthinkable to her, it really did seem to be the only way out now. Frank wouldn't have to go to Knightsbridge, and when Darcy passed on Marion's details to the police (which she certainly would), and the police raided the agency, they'd get nowhere because everyone and everything would've vanished. The only hitch, of course, was the bomb. If Darcy really was planning to plant it at the station and detonate it if Frank didn't show up, then they were back to square one. Frank *had* to go to Knightsbridge tomorrow morning and therefore, Marion realized, it was up to her to make sure he made it back alive.

Later that evening, after two somber rounds of *Cluedo* and three more lively rounds of rummy, Marion made her way to Nancy's office. The door was ajar, a spear of light cutting through the darkened corridor. After a moment's indecision, she pushed the door open.

Nancy was seated alone at her desk, a bottle of scotch in front of her. A fire burned timidly in the grate, throwing mottled golden light onto the surrounding wall of bookshelves. She seemed lost in thought, and for a while Marion wasn't even sure if she registered who was standing in front of her.

"You're not going with Frank to the station tomorrow, are you?" Marion asked abruptly. She was aware that she owed her sudden boldness to the sherry coursing through her veins, but she didn't care. This was something she had to know.

Nancy turned to look at her, unblinking, expressionless. "What makes you say that?"

"I was down in Gadgetry tonight. With Professor Bal.

He was packing a kit for Frank to take with him tomorrow. Twister Rope. A Time Lighter. Something in a burlap sack. But only one of each. I asked him if he was preparing something for you and he said no, you hadn't asked him to."

Nancy sighed, but said nothing to defend herself.

"I don't think you'll risk it," Marion went on, speaking rapidly now, her jaw tight, her shoulders hunched up near her ears. "You had planned to kill Darcy but now you know that's not an option, and so you won't risk following Frank to the station because if Darcy catches even a whiff of a setup, she'll detonate her pipe bomb. So, Frank thinks you'll be there to watch his back but really he'll be there alone, which means if he manages to resolve things with Darcy, then great. If he doesn't, and she kills him, then that's just a sacrifice you're willing to make."

There was a long, sharp silence, interrupted by the gentle tick of the carriage clock on the mantelpiece behind them and the spit and hiss of the fire. Marion felt wrung out and, mostly, disappointed. In some way it had been a relief to say everything she'd been thinking. But truthfully, what she'd hoped for was an argument. She wanted Nancy to correct her, to tell her she *was* going to the station with Frank, that they *did* have a plan to stop Darcy, and that everything would be fine. Instead, what she got was a confirmation.

"I suppose, then," Nancy said at last, her voice level, "that you believe risking potentially hundreds of lives to save one is a good idea? Or perhaps you think Miss Gibson is bluffing, and that there is no bomb at all?"

"It doesn't have to be one or the other," Marion said. "No one has to die if we're clever about it. But you're not even going to try, are you? Because this isn't about the lives of some civilians at a train station. This is about the survival of the agency. And for that, you will sacrifice anyone."

Nancy stared at her without speaking for so long that Marion felt she had to look away. And yet she didn't. A blackened log whistled in the grate, its burning amber heart split open, smoke rising like breath in the cool air.

"It is a great shame that after all these years that is what you think of me, Miss Lane," Nancy said at last. "Perhaps I have misled you. Or perhaps you have misled yourself. Either way, I ask that you remember who you are—an apprentice at *my* agency. And this…mess, although linked to you and your mother, is up to me to resolve. Now, shall I call Mr. Nicholas to escort you out—" she gestured to the office door "—or will you excuse yourself?"

18

KNIGHTSBRIDGE STATION

THERE WAS A BITE IN THE AIR, THOUGH THE early morning sky was a cloudless chasm of exquisite blue. Marion stood at the Knightsbridge station ticket hall on Brompton Road, disguised as best she could in nondescript attire—black trousers, a dull gray blouse, leather lace-up boots. Concealed under her trouser belt was her favorite multitool, the one Bill, Jessica and Kenny had given her last Christmas and beneath the cuff of her blouse, Frank's Spinner Knife. She also wore a silicone strip across her forehead and chin, and a pair of brown contact lenses and fake reading glasses that distorted the shape of her eyes. Her hair was loose, short tendrils parted subtly to conceal the shape of her face. She carried a small leather traveling case but kept no glittering gadgetry in sight. It was by no means a thorough effort, but considering the circumstances and time restraints, it'd been the best disguise she could throw together. And if she was going to be of any use, she needed to control her emotions. To think clearly, to use every skill she'd learned over the past two and a half years, to conceal herself and move unseen through the throngs of people.

Out of the corner of her eye, she spotted Frank—dressed in a long fawn coat and bowler hat. He carried a suitcase in one hand, and the other clutched a folded black umbrella. The hem of his coat swirled around his ankles as he weaved carefully but quickly through the crowd, along the pavement, through the ticket office and down the escalator.

Marion looked at her watch as she walked, following Frank across the street. It was 5:30 a.m. and the place was busier now than it'd been ten minutes ago, waves of passengers flooding in and out, bumping into one another, cursing.

She paused when she reached the top of the escalator. Several copies of Scotland Yard's *How to Identify an Inquirer* were pinned to the wall on her left. She swallowed, scanned the platform below. A group of teenagers were hovering there, passing a cigarette between themselves. Frank was lingering nearby, hands in his pockets, staring out across the platform. Had he spotted Darcy? A police officer?

"Marion Lane."

A whisper from behind her shoulder. She whipped around, heart in her throat. An elderly woman frowned at her, paused, clicked her tongue and shuffled off. Had she imagined it? Was she hearing things? Everywhere she looked, heads seemed to turn, eyes following, hands brought up to mouths and voices lowered to a whisper. Were people watching her more than usual, or had the circumstances just made her more aware? Having lived for so long in the shadowy, anonymous world of *Miss Brickett's*, she was accustomed to—and adept at—being invisible. But now, when she needed that invisibility more than ever, she got the horrible feeling it was slipping away.

She pinched her blouse, peeling it from her damp skin, adjusted her glasses and turned again to the group of teenagers at the base of the escalator, one of whom was now staring directly up at her. No, not at her, at the woman behind her. A young lady waved at the teenager, leaping down the escalator to greet him. They kissed and laughed, and Marion let out a breath.

False alarm. But still, it was time to move.

She clutched her travel case under her arm and marched down the escalator and onto platform one. Turning her head and dipping her chin, she glided past Frank without pausing, not giving him a single glance or a chance to see her. If he did, she knew he'd force her to return to the agency.

She strode eastward down the narrow platform at a brisk pace, shouldering her way through the line of harried and irritable commuters awaiting the incoming train, which rumbled faintly in the distance.

Arriving at a relatively quiet area just above the tracks, with a clear view of Frank and the escalator behind him, she paused. She settled in, drew out a newspaper, unfolded it in front of her face and leaned her shoulder against the wall.

The minutes ticked by slowly. Frank remained at the base of the escalator, staring out toward the tracks, shifting occasionally from foot to foot while incessantly fidgeting with the tip of his umbrella. A train pulled into the station, and clearly he expected Darcy to be on it because his posture stiffened as the doors split open. But among the stream of men and women and restless children, Darcy was nowhere to be seen.

His shoulders relaxed, though his fingers remained at the umbrella's tip, caressing it nervously. It was then that Marion noticed the glint of metal there, a tiny silver needlelike extension that could only be one thing. But was the dart at the tip of his umbrella filled with a tranquilizer, or something more fatal?

Her musings were interrupted by a faint ring.

She turned her head to the source of the sound, as did Frank: a grimy gray telephone attached to the wall at his left shoulder. Without hesitation, he picked up the receiver.

One second, ten.

He nodded, hung up, his eyes wide with shock.

It must have been close to five minutes that he stood there, staring vacantly at the passing commuters while Marion tried to interpret the look on his face. He was terrified, of that she was certain, but there was something else in his eyes that unsettled her further, a sort of bewilderment, or perhaps it was indecision. Who had called, and what had they said? she wondered.

She fought the urge to approach him and ask: *Was it Nancy? Was it Darcy?* But something kept her rooted in place. Maybe fear. Maybe logic.

She looked up. Darcy appeared on the escalator, moving downward. She was holding a small handbag at her stomach and was dressed in a long black coat and ruby sheath dress. As usual, she wore black leather gloves, and her blond hair was curled into perfect ringlets and pinned into a loose, low knot. When she reached the platform, she curved right, vanishing into an alcove behind the escalator.

Frank flinched, and although his back was still to the escalator, it seemed as though he could sense Darcy's presence. He placed his suitcase at his feet, slipped a hand underneath his coat.

More people pressed into the station from aboveground. Another train screeched and clamored as it pulled up. The doors opened and passengers spilled onto the platform while others pushed and shoved their way into the tightly packed cars.

Darcy finally emerged from the alcove. She looked different, though Marion couldn't pinpoint why. Frank spun around to face her. She cocked her head and smiled, slipped a gloved hand behind her back.

"Blast," Marion hissed, skin prickling. She risked a glance at the escalator, at the ticket office above and the platform around her. Nancy was nowhere to be seen. Of course she wasn't.

Marion knelt, threw open her travel case, drew out a metallic sunbird, the Distracter. Her hands were trembling so badly it took three attempts to wind up the key hidden under the bird's wing. At last, it squirmed to life in her grip, desperate to fly, but she held it tight. She didn't have a plan, only an idea. If, or rather *when*, Darcy tried something, Marion would set the Distracter free as near as possible, giving her a chance to pull Frank to safety. It would cause a scene, of course, and she wasn't sure what would happen after that. Nor did she care. All she had to do was keep Frank alive.

She slammed her case shut, rose to her feet, paused.

She took another step forward, the sunbird's wings digging painfully into her palms. She was anxious to release it, but there was something in Frank's stance that told her to wait.

While his right hand held the umbrella across his body like a sword, he used his left to retrieve something from his inside coat pocket: the small burlap sack Marion had seen Professor Bal pack last night.

Frank dangled the sack at eye level, watching it swing to and fro of its own accord. There was something inside, Marion realized, something *alive*.

Then, as if summoned out of thin air, Darcy whipped a razor blade from beneath her cuff and sprung forward at just the same moment that Frank released the drawstrings of the burlap sack and liberated an enormous swarm of…what?

"Fireflies!" Marion gasped softly. Not *real*, of course, but tiny battery-powered light bulbs adorned with lattice wings so delicate they might've been made from silk. Marion had seen them once before, she realized, the night of the Fight Club.

The winged light bulbs surged upward to the station ceiling in a blaze of moving light. Then, splitting into groups of ten or so, they swept across the train tracks and into the tunnel, toward the ticket office, along the platform, left and right and absolutely everywhere. Commuters ducked and dived and shrieked in horror as the fireflies spun around their heads and between their legs, zapping so quickly through the air that it would've been hard to decide if they were flares, bullets or some bizarre, crazed insect.

Smash. Clang. Screech.

A cluster of maybe fifty winged bulbs crashed into and under the escalator, triggering the emergency brake and stalling the contraption immediately. Passengers stuck on the stairs scrambled up toward the ticket office with such hysteria one could've been forgiven for thinking a fire had broken out on the platform below.

Meanwhile, a smaller swarm whooshed above Marion's head toward the tracks, then dipped low and doubled back through the station, flying merely two feet above the ground and picking up speed with every passing second.

Amid the chaos and confusion, Frank had sidestepped Darcy's razor, caught her wrist and pinned it behind her back. He held the umbrella loose and awkwardly at his hip, its needle tip facing upward. But Darcy was stronger and more agile than she looked. In one violent, rapid maneuver, she twisted her arm and body out of Frank's grip, then leapt backward and to the right. She said something, though her voice was drowned out by the commotion surrounding her—the shrieking commuters, the frantic beating of tiny wings, the roar of another train as it swept into the station.

Frank raised his umbrella, the tip directed at Darcy's chest.

He fumbled with a catch on the handle, then lurched forward. As he did, Darcy pulled something from under her coat. It could've been the razor, but it was more likely a gun. Frank called out, swiped the umbrella through the air.

With no choice now but to blow her cover and intervene, Marion shoved the writhing Distracter—which was obviously no longer necessary—into her bag and tumbled forward in a panic, batting away fireflies and weaving between the ever-growing number of onlookers that had filled the station. But a throng of dumbstruck commuters, who were standing in a circle staring down at a quivering mass of fireflies that had worn out their batteries and crashed to the floor, was blocking her way.

"Move. *Move!*" she urged, shoving them aside, glass and filigree wings crushing underfoot. "Out of the way! Move!"

She managed to get through the circle, breathless and burning hot, only to discover that yet another wave of passengers had hurried down the stalled escalator, drawn to the station by the chaos and glittering lights.

Something collided—sharp and hard—into her back. She stumbled forward from the impact. A small swarm of golden fireflies swept upward from where she'd been standing, their bulbs flickering weakly as their batteries began to fade. Feeling a warm trickle of blood slide down the furrow of her spine, she lifted her blouse and patted the skin, searching for the wound. Her fingers came upon something sharp and cold and delicate. Letting out a groan, she plucked the mangled wing of a single firefly from her flesh.

"Blast," she said, flicking the object to the ground and turning back to the spot where Frank and Darcy had been standing.

But both were gone.

19

A CHANGE OF PLANS

MARION TURNED TO LOOK AT THE OTHER END of platform one and, just in time, caught sight of a fawn coat slipping off the platform and onto the tracks, moving westbound. *Frank.* She wanted to call his name but stopped herself. A pair of uniformed tube drivers were standing right beside her, and the last thing she wanted was to draw attention to Frank. Or herself. After the theatrical firefly display, there was a good chance the police would soon be swarming the station searching for anyone who looked—or behaved—like an Inquirer.

She waited a beat, eyes fixed on the tracks and the darkness of the tunnel beyond, her pulse as quick as light. The station was still teeming with bemused civilians. The chaos and excitement, however, had faded somewhat now that the majority of the fireflies had either escaped aboveground, smashed themselves into smithereens or dropped to the floor, batteries depleted.

She marched toward the tracks and, once sure no one was watching, opened her travel case on her knee and drew out a coil of Twister Rope, magnetizing it immediately. It tried to curl in on itself, but she coaxed it expertly through her fingers and around her forearm. Next, she checked to ensure that the Spinner Knife was securely fastened around her wrist and her silver multitool beneath her belt, then leapt down onto the tracks, landing lightly.

Her senses acclimatized quickly to the dimness. If nothing else, she had one advantage over Darcy here. After all this time working underground, her eyes had become accustomed to the shadows, and the blackness transformed easily into distinct shapes of gray. She padded onward, in silence, leaving behind the clamor and dying pandemonium of the station.

The tunnel was dead straight for twenty yards until it reached a fork and the tracks diverged, the left curling sharply out of sight, the right running straight ahead like a thread of black yarn.

She stopped, held her breath, listened.

Something clanged up ahead—a door? Muffled voices followed. If she hadn't spent the last two and a half years of her life within a similar expanse of subterranean tunnels, she might've been fooled by the confusing acoustics. But no, the sound wasn't coming from up ahead. It was coming from behind her.

She spun round.

On the left, nestled against the wall, was a short metal ladder that led upward to a small ledge above the tracks. Beyond the ledge was a closed door and above it, a weak bulb battled the darkness, casting a faint fluorescent light onto the ladder.

She tightened her grip around the Twister Rope and patted the Spinner Knife. Reassured, she crept closer to the ladder, gliding across the tracks, no louder than a breath of wind.

The clang came again, and this time she realized it had come from behind the closed door.

Again, she wished to call Frank's name, but stopped herself. Stealth was her only advantage.

She climbed the ladder, clambered onto the ledge and pressed her ear against the door.

Silence.

She cast her eyes to the track below, around the ledge, suddenly aware of the stench of human sweat. Someone was behind the door. Was it Frank? And if so, was he alone?

She turned back to the door, skin prickling, and as she did so, the door swung inward.

"Marion?" Frank grabbed her hand, yanked her inside and closed the door with a soft click. They were thrown into complete darkness. "What are you doing here?" he hissed with an inflection she didn't recognize but which frightened her. He struck a match, held it to her face, as though he didn't quite believe what he was seeing.

The flame danced higher, then started to die. Marion opened her travel case and pulled out a light orb, flicked it on. The room was compact, less than two feet wide, the walls concrete and lined with tools and broken slats of wood, peppered with nails and flecks of old paint. Lying at Frank's feet was his suitcase, hat and poison dart umbrella—the needle tip still intact.

"Where's Darcy?" she asked, speaking quickly. "Why are you hiding here? What's going on?"

"Too bright." Frank seized the orb, turned it off. The match in his hand dwindled. He shook it out, dropped it to the ground and lit another. He seemed to regard her thoughtfully for a moment, deciding something. "Marion, I don't want you to say a word. Just listen to me very carefully and do exactly as I say. You must leave. Right this minute. You must leave the station as quickly and inconspicuously as you can."

"The bomb?" Marion asked. "Did you see it? Does she have it on her?"

"I had hoped so," he said, glancing at his umbrella. "That's why I brought that along."

Marion nodded briskly. "To drug her before she could plant it anywhere?" Frank said nothing to this, but Marion could tell by the look of dejection on his face that his plan had failed. "Okay, so she's already planted it somewhere here in the station. Is that a guess, or did she tell you?"

"She told me, and I doubt she's lying. Which is why you must leave, Marion, please. Immediately!"

She ignored this and added, "But she won't set it off unless—"

"She has already. Set the timer, I mean. I presume she's planning to deactivate it at some point, or leave the station as soon as she gets what she wants."

"Which is you!" Marion said shrilly, stopping herself before she added, *Dead*. "When...when is it due to detonate? Do you know?"

"Seconds. Minutes. An hour. She didn't tell me, of course. But that's not the only reason I need you to leave. The fireflies were my plan B, to delay Darcy, but I'm also hoping they'll have drawn them here instead. I can't be sure it worked though."

"Drawn who here?"

"The police," he said shortly.

Marion was flummoxed. Frank *wanted* the police at the station? "But...you said you're hoping to draw them here *instead*. Instead of where?"

He shook his head, placed a finger to his lips. "You must leave," he repeated curtly. "But don't go back to the agency."

He looked at his watch. "I don't know how long we have now."

"Nancy's not coming, you know that, right? She's left you to Darcy. That's why I came instead." She stopped to swallow the lump in her throat.

Frank cocked his head and frowned. But he wasn't afraid. Why wasn't he terrified?

She raised her voice to almost a scream. "We have to get you out of here before Darcy finds—"

He gripped her wrist so hard it stung. His voice cracked like a whip. Never had she seen him so filled with rage and urgency, swirling in a horrid mix that seemed to set his eyes alight.

"Quiet!" He paused. Listened. Were those footsteps? Someone panting? "You're wrong about Nancy. She *was* going to come. The fireflies, the delay. It was all her idea. But there's been a change of plan," he added. "Something unexpected has... Nancy is organizing the evacuation as we speak. There is no other option now."

Evacuation. Change of plans. Marion wouldn't allow herself to believe it meant what she thought it did.

The flame of the second match began to die and with it, Frank's temper. When he spoke next, his voice was faint, almost fragile. "But please, you must leave, Marion," he repeated for the third time. "Go anywhere, but keep away from the agency and away from Willow Street. Make sure no one follows you. Do you understand?"

"No. No, of course I don't understand! Why should I go and you stay?"

He sighed. "There isn't time to explain. I'm sorry. You just have to trust me."

She ripped herself free from his grip, opened her mouth.

Clip-clang. Clip-clang.

There could be no mistaking it now. Someone was climbing the ladder outside.

"Promise me you'll do as I say?" Frank whispered desperately, pulling his suitcase and umbrella toward him. "I'll distract her, you run."

The door flung open. A torch beam cut through the dark.

"Ah, at last. There you are," Darcy said, a pistol cocked and aimed in one hand, a torch in the other. She closed the door behind her.

Frank pulled Marion back, shoved her against the wall and planted himself squarely in front of her. He held the umbrella loose at his side. What the hell was stopping him from sending a dart right into Darcy's chest?

"We can't now," he whispered, seeming to read Marion's mind. "It's too late. We need her alive and *compos mentis*. Trust me, Marion, please."

"Funny little trick you played on me there," Darcy said, speaking over him as she placed the torch at her feet. "Can't say I saw that one coming. And I must admit, you Inquirers are as nifty as ghosts. One minute you're standing right in front of me, next thing. *Poof!* Gone. For a moment I thought you might've got the willies and scampered off, then I thought, no, he wouldn't, he wouldn't do that. He knows what's at stake." She used the gun to gesture to the room and it looked as though something had just dawned on her. "Oh, I get it now. Savvy little bugger." She smiled smugly. "You were hoping to play a bit of hide-and-seek, weren't you, sweet? Is that what those flying gadgets were for? Figured it'd take me a good while to find you? Actually, it might've done if the little princess over here hadn't been talking so loud."

Marion was momentarily distracted by the fear for whatever might happen next. Then she fell silent as the truth dawned on her.

That was why Frank had set Darcy up on a game of cat and mouse around the station. *That* was why he'd set off Professor Bal's fireflies to clear the area. *That* was why he'd tried to hide himself here, hoping Darcy would take so long to find him that she'd be forced to deactivate the bomb or risk blowing herself to smithereens. And, of course, *that* was why he'd insisted they needed to keep her alive and *compos mentis*, because Darcy was the only one who knew where the bomb was hidden.

Marion peeled herself from the wall, shuffled closer to Frank. He was standing stiffly, feet splayed, arms pinned to his sides.

"Take one more step, missy," Darcy warned. "One more! And I'll pull this trigger right now. You know I will." She examined the writhing silver cord around Marion's wrist, and her eyes flittered. "And drop that awful thing, whatever it is. *Now!*"

Marion didn't falter, terrified of the consequences. She untangled the Twister Rope and cast it aside. It wriggled and curled on the floor, gathering dust, moving as though alive. Darcy watched it curiously and with a hint of fear, head cocked, until the thing settled and was still.

"And that," Darcy added, eyes fixed on Marion's wrist, on the Spinner Knife. "Sorry, love, but I've learned all your tricks."

Again, Marion didn't hesitate. She pulled the gadget over her hand and threw it to the floor.

"Good. And one more thing," Darcy said. "The glasses, and whatever it is you have on your face. We wouldn't want anyone to be mistaking you for someone else."

Marion looked at Frank, horrified.

"Do it," he whispered.

"Now your turn, Cheevers," Darcy snarled once Marion

had peeled the silicone from her face. "Drop the umbrella and turn out your pockets. Don't make me ask twice."

Frank did as he was told, pulling a demagnetized coil of Twister Rope from under his sleeve and a Time Lighter from his breast pocket. He placed both at his feet, alongside the umbrella, and kicked them across the concrete floor to the other side of the tiny room.

Several seconds of silence passed. From somewhere not far off, near the platform, people were chattering, muttering. If only they knew what was happening here, if only they could help.

"Let Marion go, please," Frank said, breaking the quiet. "This has nothing to do with her. You've surely punished her enough. I will do as you say. Whatever you want. Just please… a compromise."

Darcy raised an eyebrow. "Compromise?"

"I'm not going anywhere," Marion said, biting down, ignoring Frank as he pleaded with her under his breath.

"*Shut it!* Both of you," Darcy snapped, the gun shaking slightly in her grip. "You ain't making no demands now, neither of you. I'm in charge, got it?"

"Darcy." Frank tried again, raising his hands as though to mollify her. "This is between the two of us. I want to explain myself. I really do. But alone. Please."

"I said shut it!" With her free hand, she drew a wallet from her coat, pulled it open and shook out two white pills. She popped them onto her tongue, knocked her head back and swallowed. She started to speak again but was stopped as an almighty racket rumbled up from the tracks below them. A blazing white glare shone through the crack under the door. The ground rattled, dust and debris lifting into the air as a train whipped through the tunnel and pulled up into the station ahead.

Chatter, voices, the conductor's whistle sounded. Time slowed, the seconds dragging on until, at last, the train's engine shuddered back to life.

As soon as the silence had returned, Frank resumed his pleading. "I know you hate me, and you're angry. You think Alice and I sent the police after you all those years ago. But I never intended…it wasn't meant to be like that. I was trying to help. I thought the police would offer you clemency. I didn't know they'd been turned." He drew a breath. "Maybe I deserve this—" he nodded at the pistol "—but please, Marion has no reason to be here. Let her go, and we'll both get what we want."

Pop.

At first, Marion thought the sound had something to do with the train that had just swept past. Then she saw Frank sink to his knees, clutching the lower part of his leg. Blood seeping through his fingers. His face was strained and pale. He made no sound.

Marion crouched beside him, shaking, numb. She faltered, then forced herself to move, tore off a piece of her blouse and tied it around his leg.

"You're okay, you're okay," she murmured desperately, propping him up against the wall as carefully as she could. She looked up, head spinning.

Darcy was standing in exactly the same spot, the gun cocked and aimed somewhere between Marion and Frank. Darcy's eyes were bright, pupils wide. "I want an apology," she said, her tone now angry, almost desperate.

Marion shivered, well aware of how long Darcy's last victim—Alan—had lived after he'd said sorry.

Frank opened his mouth. He was trying to communicate something to Marion. She got the awful feeling he was telling her—yet again—to run, to give up, to save herself. She pressed her hand harder against the bullet hole in his leg, but the bleeding wouldn't stop.

Darcy stomped her foot and shrieked. *"Say it!"*

"What...do you...want from me, Darcy?" Frank asked, the words a groan between ragged breaths. "Of course I'm sorry. You must know that... Alice and I...we didn't...we didn't know what else to do."

Darcy's face twisted into a snarl and without a moment's warning, she launched herself forward.

Marion rose to her feet, leapt into Darcy's path. But instead of curtailing the attack, she only seemed to make it worse. Darcy screamed, swiped the gun through the air, forcing Marion to back away. She kicked Frank twice in the ribs. He coughed, spluttered, curled into a fetal position.

"No!" Marion shrieked. Her limbs twitched as Darcy danced backward, leveled the gun.

Marion froze, glanced at her feet, calculating how far away the gadgets were that she and Frank had discarded. The Time Lighter was closest, but could she reach it faster than Darcy could pull the trigger? And even if she did, what use was it against a gun? Alternatively, her silver multitool was still concealed beneath her trouser belt, and if she could just turn the dial three times counterclockwise without Darcy noticing, she'd have a small serrated blade at her disposal. But again, what use was a knife in a gunfight?

Darcy moved the pistol slightly left, aiming it at Frank's temple. He tried to crawl away into the corner of the room but only managed to drag himself half a foot before collapsing with exhaustion. Marion flinched, desperate to do something, to stop what seemed inevitable now. She tried to look Frank in the eye, but his were half shut in pain. Even so, something passed between them. An understanding, a note of gratitude and sorrow and forgiveness. He lifted his head from the concrete, spat out a glob of dust and blood and saliva.

His eyes flickered to the door. Marion heard it too. A shuffle of feet. Darcy flinched but didn't turn around. The door clicked open.

Darcy pressed her forefinger to the trigger.

CHECKMATE

MARION MUST HAVE CLOSED HER EYES OR slipped into a state of shock, because the next few minutes seemed to pass in a fog, everything happening all at once.

Someone had entered the room just as Darcy had fired the gun. But in the semidarkness, it was hard to tell where the bullet had landed. Marion got onto her knees, patted the floor and at last retrieved the light at her feet. As she rose, she was knocked sideways and lost her balance. She staggered into the wall with a hard knock, steadied herself, then directed the torch beam in front of her.

To her complete surprise, *Nancy* was standing in the doorway holding Darcy's pistol while Darcy was pressed against the wall, her hands seemingly tied behind her back. Frank, however, was slumped on the ground, his head knocked back, his shirt, trousers and hair drenched in blood.

Marion felt the scream rise in her throat. Then Frank moved, clutched his shoulder and let out a guttural moan.

"Who the hell are you?" Darcy snarled, looking at Nancy, who said nothing in reply.

Marion crouched down, drew Frank into her arms, pressed her hand to the new wound in his shoulder. It made no difference, though, and hot blood pumped through her fingers with every beat of his heart.

"It's okay," she said, her voice ragged with desperation. "We'll get you to a hospital. You're going to be fine. Just hold on, just a little longer."

He smiled weakly because they both knew that was a lie. "I'm sorry, my dear," he muttered. "To have put you through this. I should never have brought you here…" He trailed off, but Marion knew what he meant. Brought her here. Not to Knightsbridge station, not to this tiny room above the tracks. To *Miss Brickett's*. "Alice made me promise…and I've failed. I promised her I'd protect you. I tried. I'm sorry."

"*Shhh, shhh*. Don't speak," she soothed, her eyes brimming with tears. He nodded while she pressed down harder on the wound and tried to console herself with the fact that at least the bullet had landed in his shoulder and not his chest or head. "I need to make a bandage," she said, looking up at Nancy. "Do you have something to wrap the wound?"

Nancy ripped the silk scarf from around Darcy's neck and threw it to Marion.

"So you came after all," Marion said as she tied the bandage. "I really thought…"

"Yes," Nancy snapped. "I know exactly what you thought. Now get him onto his feet. Quickly. Come on."

Marion slung Frank's good arm over her shoulder, lifted him onto his knees, then his feet. But the second his full weight was upon her, she staggered backward into the wall and was forced to lower him back to the ground. "I don't think I can," she panted. "I can't carry him on my own. I'll just do more harm if I try."

"Then drag him," Nancy said unhelpfully. "Once you get to the platform, ask someone to telephone for an ambulance."

"You're not coming?"

"Later."

Marion nodded at Darcy. "And what about—"

Restless, Darcy rolled her shoulders and shifted on her feet. "I was just about to ask the same thing. Are you going to shoot me now? Or later?"

"Just go," Nancy said to Marion, ignoring Darcy. "Leave her to me. And once you've found an ambulance, you must disappear. Do you understand?"

Marion swallowed, nodded. From now on, she was going to believe everything Nancy said.

Darcy grimaced, then let out a high-pitched cackle. "Oh, no, no, no. I don't think so, ladies."

Marion looked from Darcy to Nancy, confused, impatient. "Nancy?"

"Don't forget, I have myself a little insurance policy," Darcy hissed. "And I'm not afraid to use it. Catch my drift?"

Nancy flicked the pistol over in her hand, used the butt to hit Darcy in the jaw. Blood trickled down her chin.

"That's going to leave a mark, you bitch!" Darcy seethed.

"Tell me where it is," Nancy said. "There's no point in me keeping you alive if we're all going to die anyway. I'm not playing games here, Gibson. I *will* pull this trigger. You have five seconds."

Darcy squirmed. It *was* a game, no matter what Nancy said. A game of lies and deception. But who was better at bluffing?

"Kill me then," Darcy said, "if that's really what you want, go ahead."

Nancy threw her against the wall so hard Marion thought

she might've knocked her unconscious. Her eyes lolled, her head slumped. Nancy twitched, lowering the gun, then brought it back up again as Darcy opened her eyes and rattled on, fast and maniacal.

"Go on, go ahead, kill me. Do it. Do it. Do it!" She smiled, cackled. "No? It ain't such a good plan after all, huh? The bomb will go off quite soon, I think. It's not too big, but in such a confined space, well, you just can't imagine the damage it'll do. Are you willing to let innocent people die?"

There was a short silence, punctuated only by Frank's shallow, unsteady breathing.

"He's fading," Marion said, attempting to haul Frank to his knees a second time.

Nancy nodded quickly. "Yes, I know. So get moving! I'll deal with this."

"No!" Darcy screamed, spraying blood and spittle onto the floor. "He stays, or I'll never tell you where it is. I mean it. I don't care if I die. I've already done what I came here to do." She nodded at Frank, and Marion knew it was true. She'd come to kill him, and she was now just minutes away from success. "I've got nothing left to live for. I'll let that bomb go off, swear to God I will. I never planned to leave this station alive anyway." She looked at the pistol in Nancy's hand, almost longingly. "As long as it's on my own terms, I don't care how I go."

"Fine. He stays," Nancy said. "Now spit it out, Gibson. Where have you hidden the bomb?"

Darcy dithered, watching Frank shiver and moan in agony. "Okay, deal," she said on a theatrical sigh. "I'll tell you." She craned her neck to check the time on Marion's wrist. "But just give me a moment. Let's say…thirty minutes, eh?"

"He won't make it," Marion whispered, hoping Frank couldn't hear her. She tightened the scarf she'd used to ban-

dage the wound on his shoulder. But it was soaked through. And the wound on his leg, dressed by the flimsy strip of cotton she'd ripped from her blouse, was no better (or possibly worse). But what worried her the most was the way his skin had turned gray and cold. She looked up at Darcy pleadingly, though she knew it was futile. "He doesn't have thirty minutes. I need to get him to a hospital right now."

"Exactly," Darcy cooed. "Checkmate, sweet."

INTO THE DARK

TIME LANGUISHED AS FRANK'S BREATHING grew ragged and shallow. The room was still, no one moved or said a thing. Nancy held the pistol cocked and aimed at Darcy's forehead, but everyone knew it was an empty threat. If she pulled the trigger, she'd die along with Frank, Marion and possibly hundreds of innocent people.

"Get down onto your knees," Nancy said to Darcy, breaking the quiet a moment later.

Darcy spat at her feet. "Piss off."

The bulb on the ledge outside flickered, hissed. Marion held a finger to Frank's neck feeling for his pulse and tried to convince herself he still had time. But the beat was getting weaker by the minute.

"I might not be able to kill you," Nancy went on, "but there are worse things than death, I can assure you. Do you really want to test me? Get onto your knees. Now!"

Nancy loomed over her and repeated the question she'd

been asking for the past fifteen minutes. "Tell me where you've hidden the bomb."

Darcy offered nothing but a wicked smile in response.

Marion shook her head, coming to a decision. "Nancy, stop. She isn't going to tell you anything and we're wasting time trying." She got to her feet, dusted the gravel and grit from her trousers. "I'm going back to the platform. I'll get someone to telephone an ambulance, then I'll start looking for the bomb. There're only so many places it could be. In the meantime, you evacuate the station." How Nancy was going to pull that off, Marion had no idea. But it was all she had.

Nancy seemed uncertain. "This is a big station. That bomb could be anywhere. And as for evacuating the place...there're hundreds of people on the platform, in the train, on the escalator and we don't know how much time we have."

"Well, if you have a better plan, I'd love to hear it."

"I do, in fact." Without breaking focus, or moving the pistol from Darcy's face, Nancy pointed to a handbag lying on the floor near the door. "There's a Liar's Eyeglass in there. Pass it to me."

Marion stalled. Not because Nancy had thought to bring along a Liar's Eyeglass, the very same barbaric lie-detecting gadget that had caused so much trauma and turmoil last year, but because...

Handbag.

Marion retrieved the gadget, handed it over, then stepped through the door, onto the ledge, her mind spinning. Nancy protested, spat out a string of commands, but Marion didn't hear a word. The tunnel beyond was black and quiet, the only light the flickering bulb above the ledge. From up ahead, where the tunnel wandered into the dark, a distant sound echoed, low and deep, like a growl. Her mind was ticking, a thought rising, unfurling.

She tilted her head to the side, forcing the memory to shift into place.

Long black coat. Ruby sheath dress. Leather gloves. And a handbag.

"The handbag!" She turned back to the room, stepped inside.

Darcy was still standing, slumped against the wall. Her hands still concealed behind her back.

"You had a handbag. When you arrived at the station. I saw it," Marion blurted, her mind working faster than her tongue. "You came down the escalator. And then...and then..." She paused, mouth agape, throat dry. *Think*, she urged herself. *Think. What happened next? What happened to the handbag?* "The alcove! You disappeared into the alcove under the escalator. And when you reemerged, I knew there was something different, something missing."

"What are you talking about?" Nancy said, the slightest shift in her expression from control to confusion. She backed away from Darcy, pausing at Marion's side.

"The bomb must've been in her handbag," Marion explained impatiently. "She hid it under the escalator. I'm almost certain of it." She forced herself to look again at Frank and waited, numb, to see the shallow rise and fall of his chest. It was subtle, but it was still there. They had time. She stared at Darcy, her hands were moving behind her back, something looked wrong, but Marion was too distracted by the adrenaline surging through her body, sparking the tiniest flicker of hope.

Nancy, in shock, lowered the gun a fraction. She turned her head to look at Marion. "What are you waiting for then? Go! Now!"

Marion nodded, started for the door. Then stopped.

Frank winced, tried to scream.

Darcy's hands were no longer behind her back, no longer bound in Twister Rope. She leapt forward, brandishing the weapon she'd been holding in secret—a thick wooden slat, several inches long.

Marion ducked. But the assault hadn't been aimed at her.

There was a sickening whack, followed by a muffled whimper and a heavy thud as Nancy collapsed to the floor. The gun tumbled from her hand. Darcy dropped the slat, reached for the gun instead.

As did Marion.

The pair swept through the dark, arms thrashing. Marion got to her knees, felt gravel, dirt, wood, then—finally—metal. She wrapped her fingers around the barrel of the gun as Darcy grabbed her collar and dragged her backward.

Marion coughed, clutched her throat and was forced to release the gun. A sharp, deep pain hit her midspine and she folded over her knees, gasping for breath. Her vision began to tunnel, but she willed herself back, gulping down mouthfuls of air with rib-splitting force.

She looked up.

Darcy, too, was on her knees and crawling back toward the gun, which now lay on Marion's left side.

Marion kicked out her leg, sending the gun flying through the door, over the ledge.

Clang. It landed on the tracks below.

The two women froze, both still on their knees, panting hard.

Something rumbled in the near distance. The air tasted of dust and sweat and petroleum.

Darcy lumbered to her feet, staggered forward, baring her teeth. Marion mirrored her, blocking the way. Darcy turned her body to the side, flung her shoulder at Marion's chest, seized her arm with a vise grip. Desperate to release herself, Marion twirled once, then ducked. Darcy let go and Marion stumbled backward. One step. Two. She stopped, swayed, realizing where she was—teetering on the edge of the ledge, above the tracks.

The distant rumble was close now.

The blackness in the tunnel lifted. Two glaring lights appeared in the distance.

Eyes.

Headlights.

Darcy and Marion turned to the glare, squinting. Marion's heart felt as though it were beating in her throat. She couldn't feel her body, but her mind was clear.

The engine roared and rumbled and coughed. The train was coming closer, rattling along the tracks at an unthinkable speed.

The two women locked eyes. Darcy's were cold and spiritless, like pits of ice.

"I'm sorry," Marion muttered. "I'm sorry for what happened to you. I'm sorry you felt betrayed and alone. I know Alice was sorry too."

The noise in the tunnel was almost deafening now.

Darcy nodded subtly, then said, "Maybe. But the damage is done. I have nothing to live for now."

The train thundered onward. Closer. Seconds away, the headlights a bright white that blurred everything else around them.

"The bomb goes off in ten minutes," Darcy whispered, then jumped.

THE FOLD

MARION WAITED FOR THE SPARKS OF LIGHT IN her vision to dissipate, then staggered away from the ledge, legs like rubber. She stared, horrified, at the mangled shadow lying on the tracks, at the train flying past, brakes screeching. Just a few inches, just one more step or one tap on the shoulder and it would've been her.

Bewildered and dazed, she stumbled back across the ledge and through the door, pausing just beyond the threshold. Two bodies lay motionless in opposite corners of the room. She faltered, trembling, then sank to her knees beside Nancy. She wasn't moving and was cold to the touch. Her hair was sticky with blood. Marion fumbled for an artery in Nancy's wrist, then her neck. She tried several times, but felt only the thud of her own pulse, hot and quick, beneath her fingers.

No, she mouthed, tears blurring her eyes. *No. Not you too. Not you…*

For a second, maybe more, she wasn't able to move. Was

this real? Could Darcy really have killed her with a single blow to the head? Was Marion now the only one left alive in the tunnel?

She heard a voice croak from behind her right shoulder.

"Bomb…"

She crawled over to Frank. His eyes were half-open, and his lips parted helplessly.

"Disarm," he croaked again. "You must go before…"

"You're alive," she breathed. "Thank you. Thank you."

"Bomb," he repeated. "Then…you must…you must leave. Don't…go back to…the bookshop. Don't ever go back. The police…are…looking for you. You must run."

She picked up her travel case, but didn't have time to collect the array of gadgets strewn across the floor from earlier. She kissed Frank on the cheek. "Don't worry about me. Everything will be fine."

He reached out to touch her on the shoulder, as he always used to, but his hand fell short. "You are the best Inquirer we…ever hired. You have a gift. Remember that—"

"I'm coming back," she said, cutting him off. "Don't try to move. And don't…" She gulped. "Don't close your eyes. Promise me?"

He didn't acknowledge the request, he didn't even blink, and only a subtle twitch of his fingers, as though reaching out for her hand once more, suggested he might've heard.

He mumbled something as she got to her feet. It sounded like "Goodbye."

She took a ragged breath, gave him one last glance, then clambered down the ladder.

The train had stopped up ahead, just shy of platform one, and several official looking men and women were patrolling the tracks, guiding flustered passengers into the station while spewing some vague excuse about what had happened.

"Nothing to worry about. Just a mechanical error," an official said to a group of passengers as he shepherded them onto the platform.

"But I felt something!" one of the group insisted. "Something hit the train, I'm sure of it."

"Everyone's saying it's *them*," another said. "The Inquirers. They were here, you know, at the station."

A third passenger nodded excitedly at the suggestion. "Yes, yes, you're right! That must've been what it was. They've been setting gadgets off all morning, haven't they? I bet that's what hit us."

"Must've been something bloody huge, though," the first said.

"Well, you never know…"

The official was mum, but he gave his colleague a worried sidelong glance.

Marion waited until the group was out of sight, then slipped past the train, along the tracks, shifting from shadow to shadow, sleeper to sleeper. With less than ten minutes to find and deactivate the bomb, she simply couldn't afford to be seen, questioned or—worst of all—apprehended. No one would believe her if she told them what was at stake, especially if they suspected she was an Inquirer.

It must have taken her only a few minutes to reach the platform and climb up, but already the station was crawling with police. A pair of officers near the escalator glanced in Marion's direction, frowned. Had they seen her clamber up from the tracks? Could they see her bloodstained blouse, the soot and grit on her face? Could they sense her urgency and panic?

She touched her cheek subconsciously, then drew a sharp breath. In her haste to get to the platform, she'd forgotten to reapply the glasses and silicone face strips that Darcy had forced her to remove. Speaking of which: *Why* had Darcy insisted she remove them? She shook her head—with time slipping through her fingers, she had no choice but to hope for the best and continue on without a disguise.

She dipped her head, counted to five as she pretended to fiddle with her watch strap, then looked up. The officers were moving up the escalator (which had now been repaired) and out of sight. As she walked, she plucked her custom multitool from beneath her trouser belt.

Arriving at the alcove Darcy had disappeared into, she realized it was not, in fact, an alcove at all. Instead, it was simply a bare nook on the underside of the escalator, no bigger than two square feet. And as she scanned the tight space twice over, her heart sunk.

No handbag. No bomb.

"Dammit."

Sweat poured down the furrow of her spine, down her chest. She didn't dare look at her watch but, at a guess, there couldn't have been more than five minutes left on the clock.

"I saw you," she said to herself, recalling the moment Darcy had stepped off the escalator, clutching the handbag at her stomach. There wasn't anywhere else she could've disappeared to from here, but if she hadn't come to deposit the bomb, what had she been doing all that time? And where had she left her handbag?

Anxiously, Marion glanced left and right over her shoulder, ran her hands along the wall behind the escalator, hoping to feel something give way. But this wasn't *Miss Brickett's*, a subterranean labyrinth peppered with secret passageways and concealed rooms.

There was nothing.

She placed her travel case on the floor, pushed the hair from her face, sick with dread. How many people were going to die if she couldn't figure out what Darcy had done with the bomb?

A young boy—sipping from a bottle of lemonade—sauntered past and gave her a suspicious look, which was only fair, considering the state of her attire, the sweat pouring down her face and the wild tremble in her hands. He flung the empty bottle into the rubbish bin a few feet away from the "alcove," then, giving her the side-eye, turned around and rushed up the escalator.

Marion stared at the rubbish bin for a split second, then leapt forward. Gently, slowly, she tipped the thing onto its side and cursed under her breath as she shifted through its contents: soiled paper towels, food wrappers, bottles, cans, tissues.

And then, at last. Right at the very bottom of the bin, covered in all manner of dirt and grime was a small black handbag.

Delicately, she laid the bag on the floor, unclipped the front button and peeled it open.

Rolled inside a brown paper packet was a short steel tube, sealed on both ends with a brass cap. Even in the clamor and chaos surrounding her, she could hear it—the steady, certain tick of a timer from within.

Working quickly, she pulled the latch on her multitool, spun the dial five times clockwise and a set of pliers sprung out from the handle.

Holding her breath, she begun to unfasten the brass cap from the steel pipe.

Just three turns and it came loose.

Penlight clamped between her teeth, she examined the pipe's open end, the timer now as loud as gunfire in her ear. She'd never seen a pipe bomb before, but it was exactly what she'd expected: gunpowder, nails, wires, a detonator, a battery and a timer.

Now what?

She placed the pipe as carefully as she could on the concrete floor, wiped the sweat from her hands, drew a breath and held it. If she moved too quickly, she would create static or friction, which could set off a spark and ignite the gunpowder. If she moved too slowly...

She cut off that thought midstream and instead reexamined the bomb's components, paying close attention to the two black wires that extended from the battery pack, one attaching to the detonator and one to what appeared to be a small kitchen timer. She resisted a gasp as she realized there was less than a minute remaining on the clock.

"Okay...okay. So, detach the wire running to the detonator?" She might've said it out loud, or just thought it. "Or remove the timer?"

A drip of sweat fell from her forehead. *Plop*, onto the pipe's outer casing.

A shadow loomed behind her. She could sense someone watching, breathing down her neck.

Voices grew louder, footsteps beating on the platform, someone shouting.

Either it was her imagination, or the ticking from inside the pipe had stopped. She didn't dare glance at the timer and instead, using a set of cutters from her custom tool, snipped the wire attached to the detonator.

She froze. A swift silence seemed to fall like a veil around her. She felt nothing, saw nothing and then, *"Schnell, bitte!"*

She turned to see a well-dressed gentleman in thick-rimmed spectacles and a green-and-brown-checkered waistcoat.

"Mr. Zimmerman?" she muttered, startled, her mouth so dry she wasn't sure the words had been audible. "What... what are you—"

He held her gaze for a second, then looked down at the

bomb in her lap. It hadn't gone off, obviously, and the ticking had stopped. She placed it on the floor.

"It's cold, I think," she said, partly to herself. "But the gunpowder...it could still go off, even without the detonator."

Zimmerman nodded, then looked eastward down the platform, toward the tracks and the stationary train.

"Frank!" Marion blurted. In the terror-filled minutes she'd been dealing with the bomb, she had actually forgotten. "He's injured, very badly. I don't know how much time he has. And Nancy..."

Zimmerman nodded again. "I have called an ambulance already," he said in English, his accent thick and gruff, quite in contrast to his demure appearance. "But we don't have long." He extended a hand, and for a moment she thought he was offering to help her to her feet. "The wire is cut, yes?" His eyes were fixed on the metal pipe.

She picked up the bomb, handed it over. "Yes. But like I said, we should dispose of it. Just in case."

"Leave it to me."

"I'll wait with Frank, then. He's just a few yards down the tracks. That way."

"*Nein!*" Zimmerman said, resolute. "*Dieser Weg.*" He jabbed a finger at the escalator. "You must leave."

"Not yet. I have to make sure Frank is—"

"No! No time. Look." He inclined his head, cast his eyes to the center of the platform. A circle of twenty policemen were gathered there, and alongside them, a pack of dogs, yanking at their leads. "You leave now, or you leave with them. Understand?"

"But I told Frank I was coming back! I must make sure the ambulance—"

"It will come," Zimmerman said impatiently. "I will wait here until it does."

"But what about the gun? There's a gun on the tracks. And all our gadgets lying around. We have to collect them before the police—"

"Yes, of course. I will make sure nothing of yours is left behind." Carefully, Zimmerman rewrapped the bomb in its brown paper bag, placed it into the satchel slung over his shoulder and pushed his spectacles farther up his nose.

A group of five policemen and their dogs had now broken off from the circle and were patrolling the tracks, while a smaller group took the eastern end of the platform. But what concerned Marion the most wasn't the sheer number of policemen in the station, but the fact that they appeared to know exactly *who* they were looking for. She watched in horror as an officer not more than ten yards away pulled an elderly woman aside and showed her a photograph.

"It is over now," Zimmerman said, confirming Marion's fears. "They know who you are. And what you look like."

"*How?*" It was a stupid question. She knew exactly how. What she'd meant to say was *good Lord.* Darcy had called checkmate on the ledge above the tracks, but really she'd had everyone cornered long before.

"Your photograph, along with some information, was handed to Scotland Yard this morning by a Fräulein Ferg," Zimmerman answered.

"Information?"

"*Ich weiß nicht.* Something that links you to Oscar Biggar's murder. It is…damning, they say. You will be convicted if they catch you. *Bestimmt.* Definitely." He paused a moment. "Your *friend,* Constable Redding, informed Nancy just one hour ago. She called Frank here on the telephone, thinking you were still at the agency but—"

"The delay," Marion mumbled flatly, recalling what Frank had told her in the room above the train tracks: *I'm hoping they'll have drawn them here instead.* "He didn't just set off the fireflies to delay Darcy, he set them off to draw the police to the station. To draw them away from the bookshop, and therefore me!" She faltered and for a moment she wasn't sure she even wanted to know the answer to her next question. Unfortunately, she'd a feeling she already did. "The bookshop... has it, has it shut down?"

Zimmerman nodded solemnly. "The Fold. You know about it, yes?"

Marion tried to dismiss the horrid ache in her chest, the coldness curling in her stomach. She couldn't accept that this was really it—the absolute end—and that she'd never again see the inside of *Miss Brickett's*. There had to be another way. There *had* to be hope.

"Do you know where they've gone," she asked, "the others?"

Zimmerman spread his hands and shrugged.

A trio of senior looking officers, each bearing the same photograph—which Marion could now see was a hazy close-up of her face, one from Darcy's collection no doubt—turned toward the escalator. Marion dropped her head while Zimmerman shuffled expertly and swiftly in front of her.

"What will happen to Frank?" she asked, aware of the officers' gaze burning into the back of her head. "If I run. What will happen to him?"

"No one knows his face. Or who he is. He is just a commuter who got caught in your way. And I will make sure he gets the treatment he needs."

Marion closed her eyes for a brief moment, picturing Frank as he lay in the darkened room above the tracks, alone and on the brink. It felt so utterly wrong to leave before she knew he was safe. But even if she wanted to, she couldn't make her way back along the tracks without being seen.

"Nancy is dead," Zimmerman said, breaking her from her thoughts. Was it a question? It didn't sound like one.

"Y-yes," she answered uncertainly.

"But not here, okay?"

"What?"

Zimmerman went on rapidly, "You must not tell anyone she died here in the station. She died before she left the agency. An accident. You don't know the details."

"But the body…" Marion fumbled. "It's there…with Frank, above the tracks."

Zimmerman shook his head and mumbled, "Not for long."

Her focus broken, she looked left. The trio of policemen were now questioning a couple of passengers just a foot away, so close she could hear every word.

"Excuse me, ma'am. Have you seen this woman?" the one officer asked. "We were told she was here an hour ago."

"Not seen her, sorry."

The officer nodded, moved on to the next. "Excuse me, sir. Have you seen this woman?"

Zimmerman drew Marion a step to the left, just as one of the other officers turned to look their way. He placed a hand on her shoulder and whispered more urgently than ever, "There's no more time! *Schnell, bitte. Go!*"

Like a film reel unraveling before her, she watched the officers draw nearer, so close she could clearly see the photograph, the smile on her face, the bookshop's bow-fronted windows in the background. She knew exactly the moment the picture had been taken—Good Friday, the night of the *Miss Brickett's* Fight Club, the moment she'd spotted Kenny, Bill and Jessica strolling toward her down the cul-de-sac, the moment she'd seen the flash of white from the shadows, the moment this had all begun.

She took a breath, glanced at Zimmerman once more. He

was right: the only thing worse than leaving Frank was leaving the station in handcuffs. So, without giving herself a chance to change her mind, she picked up her travel case, dipped her head, hunched her shoulders and stepped onto the escalator.

She marched without pause down Brompton Road, past Harrods' glittering window displays, past the chattering patrons who'd merged onto the pavement to observe the chaos unfolding down the street. A wailing ambulance drove past, then screeched to a halt outside the station. She watched, bereft, as Frank was carried through the ticket office on a stretcher. It was too far away for her to see his face, but the paramedics were moving quickly, which she took as a good sign. He was still alive.

Only once the ambulance had pulled away, with Frank safely inside it, did she allow herself to feel the sheer exhaustion and dread that had been building inside her for days. Everything blurred and slowed, like an awful, vivid nightmare. Where was she supposed to go now? What was she supposed to do? If the bookshop had been sealed, as Zimmerman insisted, and *The Fold* protocol set in motion, then everyone she knew and loved would've already vanished, transformed into their *noms de plume* and disappeared into London and beyond like wisps of smoke. She could go after them, of course, track down Kenny and Bill and Jessica. Indeed, there was nothing in the world she wanted more. But with the entirety of London's police force on her tail, anyone she was seen with now would be marked as aiding and abetting a wanted fugitive.

"Ay, out the way!" Someone bumped into her from behind, a gruff-looking hooligan with a scar across his lower lip and a missing front tooth. He paused to examine her face. His brow knotted, recognizing something. "Hold on a minute. Aren't you...you're the one they've been looking—"

Marion didn't wait for him to finish. She dashed left, into

the nearest side street, pinned her back against the wall, her heart hammering. Now she knew why Darcy had been so insistent that she remove her disguise.

Footsteps thumped in her wake, then stopped. She ripped open her travel case, pulled out a gray wool scarf, wrapped it around her head, nose and mouth and turned back toward Brompton Road, hoping to blend in with the crowds and slip away.

But as she did, a wall of six uniformed officers appeared in front of her, blocking the way.

Standing in the center was a short and spindly man with a long, pointed nose, thick red hair and a sparse orange beard. She recognized him immediately from the headshot stapled to a file she'd paged through countless times in the Intelligence Department, labeled: *Collaborators. Redding, M: Metropolitan Police.*

She turned around, sprinted down the side street. Boots beat hard against the tarmac behind her, voices rose. Someone was shouting for her to stop. Someone else was calling for backup. Ahead, the street forked left and right. She had less than a second to choose. Half a second.

Smack.

An officer collided with her from the left. She fell onto her side, rolled over and staggered back to her feet in one fluid movement. The officer followed, leapt forward and gripped her by the thigh. She kicked him off but with three of the five officers having now caught up, she was surrounded.

"Drop your bag and put your hands in the air!" one of the officers demanded.

She dropped the travel case but kept her arms pinned to her sides, fists balled. The officers closed in. One of them drew a baton from his belt and swiped it through the air with a snigger.

She looked up, back toward Brompton Road and the moving crowds, the sea of faces and bodies, some of whom had paused, turned to the scene. Among them was Constable Redding, charging down the side street toward her. And unbeknownst to him, trailing several yards behind and partly in disguise, were Kenny and Bill.

Bill caught Marion's eye. Kenny drew a pistol from his belt. Everything inside her clenched with fear.

A crowd had formed at the end of the road, one hundred keen eyes, fifty witnesses. And if Kenny pulled the trigger, if he felled an officer right here in front of everyone, his life would be over.

She waited for Redding to reach the scene, then lifted her hands into the air. Kenny skidded to a halt a few feet away, forcing Bill to do the same. Marion and Kenny locked eyes. She wished she could've said it then, the thing she'd been wanting to say for months. Instead, she shook her head, and he lowered his gun with a trembling hand, slipped into the shadows and out of sight.

Marion blinked and turned back to Redding. He gesticulated furiously at the officer who'd drawn out a set of handcuffs. "That won't be necessary, Peterson. I'll handle things from here."

The officer nodded and slinked back, looking mildly confused and somewhat incredulous.

Redding passed his gaze over Marion's bloodied, soiled blouse. "Are you hurt, Miss Lane?"

She might've been, but she couldn't feel a thing now. "I'm fine."

"And you're on your own?" Redding asked, looking over his shoulder, as though he sensed someone near. But Kenny and Bill were nowhere to be seen.

"Yes," she said. "I'm alone."

Redding instructed the remaining officers to back off, then came to Marion's side and spoke in a whisper. "Miss Lane, you are one crafty lady, I'll give you that! My fellas here have been searching this place for over an hour." Furtively, he pushed a hand into his pocket and pulled out an unlit bulb adorned with filigree wings. "What were you lot *thinking*?" he hissed, crushing the firefly between his fingers. "I have always protected you and lied for you. But *this*?" He opened his hands and let the crushed glass fall to the pavement like golden glitter. "There is nothing I can do for you this time. Nothing. I'm sorry. It really is over now."

23

THE GHOST OF DARCY GIBSON

IT WAS SEVERAL LONG AND PAINFUL HOURS, OR
perhaps even an entire day, since Marion had been arrested by
Constable Redding. She'd given her statement on what happened at Knightsbridge station, claiming that a woman named
Darcy Gibson—who had framed her for the murder of Alan
Biggar—had tried to kill her and a stranger by the name of
Phillip Cheevers (who she'd just discovered was in a critical
but stable condition at St. Thomas Hospital). She then went on
to embellish her backstory, explaining how Darcy had known
Alice Lane and the Biggar brothers, against whom she'd sought
a bloody revenge. She suggested an inquest into the Biggars'
clothing chain enterprise and their previous drug trafficking
operation, hopeful that somehow someone would uncover
the dirty secrets that lay beneath the brothers' apparent "phi-
lanthropy." For as long as possible, Marion kept to the facts.
But when it came to the involvement of Frank or anyone else

who'd worked at *Miss Brickett's Investigations and Inquiries*, she was vague and occasionally misleading.

Seven members of Scotland Yard had been present, including lead investigator, Detective Inspector Donald Knead and a fidgety, sweaty Constable Redding. They'd listened dutifully to her monologue, puffing cigars and sipping tea, glancing at one another with raised eyebrows and dubious expressions and offering Marion no hope whatsoever that she'd ever again see the light of day. And just when she thought her chances of escaping a life in prison (or the noose) couldn't possibly get any worse, a large and morose looking officer with a stupid grin waltzed into the interrogation room with an item in an evidence bag. He handed the item to Detective Inspector Knead, gave Marion a knowing look, then left.

Your photograph, along with some information, was handed to Scotland Yard this morning by a Fräulein Ferg…

Marion's mind began to spin a thousand miles a minute as she realized what the *evidence* bag contained—her bespoke leather belt with a crescent moon buckle, the one Darcy had borrowed then given back to her at the Mayflower the first time they'd met.

Something that links you to Oscar Biggar's murder.

All along she'd known there was something she'd missed in Darcy's flawless plan. Well, here it was. *Wonderful.*

"Does this belong to you, Miss Lane?" Detective Inspector Knead asked coldly, while Redding paced back and forth behind him chewing his nails, as if *he* were the one being accused of murder.

"No," she lied blandly. "I've never seen it before."

"Really? Never ever? You sure about that?"

Marion nodded.

The Detective Inspector curled in his lips maliciously. "As

you know, we received a tip-off this morning from an anon-ymous source—"

"From Darcy Gibson, you mean," Marion interrupted irri-tably. "Miss Ferg was either Gibson's alias or a friend of hers. But go on."

"Among another things," the Detective Inspector continued in a snarl, "the tip-off informed us that we might find some-thing rather interesting at Number 16 Willow Street, your home, something related to the murder of Oscar Biggar. And this," he added unnecessarily, nodding at the belt, "is what we found. So, Miss Lane, if indeed you have never seen this belt before, can you please explain to me how it ended up in your house?"

She gave him a blank stare and crossed her arms. She was already up to her neck in incriminating evidence. The only thing she could do now was deny it all.

The Detective Inspector waved the belt in front of her face, then jabbed a finger at the buckle. "A fascinating shape, isn't it?"

She squinted at the thing, shook her head. "Not really. It looks like a half moon to me. Ever seen one of those before?"

He scowled. Not in the mood for wisecracks, then. "Our fo-rensics department has confirmed that the shape of this buckle matches the impression found on Oscar Biggar's neck." He paused, giving Marion a chance to catch her breath before the final nail was hammered securely into her coffin. "Must I spell it out for you, Miss Lane, or do you understand what I'm implying?"

"I do, unfortunately," she retorted. "But, like I told you, Darcy Gibson set me up. If she used that belt to kill Oscar Biggar, as you're suggesting—"

"I'm not suggesting that at all. I'm suggesting *you* used it to kill—"

"—then she planted it in my house to frame me," Marion interrupted curtly. "I don't understand what else you want me to say. I'm innocent."

Constable Redding raised a hand to placate her, and after a hushed conversation with the Detective Inspector, a heavy silence filled the room.

Marion slipped into a fog of bewilderment and exhaustion, replaying the sequence of events that had brought her here, every meticulous step Darcy had plotted out to get away with the murders of the men who'd wronged her and, while she was at it, ruin Marion's life as some sort of wretched, posthumous revenge on Alice. If the whole thing wasn't so utterly awful, she would have almost been impressed.

"W-well, there we a-are, Miss Lane," Redding said with a stammer as soon as Detective Inspector Knead had left and the pair of them were alone in the interrogation room.

Marion watched him pour another cup of tea with trembling fingers, lower himself into the chair opposite her. Knightsbridge station was the first time either of them had met. It was also the first time Redding had seen an Inquirer in the flesh. And while he'd known Marion's face from the infamous photograph his pals at the Yard had been passing around, she did wonder if perhaps he'd been surprised to note how ordinary and unexceptional she looked in person. Not quite the troublesome, gadget-wielding agent of chaos he might've imagined.

"Why did you do it?" she asked. "Why did you throw us under the bus like that? Leaking all our secrets to the newspapers? I know it was you." She did *not* know, in fact, but it was a calculated guess, and judging by Redding's reaction, she was spot on.

After taking a long sip of tea, he drummed his stubby fingers on the table and fixed her with a skittish look. "I—I didn't have a choice. Knead knew I'd been dealing w-with you lot, and he wanted information to leak to the papers. It was jump off the sinking ship or go down with it."

"You could've lied."

"He put me on a polygraph."

Marion was too exhausted to retort. She sighed instead. What was done was done, and there was certainly no going back now.

"You k-know h-how it is with the boys in blue," Redding rambled on, a hint of shame coloring his tone now. "H-hate the Inquirers, always have. Especially Knead. He's b-been waiting for years to blab to the p-papers about you lot, just n-never had anything d-damning enough to make it worth his while. Then this murder rumor c-comes up and, well…" He shook his head vehemently, took another sip of tea and choked on it.

Marion stretched out her neck, which sent a shot of pain through her shoulders. She'd been sitting in this tiny windowless room for so long it almost felt as though everything that had happened at Knightsbridge station had occurred in a previous lifetime. Unfortunately not.

Recovered from his choking fit, Redding leaned across the desk, cleared his throat and calmed his stammer. "You know, if only you lot had offered me a position at your agency, I wouldn't have had to spill the beans like this."

Marion took a sip of water. She was so very tired of talking and felt entirely devoid of emotion, but this required a rebuttal. "Why on earth would we have hired someone like you?"

Redding straightened awkwardly in his seat. "Well, I'm… I have *experience*. Knowledge! I would've made a brilliant Inquirer, though I say so myself." He tugged irritably at his spindly beard, pulling out a clump of frizzy orange hair. "But never mind. No chance of that now. You really have gotten yourself into a fix. Good and proper."

"I didn't kill anyone," Marion repeated for the hundredth time. "It was a setup. Right from the beginning."

"Yes, yes. So you say." He was becoming more emboldened by the minute, and Marion didn't like it one bit. "A setup by this mysterious Gibson character who conveniently kicked the bucket before she could defend herself. That's the gist of it, eh?"

"Darcy Gibson is a convicted criminal who was in prison for eight years. Surely it's not so hard to believe—"

Redding interrupted brusquely. "By the way, this Miss Gibson woman, how did you say she died?"

Marion felt a prickle at the back of her neck as the memory flashed across her mind. "She jumped in front of a train."

"Ah, yes. Strange though, isn't it? The train driver *did* see someone jumping. A woman, he was sure. Of course, he can't tell us what she looked like."

"What's strange about that?"

Redding's mustache twitched, as did his right eye. "The body, Miss Lane. There was none."

Marion stopped breathing. Stopped blinking. Even her heart might've stopped beating. Darcy had jumped. Darcy was dead. Frank was in hospital, safe. "She jumped," she said shrilly. "I *saw* her jump. Right in front of the train!"

Redding's cheeks turned pink as he slammed a hand on the desk and barked, "Then where's the blasted body? Zapped up by little green men? Dissolved by one of your ridiculous gizmos? Carried off by an army of ants?"

"I... I don't know. How well did they search for it? The train was going very fast." The train *had* been going very fast. Not fast enough to make a body disappear, though.

Redding's expression suggested he was on the verge of a

tectonic meltdown. "Now you listen here, young lady! I won't
have you make a fool of me any longer. I am trying to help
you, but I can't do that if all you feed me is a bunch of im-
plausible, ridiculous lies! An innocent civilian was shot twice
at point-blank range in Knightsbridge station. Not by you,
apparently, and yet you were the only one there with him in
that tunnel."

"But I wasn't!" she repeated, desperate now. "Darcy Gibson was there and—" She stopped herself just before she mentioned who else was with her at Knightsbridge.

You must not tell anyone she died here in the station. She died
before she left the agency. An accident. You don't know the details.

"You do realize how this looks?" Redding went on. "You
realize how little hope you have if this case goes to trial?" He
raised a finger as he began to count the very many reasons
Marion was absolutely done for. "One, you have an indis-
putable motive for the murders." He raised a second finger.
"Two, the only people anyone saw in that train tunnel were
you and the man you shot, Mr. Phillip Cheevers." He raised
a third finger. "Three, your fingerprints were discovered on
the revolver used to kill Alan Biggar, as well as on the belt
used to—"

Thank the sweet heavens, before he could take his unprovoked diatribe any further, the door swung open and the
portly, morose looking officer returned, this time bearing a
notepad and several case files. He scuttled across the room and
whispered something in Redding's ear.

"She's *what!*" Redding spat at the officer, who now looked
as affronted as Redding looked shocked. "Since when? No…
no, that's impossible. Absolutely impossible!"

The officer shrugged, then pointed at the door. "Just passing on the message, sir. You can come and see for yourself if
you don't believe me."

Redding pushed back his chair, got to his feet. "You'll ex-cuse me for a moment, Miss Lane."

The door clicked shut and, just like that, Marion was left alone to wallow in her misery. She looked up at the plain white ceiling and tried not to think about what was going to hap-pen to her (a life behind bars, at best). But how had it come to this? How had she gone from in love, confident and joyous to handcuffed, alone and accused of murder, all in the space of two weeks? She thought of Bill, Kenny, Jessica, and where they were. She thought of Frank, his injuries, and whether he'd survive the night. She wondered, too, about trivial things, such as what she'd left behind in her room in the staff quar-ters—her clothes, her beloved gadgets and tools and treasured memorabilia, her well-thumbed copy of *The Basic Workshop Manual*. But, mostly, she thought of her mother. Would Alice have been proud of her for what she'd tried to make of her life, or disappointed at how it had all come tumbling down?

At least forty minutes elapsed before Redding reappeared, looking marginally more startled than when he'd left and a good deal more confused.

"There's been a, well, I suppose you could call it a *develop-ment*," he announced abruptly, hovering at her side, his hands wringing together at his waist.

"A good one?"

Redding looked at the door, as though to check that it was closed. "I don't…well, maybe." He inhaled, fidgeted. "I don't want this case to go to the Old Bailey any more than you do, Miss Lane. It would be a disaster for the Yard. For me, espe-cially, for reasons I'm sure you can puzzle out. No one likes to harp on about the past, you know. We've all done things we regret. I certainly regret getting involved with you lot, that's for bleeding sure!"

Marion frowned at him, her heart rapping a little faster than before. "If you don't want the case to go to trial then what—"

Redding sat down, leaned across the table, and whispered furtively, "The issue is the confession itself, you see. It must be tested, according to the lawyers—"

Marion bristled. "*Confession?* I said I'm innocent!"

Redding went on as if he hadn't heard her, "—tested to make sure she was actually there, you see. Then there's the matter of your fingerprints, but I suppose the gloves explain that away." He paused to take a breath, then went on as if he was talking to himself. "We do have her file, though. Would that be a problem? Her photograph too, yes, yes. Oh dear. But this is close enough, I suppose. And it's better for all of us." He blinked at Marion. "You understand?"

"Not in the least. What's going on?"

He flapped his hands irritably. "I'll explain in a moment." He pushed back his shoulders in an effort to compose himself, though it didn't seem to make the slightest difference to his nerves. "Just listen. Don't argue with anything I say, don't ask questions and for heaven's sake don't say she isn't who she says she is."

"She?"

Redding continued frantically, "I've spent the last half an hour negotiating a deal on your behalf, and this is quite frankly your last chance."

Marion wasn't buying it (or understanding it). "How kind. But what sort of deal are we talking about here? And what's the catch?"

Redding moved forward in his seat. Crossed his legs, uncrossed them. "There are two, actually. Number one, you must hand over the keys to the bookshop. And show us the rest."

"The rest of what?"

"Everything. You weren't just operating from the bookshop, that's obvious enough. We'd have to see the other part. The secret section," he added in a whisper.

Marion forced her weary brain to contemplate the implications of this. There was no way she'd be able to take Redding and his mates down through the trapdoor and into the Grand Corridor, now that it was sealed, even if she wanted to, even if she *had* to. If Nancy had done things Nancy-style, then it was likely the trapdoor was entirely invisible, the floorboards covering it utterly flush. No one, no matter how hard they searched, would ever find what had once been the portal to the world of *Miss Brickett's*.

"All right," she said, coming to a decision. Her tour of the bookshop would require a little creativity and a good bit of imagination from all parties, but since neither Redding nor any of his colleagues had ever entered the "secret section" of *Miss Brickett's* before, they'd really have no idea whether she was showing them all of it or not. Easy. "But you might be disappointed," she warned.

"Yes, well, we'll see about that."

"And what's the second condition?"

Redding folded his arms across his chest and scowled. "Nancy Brickett. Tell me where she is."

A drip of perspiration slipped down Marion's neck. She moved uncomfortably in her seat. "She's dead."

Redding drew back, his mouth open. Was he sad to hear it, or just shocked? "Dead? Nonsense. I telephoned her just this morning to warn her about the tip-off. She told me she was making her way to Knightsbridge to sort things out."

Marion nodded sadly. "Yes. I know. But she died before she left the agency," she lied, exactly as Zimmerman had insisted. "I am, *was*, only an apprentice there, so I don't know the details. It was an accident, apparently. Something with the gadgets I think. The council got rid of the body," she added, just because. "You know, like they've done before with—"

Redding broke in with a snap, "No! She can't be dead! As head of your operation, your *illegal* operation, Nancy Brickett must face charges. That's the deal I've just made with my colleagues and I can't go back on it now!"

"Well, that's your mistake," Marion replied calmly.

Redding sucked in a furious breath. "My superiors will insist that you take a polygraph test to prove it."

Marion gave him a one-shoulder shrug. He and his pals could question her till kingdom come and it would make no difference to anyone. Nancy might not have died in the way or place Marion had said, but she'd seen the body, she'd felt the cold, clammy skin and nonexistent pulse. Nancy was dead, and if Marion had to take a polygraph test to prove it, so be it.

"Fine," she said.

There was a moment of silence. Redding paced the length of the interrogation room and Marion stared blankly at the wall, thinking of absolutely nothing. She still wasn't sure what Redding was offering her in exchange for a bookshop tour and a polygraph test. Maybe a shorter sentence, maybe a more comfortable cell. Did she even care?

Eventually, the door opened and the portly officer reappeared, this time accompanied by a petite blonde in handcuffs, wearing a long dark coat and sporting a cut and bruise on her jaw.

"So..." Redding said to Marion, gesturing to the blonde, "here she is. In good shape for someone who jumped in front of a moving train just hours ago, don't you think?"

Marion's mouth went dry and her limbs weak. She blinked several times, trying to decide if Redding was right and the woman standing in front of her was Darcy Gibson. She squinted, cocked her head. The eyes were Darcy's—silver-

gray, alluring, almost threatening. The face was Darcy's—
heart-shaped and innocent. The hair was Darcy's—neat
ringlets of champagne blond. Even the wound on her jaw
was Darcy's—broken skin and delicate bruising from where
Nancy had hit her with the butt of her gun just hours ago.

But there was something not quite right.

Darcy was tall and wide set, while the woman standing
in front of Marion was petite and narrow hipped. And if she
looked closely, very closely, she could just make out the pale
tan line of a silicone flesh strip running the length of the
woman's jaw.

"It's your lucky day, Miss Lane. Miss Gibson here," Redding
said, tapping the woman on the shoulder, "has confessed to
murdering Oscar and Alan Biggar and has even confirmed that
she tried to set you up for the whole thing. Isn't that fantastic?"

Marion gripped the edge of her chair, just before she top-
pled over. "I don't understand—"

"You're free as a bird," Redding explained, excitement in
his voice. "Off the hook, innocent as a lamp. Etcetera, etcetera—" He raised a cautionary hand, interrupting himself.
"That is, provided you take us on a tour of the bookshop. And
provided you pass your polygraph."

Even if she could somehow get her lips to move, Marion
wouldn't have known what to say. She thought for a moment
that she must be hallucinating, and that the woman standing
in front of her was an invention of her very exhausted and an-
guished brain. But when Redding and this pal were distracted
by the arrival of Detective Inspector Knead, the blonde locked
her false gray eyes on Marion, winked and mouthed, *Trust me.*

AN END AND A BEGINNING

MARION WATCHED LONDON SLIP BY IN A BLUR through the bus window. It was two weeks after the events at Knightsbridge station and the sun, just risen, was barely peeking through an impassible fortress of gray, casting the city in an eerie gloom. Strangely, it almost felt as though this were the very first time she was seeing London like everyone else. Dull, hopeless.

The bus pulled up at a traffic light in Chelsea, and she watched as a knot of pedestrians clambered off, split up and scurried down the street. Everyone was wearing the same expression: their eyes were listless, postures slumped as they, like Marion, trudged through another day, an endless procession of minutes and hours that added up to nothing at all. But actually, now that she thought about it, this wasn't the first time she'd seen London in all its gloom and depression. She'd observed it just the same when she was younger, staring out through her bedroom window at Willow Street in the days before her life had meaning, in the days before Frank and Kenny and Bill and Jessica and *Miss Brickett's*. Were things better now than then? Or worse? Was it worse to finally get the thing you've always wanted, only to have it snatched away, or to never have had it at all?

On the plus side, she'd escaped life behind bars—albeit by the skin of her teeth. Following her polygraph test at the police station (which, much to Constable Redding's displeasure, proved Nancy *was* dead) and her tour of the bookshop (which left Scotland Yard with a number of theories and suspicions but no concrete answers), all charges against Marion were dropped and "Darcy Gibson" was bundled up in the back of a police van and driven off to Holloway prison. It was truly the most astonishing end to the whole thing, but what made it even more bizarre was that the car transporting "Darcy" from the station to the prison mysteriously burst into flames *en route*, killing "Darcy" (for the second time) and injuring three wardens. Still, with "Darcy's" full confession down on paper, and Scotland Yard keen to put the messy ordeal behind them, Marion was given the green light to return to her old house in Willow Street and "live a normal life," as Constable Redding had put it, in an almost pleading tone.

She was free. Free to leave the interrogation room, collect her travel case and dodge the pack of photographers and journalists waiting like starved wolves outside the police station.

But then what?

Her first instinct had been to take a taxi straight to St. Thomas Hospital. She needed to see with her own eyes that Frank was alive and well. But could she? Should she? Constable Redding had assured her that apart from the commuters who'd been questioned at Knightsbridge station, no one had any idea what she looked like. He also insisted that no one at Scotland Yard had given, or would ever give, her photograph to the newspapers. But what if Darcy had, or her friend Miss Ferg? What if the journalists waiting outside the station *had* actually managed to get a picture of her?

She was innocent as far as the law was concerned, but until Scotland Yard released a statement explaining things (such as who the Biggar Brothers really were and who had killed them), she and all the Inquirers were public enemy number one. Therefore, the last thing she wanted was for Phillip Cheevers—a blameless commuter—to be seen in her company. So, instead of taking a taxi to St. Thomas, she took one to Willow Street, locked the door and didn't leave for fourteen days.

There was, of course, a lot to think about in that time: What had happened to Bill and Kenny after they'd witnessed her arrest at Knightsbridge? Would she ever see them again? What had happened to the others—Jessica, Maud, Preston, David, Professor Bal? Did they know she was free, or did they think she was still in prison awaiting trial? Who was this mysterious Darcy impersonator, and why in heaven's name had she confessed to everything? What had really happened in that police van? What had happened to the body of the *real* Darcy Gibson? Would Frank make a full recovery? What was she, Marion, going to do with her life now that everything she knew was broken and everyone she loved had vanished? But she didn't think about any of that. She couldn't. Her mind was blank. Dark. A grim, wide chasm of nothing. And when she finally managed to haul herself from bed and venture outside, there was only one place she wanted to go.

Now, on the bus there, a flash of silver caught her eye. She glanced right to see a young girl, perhaps in her early teens, sitting on the opposite side of the aisle and turning a glittering object over in her hand. Marion squinted at the thing, which had reflected a ray of pale sun streaming in through the bus window. It was a sunbird, all metal, wings, claws and beak.

The girl's mother, noticing Marion's gaze, slipped a hand over her daughter's, concealing the bird. "Put that away, dear," she whispered. "Remember what I told you?"

Marion cocked her head and asked, "Where did you get that?"

The woman looked around nervously, but her daughter was not so distressed.

"It's a replica Distracter," the girl answered happily, despite her mother's frantic *shushing*. "From the shop in Fulham. They have light orbs too, and funny looking keys and watches and—"

"It's just for fun," the mother interrupted hurriedly. "Though for some it's a show of support, I suppose." She waited for Marion to nod approvingly, then went on, "Ever since that...*event* at Knightsbridge station, these replicas have been popping up all over the place. I can't walk five minutes without seeing someone carrying something that looks like a, eh, well, you know..." She gestured at the sunbird in her daughter's lap. "The Inquirers were good for this city, and I'm not the only one who thinks so."

The bus finally jerked to a stop. Marion got to her feet, bid the girl with the sunbird farewell and climbed off. She trailed down the familiar Musgrave Crescent, around the boundary of Eel Brook Common, turning southeast. She slowed as she approached a cul-de-sac that split off from the common, dimmer than any of the surrounding streets, as though cowering in its own shadow, hoping not to be seen. The road was quiet and deserted, no different from how it had been in the days of the Inquirers.

She padded down the street, her gaze fixed ahead. As she'd expected, the bow-fronted windows were boarded up, the steel door crisscrossed with two wooden planks nailed to the wall. The old sign that had once read *Miss Brickett's Second-hand Books & Curiosities* had been painted over and replaced by faded lettering, as though not quite sure of itself just yet: *Mr. Kingston's Meats and Eats.*

She wasn't sure why she'd felt the need to come here. Did she expect to see Bill, Professor Bal, or some other familiar face peering out through the window, ready to tell her everything had been a ruse and *Miss Brickett's* was, in fact, still in operation? Or perhaps she hoped to catch a glimpse of Mr. Kingston, whoever he was, and ask him if he knew there was a trapdoor in the floor of his shop that used to lead down to a vast labyrinth?

The past three years of her life had been like a dream. Strange, bizarre, terrifying and wondrous. Sometimes, she'd stand in front of the mirror, stare at the pale, blue-eyed face looking back at her and wonder if she'd just experienced some sort of prolonged episode of madness, during which she'd become an apprentice detective, lived underground, fallen in love and created magical gadgets.

A soft breeze whistled down the cul-de-sac, and the freshly painted sign creaked above her head. She'd always felt that this shop, and what lay beneath it, was a living thing. Alive. Ever-changing. Perhaps, then, this was just a reincarnation of sorts, and one day the magic beneath Mr. Kingston's feet would seep through the floorboards and change his life, just like it had done for Marion and so many others before her.

One last look at the peeling black paint, the old door and frosted windows, and she turned away for the very last time. She wouldn't come back here, she promised herself. It was time for new things, to embrace a life that perhaps she didn't want, but which she'd one day understand was meant for her.

The very next day, Marion was back in her living room at Willow Street, downtrodden as ever, though perhaps entering the first stage of acceptance of her new life. Dressed casually in a plaid wool cardigan and gray slacks, she'd been trying to rearrange a set of vases on the mantlepiece for nearly twenty minutes. The vases, all from her grandmother, had arrived just that morning, along with a short note.

> *Darling,*
> *I heard about the bookshop closing. I'm terribly sorry, though I'm certain it's for the best, especially now that you're courting that young gentleman, Mr. Hugo. How lovely! A man to keep you company at last! I suspect you will fall into domestic bliss, now that you're giving it a chance.*
>
> *Sincerely,*
> *Your loving grandmother.*
> *PS Do come and visit me in Ohio as soon as you get the chance.*

She tore the card in two and lobbed it into the wastepaper basket. Her grandmother, Dolores Hacksworth, had lived with Marion from the time of Alice's death to the time of Marion's recruitment at *Miss Brickett's*—a long, excruciating period during which Dolores had tried to transform her only granddaughter into the perfect little housewife she was never going to be (especially now that the only man she'd ever loved had disappeared).

She was considering holding a match to the note for good measure when the doorbell rang.

She tensed, held her breath. Had the police changed their minds? Had reporters tracked her down? She shuffled to the door, reached for the handle, paused, then steeled herself and opened it.

She gasped.

Kenny, Bill and Frank were standing in front of her.

"Sorry for the intrusion, my dear," Frank said as he led the foursome into the living room, Bill dragging several suitcases behind him—one of which, Marion was quite sure, belonged to her. "Perhaps we should've telephoned beforehand."

Marion stared at him, unable to speak. Was this another potential hallucination? She eyed Frank's attire—a gray flannel suit and matching fedora, a polished steel cane at his side. He walked with a prominent limp, his skin was gray and his eyes lackluster, but there was no doubt he looked at least five hundred times better than the last time she'd seen him.

"Ah, yes," Frank said, watching her eyes drift back to the pile of suitcases. "I had your things brought up from your room in the *Miss Brickett's* staff quarters before we closed down. Everything should be there, including, of course, your mother's raven." He smiled and added, just loud enough for her alone to hear, "She is always with you, my dear, remember that."

Still too overwhelmed to speak, she turned to Kenny—dapper in a denim jacket and black jeans, only one small scar remaining on his forehead from the incident at the boardinghouse. She then looked at Bill—dressed in loose beige trousers and a nondescript pullover, his expression one of deep concern.

"Mari? You look really pale. You feeling all right?"

"Let's make some tea, shall we?" Frank suggested. "With lots of sugar."

"I'm so sorry we left you alone like this," Kenny told her. "I knew it was a bad idea, dammit! Lane, please, say something? Tell us you're okay?"

"I, eh, yes. Yes. I'm fine—" She heaved a breath, then burst into tears. "It's just been so long, and I wasn't sure I'd ever see you again. Any of you," she spluttered. "I was so afraid."

"I'm terribly sorry, Marion," Frank said, returning with a tray of tea and stale biscuits from the pantry. "I was only discharged from hospital this morning—"

"And Kenny and I had no idea you'd been let off," Bill added hastily. "We telephoned Redding at the station every single day since your arrest, but he wouldn't tell us anything. Guess it's because he didn't know who we were, and we couldn't exactly say we were *Miss Brickett's* employees. He just said there'd been a development and Scotland Yard would be making an announcement soon. Well, as you know, they only announced it yesterday." He produced a newspaper from inside one of the suitcases he'd dragged in, the headline of which read: *"Shocking Development in Biggar Murder Case: Charges Dropped Against Arrested Inquirer after Stunning Confession from Second Suspect, Darcy Gibson."*

"She's dead," Marion croaked, after gulping down a mouthful of burning hot tea. "Not Darcy-Darcy. I mean, the real Darcy too, obviously, but also the woman who—"

Bill cut in, saving her from a long-winded explanation. "Yeah, we know all about that. It was Anneliese."

Marion gasped a second time. She took another sip of tea. "Anneliese? You mean the woman I met the night of the Fight Club?"

Frank nodded, but instead of looking sad or shocked, he was smiling. As were Kenny and Bill.

"What am I missing here?" Marion blurted out. "She confessed to a crime she didn't commit to save me from a life in prison and now she's dead and you're all smiling about it?"

"Dead?" Frank said. "No, Marion. Anneliese is very much alive."

Marion almost dropped her teacup. "But the van...there was a fire, and a body inside! Redding telephoned to tell me."

"Yes, indeed," Frank said mysteriously. "But Zimmerman and the members of *Der Schatten* are, if nothing else, brilliant at that sort of thing. Aren't they?" He got to his feet, groaned, checked the time. "Anyway, it was wonderful to see you, Marion. But I'm afraid I must be on my way. I've a train to catch."

"You're leaving? But you only just got here. And I have questions. Hundreds of questions! I want to know about Anneliese. And Zimmerman. I met him at the station after I left you. He told me something very strange about Nancy."

Frank leaned over with a wince, put a hand on her shoulder and smiled warmly. "Of course, my dear, I understand. You want to know everything. And you will, in time. I assure you."

"But—"

"*But,*" he interrupted, "I cannot miss my train. Here." He reached into his coat pocket and pulled out three sealed envelopes. One addressed to her, the other two to Kenny and Bill. He handed them over, turned and was gone.

25

LAST ROUNDS

THE SECOND FRANK HAD CLOSED THE DOOR, Marion, Kenny and Bill tore open their envelopes.

Inside was a letter the color of charcoal, lined with silver script.

Marion could hardly hear for the blood gushing in her ears. Her hands trembled as she ran a finger down the lines.

Dear Miss Lane,
On April 19 of this year, Mr. Lance Zimmerman of Der Schatten signed an agreement with Miss Brickett's Investigations and Inquiries on your behalf (as a consequence of your decision to "borrow" Mr. Zimmerman's prize money). The agreement is as such:

Miss Marion Lane, Inquirer, will undergo a mandatory twelve-month pro bono shift at Der Schatten, including but not limited to:

Case filing, documentation, presentations and archiving.
Fieldwork (in and around West Berlin).

Gadgetry repair and design (under the guidance of Mr. Zimmerman).

Further details of this agreement shall be provided to you upon your arrival.

Please meet us at the stated location, at the stated time. Exactly.

May 9, 1960. 2:00 a.m. 4 Triftstrasse, West Berlin. Der Schwarze Hund.

Order one "Dunkel mit Silber" and wait.

We look forward to seeing you.

Marion reread the letter three times, muttering to herself. "*Dunkel mit Silbur... Der Schwarze Hund.*"

"Dark with silver," Kenny stated, holding up his own letter. "The Black Dog, Berlin."

"Yours says the same?"

He smiled, handed her his letter.

Dear Kenneth Louis Hugo,
We are pleased to inform you that you have been selected to join Der Schatten, West Berlin, in the position of senior investigator.

Should you accept this invitation, we ask that you meet us at the stated location, at the stated time. Exactly.

May 9, 1960. 2:00 a.m. 4 Triftstrasse, West Berlin. Der Schwarze Hund.

Order one "Dunkel mit Silber" and wait.

We look forward to seeing you.

"I can't believe it!" Marion gushed, buzzing with enough adrenaline to set her nerves alight. "*Der Schatten.* Berlin? You don't think it's a joke, do you? Bill? What does yours say?"

He looked up with a wide smile. "Same as Kenny's, pretty much. Looks like we've all been recruited. Um, except," he added, reading Marion's letter over her shoulder, "you're going to work *pro bono* for twelve months."

"I'll work there *pro bono* for the rest of my life if it means seeing everyone again. And getting back to work. Do you think the others have been recruited too? Jess? Maud? Preston? And what about Professor Bal?"

Bill shrugged. "Guess we'll find out in—" he reexamined his letter "—exactly thirty-three hours."

Marion pinched herself on the arm, just in case. It was *not* a dream.

"All right then," Kenny said, getting to his feet. He surveyed Marion with a slight frown. "How about a drink? You definitely look like you could use one."

Marion stared at him without saying anything. His perfect sandy hair, tanned skin, brown eyes, the scar on his forehead that reminded her just what he was willing to do to protect the people she loved. How could she ever have doubted him? Bill was right—her love for him was worth the risk. A thousand times over.

"Lane? What is it?"

She reached for his hand, smiled. Had she ever felt this happy? "I've been meaning to tell you this for a while now but, you know, things got a bit complicated, and I just never found the—" She broke off, thinking of the metallic rose he'd made for her, yet another sign of the lengths he'd gone to to prove himself. "I love you, Kenny Hugo."

He kissed her on the forehead. "I love you back, Marion Lane."

The entrance to *Der Schwarze Hund* was located at the bottom of a filthy stairwell that spiraled through the pavement and into what appeared to be an out-of-use sewer system. Marion,

Kenny and Bill turned to one another warily as they stepped through an arched doorway at the base of the stairwell and into a short tunnel that reeked of urine. They trudged on for several yards, eventually reaching a second door that opened up into *Der Schwarze Hund* beer hall. The space was low-roofed and smelled nearly as bad as the passageway outside, the walls on all sides made of jagged stone and decorated with hundreds of tapestries, paintings and sculptures of black dogs in various settings. Lining the hall from wall to wall were twenty long wooden tables, rustically lit by candles in grimy, frosted jars.

It was one fifteen in the morning, but you might not have guessed it by the vast number of patrons packed inside, mostly elderly men in gray trench coats and felt hats embellished with long feathers, sipping their beers and grumbling under their breath. The air was hot and thick, and Marion shrugged off her coat as the trio made its way to the bar counter.

"Guten Abend," she said in her best accent, speaking to the middle-aged man behind the bar, who'd been watching them with a scowl ever since they'd arrived. "Ah, three *Dunkel mit Silbur, bitte."*

The barman's forehead creased, he tilted his head. *"Was?"*

Marion cleared her throat and tried again, speaking slowly, "Three *Dunkel mit Silbur, bitte."*

"Nein!" he spat, then cursed, waved his hands in what Marion assumed was a rather unpleasant gesture and stumbled off to serve someone else.

"Oh, okay," she said. "That went well."

"I don't know if you said it right," Bill told her.

Marion shot him a look. "Would you like to try, then?"

Bill gulped, shuffled over to the other end of the bar and repeated the phrase to no avail.

Kenny was silent for a moment, then said under his breath, "I swear to God, if this is a prank, I'll be out for blood."

"If it's a prank," Marion said, "that means Frank's in on it. Which I very much doubt."

Bill shrugged. "Stranger things have happened."

Marion didn't answer only because her focus had fallen instead on a well-dressed blonde, seated alone at the far end of a table on the other side of the hall. Her back was to Marion, but there was something distinctly familiar about the gentle slope of her shoulders, her thin neck.

"What?" Kenny asked, following her line of sight.

"Wait here. Back in a sec."

She padded over to the table, and when the blonde looked up and smiled, she took a seat opposite her.

"Anneliese?"

"Marion Lane," the woman replied with a thick accent that threw Marion off guard. "Very nice to see you here. I was hoping you'd get an invitation."

Marion had a million questions on the tip of her tongue but suddenly found she couldn't remember any of them. Instead, she said, "You're very... German."

Anneliese laughed softly. "*Ja*, of course."

"But Constable Redding...the entire Scotland Yard...you had them fooled!"

"Accents ain't a problem for a member of *Der Schatten*, sweet," Anneliese said in a perfect imitation of Darcy's cockney inflection. So perfect, in fact, that it made the hairs on the back of Marion's neck stand up.

"What about the rest of it, though?" Marion asked. "The van. The fire."

Anneliese nodded, then drew out a small tan-colored object from behind her ear. It looked like a very small pen, sort of. "Tranquilizer pins on one end, Time Lighter on the other. Fits perfectly under a silicone face strip, too."

Marion blinked. "Oh..." was all she managed. "But what

about the body they found in the van? Where'd you get that from?"

Anneliese shrugged. "There wasn't a body on the tracks in Knightsbridge, yes?"

Marion gasped, recalling what Redding had told her in the interrogation room about Darcy's body: ...*there was none*. "But I still don't get it. Did you need two?"

"Two?"

Marion was beginning to feel light-headed. Actually, she was close to keeling over. "There were two bodies in the tunnel that day. Darcy's and Nancy's. But the police never found either." She gripped the edge of the table, just in case she really was about to faint. "So...what? You needed *both* for the van setup? Surely not?"

A look of comprehension came over Anneliese's face. She smiled, raised her stein and winked. "You will understand soon, I think."

Marion had every intention of pressing Anneliese for more, but the woman was on her feet and gliding over to the bar before she could get another word out.

"Mari!" called a voice from the entrance, forcing Marion's attention away from Anneliese. Jessica was wrapped in a red wool coat and a white knit scarf. She raised her hands in delight as she bounded over. Trailing her was Preston, who carried a haversack slung over his shoulder and a suitcase at each hip.

"This one does *not* travel light, let me tell you," Preston said, lowering the suitcases to the floor with a groan.

"Well, what did you expect, darling?" Jessica tapped the largest case with the tip of her boot. "It's my entire life in there."

"*God*, it's good to see you," Marion gushed, wrapping her arms around Jessica.

"Pres, my man!" Kenny cheered, slapping Preston on the back.

"You got a letter, then?" Marion asked. "The both of you?"

Jessica nodded as she took off her coat and threw it over her suitcase. "I was tempted to telephone you as soon as I did. But then I thought it might be an awkward conversation if you *hadn't* received one. And heaven knows what the consequences might've been for loose lips. You know how these people are about secrecy."

"And lucky for Jess," Preston added, "I caught up with her at the train station, because by the looks of it, she was about to head east to the Russians with a suitcase full of our replica gadgets."

"It's true," Jessica confirmed with a wary smile. "Your first investigation might've been a missing persons case." She unclipped her bag and drew out a small silver sunbird, identical to the one Marion had seen the young girl holding on the bus a while back.

"What the blazes did you bring that here for?" Kenny asked, glowering at the sunbird. Clearly, he'd hoped never to see another bizarre gadget as long as he lived.

"I've been collecting them for Professor Bal," Jessica said. "Long story."

"You've seen the professor?" Marion asked, gobsmacked and a little affronted.

"Well, no. Not exactly. He's been—"

Bill interrupted as he glanced around the bar with a frown. "Who are we supposed to be meeting here anyway? You reckon it's Zimmerman?"

Marion scanned the hall for Anneliese, but she'd vanished.

"*Hmm*, I'm not sure," Jessica said thoughtfully, climbing onto the stool Kenny had pulled out for her. "More likely Frank, don't you think?"

"I wonder who else will show," Marion mused. "Do you think everyone got a letter, or just a few of us?"

"Definitely *not* everyone," Jessica said carefully. "I bumped into David at King's Cross yesterday. Actually, it wasn't a chance encounter. He asked to see me for lunch, and since I was leaving that afternoon, a station sandwich was all I could offer him." She waited for a group of patrons to pass, then went on, "He's moving to Glasgow. Some distant relative offered him a place to stay and a job at the Royal Automobile Club. No idea what he'll be doing there, but he seemed quite happy about it."

"A fresh start," Marion said with a nod. "Just what he always wanted."

"My thoughts exactly. Anyway, I didn't ask him if he'd received a letter from *Der Schatten*, but since he didn't mention it, I think it's safe to say he didn't make the cut."

Just then, two figures appeared at the entrance. Maud and, wearing a green checkered coat and tattered beret, Professor Uday Bal.

Marion kissed Maud on the cheek, drew the professor into a bony hug. "Professor!" she said, guiding the pair over to the table where Kenny, Jessica, Bill and Preston were seated. "Where have you been these past weeks?" Marion asked, directing the question mostly at Bal.

"I've been…around." The professor touched his old beret and smiled sheepishly as he sat down next to Marion. "I'm sorry I didn't contact you but it was all so very complicated in the beginning, you know, with your arrest and *The Fold* and besides—" he swallowed, twisted his hands together "—I, well, I've been very busy."

Marion raised an eyebrow. "With?"

The professor stalled, but Bill answered for him. He grabbed the replica Distracter from Jessica's hand and planted it in on the table. "Ripping off your own inventions?"

"These were all *you*?" Marion asked.

The professor threw a handkerchief over the sunbird. "Careful, kids. This isn't London. You've got to be a bit more… discreet here." After scouring the bar for eavesdroppers, he lowered his voice and added with a smile, "But yes, it was all me. Earning a bit of money here and there. Quite fun, actually. Until N—" He stopped, cleared his throat. "Until some of the High Council found out. Which is why I've been trying to buy back all of my stock." He inclined his head at Jessica, who smiled in reply.

"Right, makes sense," Marion lied, still confused but quite used to the feeling now.

"Anyway, enough of that," Maud said from the other side of the table. "The important question is, has anyone tried to order a bloody *Dunkel*?"

Bill shook his head vehemently. He glanced at the barman, who was watching them again, arms crossed, with an expression of irritation. "I think if we try again, he might throw us out."

"So what, then?" Maud asked. "We just sit around? We don't even know who we're waiting for."

The group turned to Professor Bal, who fiddled with his beret and tapped his foot as he answered, "Almost time, almost…"

As the night lumbered onward, several more former *Miss Brickett's* apprentices and Inquirers—including Quinn and Proctor—arrived at the beer hall, each as bewildered and jittery as the next. Everyone took their turn ordering a *"Dunkel mit Silbur,"* (to no avail), and soon the locals, unsettled and irritable, filed from the hall one by one.

When the very last had climbed their way up the spiral stairwell and back onto the street above, the lights in the bar were dimmed.

Marion turned to Professor Bal with a questioning look.

He nodded subtly. "It's time."

"Right, let's give this another go." She got to her feet, everyone watching, and padded over to the deserted bar. As she approached, she heard a shuffling of feet, a click, a clang.

The barman reappeared through a door hidden somewhere in the shadows. He had changed his clothes and was now wearing a slick black suit and silver tie, his hair smooth against his scalp and a bunch of keys dangling from his fingers.

"Can I help you?" he asked in perfect English.

"*One Dunkel mit Silbur, bitte,*" Marion said.

The barman inclined his head, then pressed a button on the wall behind him.

There was a creak; something moved.

She stepped forward, cocked her head. A tiny white light flickered on behind the bar, illuminating an open door and beyond, a corridor that fed into the blackness. She looked over her shoulder to see Jessica, Bill, Kenny and Professor Bal already on their feet, and the others following closely behind.

"This way, please," the barman said, gesturing to the corridor. "Mr. Stone and Mr. Zimmerman are expecting you."

EPILOGUE

FIVE MONTHS LATER
Der Schatten Headquarters,
West Berlin

"PERFECT!" JESSICA SAID, STRAIGHTENING THE collar of Marion's cropped gunmetal blouse, which she'd paired with pleated high-waisted trousers in black and a smart blazer with epaulettes and silver buttons.

Marion examined herself in the mirror—her shoulder-length hair framing her face in soft, brown curls, her lips a bold red, her blue eyes outlined in kohl. But it wasn't just the uniform that made her small, dainty frame seem commanding now.

"Do you remember what you said to me while we were getting dressed the night of the first Induction Ceremony we ever watched?" she asked, fastening her watch around her wrist.

Jessica was quiet for a moment, then smiled knowingly. "I said we'd be pinning an *I* to our chests in two years' time, full-fledged Inquirers."

Marion clipped a shimmering pink pearl to each ear. "I didn't believe it, you know. After Michelle White's murder, I had a feeling things were going to turn sour and we'd never get our badges."

"Well, you hit a bull's-eye there," Jessica laughed as they left the changing rooms and stepped inside *Der Schatten's* colossal auditorium. "But when does life ever work out the way we plan? Sometimes it turns out worse than we imagine. And sometimes—" she looked up at the thousands of tiny battery-powered bulbs in gray frosted glass hovering just below the ceiling, then at the towering mechanical pine trees that stood like pillars around an oval-shaped stadium. "—far, far better."

They took their seats in the front row, alongside Bill, Preston, Maud, Kenny, Anneliese and several other *Der Schatten* and former *Miss Brickett's* employees. In the center of the stadium, guarded on each side by a large hound wrought of gleaming black steel, was Mr. Zimmerman and standing just behind him, Frank and Professor Bal.

The hovering bulbs in the ceiling dimmed. Zimmerman's hounds shivered, and the hall fell silent.

"Tonight," Zimmerman announced, "we formally welcome our British compatriots and friends, who will work alongside us to protect and serve the peoples of West Berlin and greater Europe. *Der Schatten schaut zu!* The shadow is watching." A slim pillar rose from the floor, attached to which was a small black box. Mr. Zimmerman opened the box, picked out an S-shaped breast pin, crossed diagonally with a silver dagger.

Jessica squealed under her breath, squeezed Marion's hand. "Here we go!"

As the ceremony drew to a close, Marion bid farewell to the others, straightened the new S-shaped pin on her chest and left the hall. She turned right down a narrow, tiled passage. Halfway along, a swarm of sleek metallic spiders emerged from the walls. Coolly and without pausing, she drew a Time

Lighter from her trouser pocket, clicked it on. A small green-tinted flame danced from the tip and the spiders vanished.

At the end of the passage, she reached a lift—the floor, ceiling and every wall made of glass. The doors slid shut with a soft whoosh, and the lift moved swiftly upward until it reached the top floor and a door marked: *M. Lane: Head Mechanic.*

She punched in a code, and the door parted to reveal a plushly furnished office. There was a settee, a large rosewood desk and leatherback chair, a teak workbench—covered in an assortment of ticking, whirling contraptions—and, finally, a glass display cabinet just behind. She paused for a moment in front of the cabinet—the top row lined with three objects: a brass raven, a ragged rose and a silver sunbird. Pieces of her old life, reminders of how far she'd come.

There was a knock at the door. She turned as it swung open.

A woman stepped inside, dressed like Marion in formal black and silver, adorned with epaulettes and shiny buttons. She looked at the brass raven in the cabinet, then at the silver S pinned to Marion's chest.

Nancy Brickett had been one of the first people to welcome Marion and the others to *Der Schatten* five months ago. The sight of her then had nearly caused Marion to keel over with shock, even though there had always been some small part of her that believed—or simply hoped—she was alive. Since then, Nancy had been a constant presence in Marion's life, guiding her through her new career at *Der Schatten* with perhaps a fraction more warmth than Marion had expected. And in return, Marion fostered a deep admiration for the woman she had for so long misunderstood.

"Congratulations, Miss Lane," Nancy said, extending a hand. "You are an Inquirer now, at last."

★ ★ ★ ★ ★

ACKNOWLEDGMENTS

HAYLEY STEED AND LAURA BROWN, TO WHOM this book is dedicated—thank you for being there every step of the way, and for believing in me and Marion from day one. It is certainly no exaggeration to say these books would not exist without you.

To the rest of the Madeleine Milburn team, particularly Elinor, for answering all my anxious after-hour emails; Liane-Louise and Valentina from the foreign rights department; and Georgia for your editorial assistance and support.

Thank you to the Park Row and wider HarperCollins teams for turning this manuscript into a book, particularly Erika Imranyi, Emer Flounders, Lindsey Reeder, Rachel Haller and my brilliant copy editor, Cathy Joyce.

Micaela Alcaino—you've done it again! What a privilege it has been to have you on Team Marion. Thank you for this bewitching, enchanting, perfect cover. It might be my favorite yet.

I have such admiration and gratitude for my ever enthusiastic and supportive reader/reviewer community on Instagram and Twitter, who have helped me spread the word about Marion Lane over the past three years. Namely, @pricetom (did you spot it?), @bookishreadsandme, @bookish_girl_in_bookish_world, @covers_and_cocktails, @bookish.bex,

@mrsdez6207, @aprilslibrary, @bookmarkonthewall, @the thoughtsofabibliophile, @franzencomesalive, @readerpenguin_, @bookoholicme, @prairiegrownreviews, @liztheliterary, @crazee4books, @acottageofbooks, @saika.reads.andreviews_, @husnas_library, @careful_of_books, @libraryofcaley, @michellesreadingcorner (I know I'm forgetting people here—I'm sorry!). I love you all. Drinks at the library bar on me?

To my family and friends for their tireless support and encouragement, thank you! I love you guys.

And Will: you, more than anyone else, have been there for the not-so-pretty side of the writing process, through the long, hard hours and occasional breakdowns. Thank you for always reminding me why I do this, and that I can.